GLOBAL DAWN

a novel by
Deborah Gelbard

PENDIUM

PUBLISHING HOUSE

514-201 Daniels Street
Raleigh, NC 27605
For information, please visit our Web site at
www.pendiumpublishing.com

PENDIUM Publishing and its logo are registered trademarks.

PUBLISHER'S NOTE

This is a work of fiction. Names, characters, places, and incidents either are the product of the author's imagination or are used fictitiously, and any resemblance to actual persons, living or dead, events, or locales is entirely coincidental.

This book is printed on acid-free paper.

This book is dedicated to my two sons, Meron and Amir.

Table of Contents

Acknowledgments

I am deeply grateful to the following:

Evan Fallenberg and Judy Labensohn for their expert guidance, encouragement and friendship; Robert A. diCurcio (author of 'Vermeer's Riddle Revealed' Aeternium Publishing, April, 2002, ISBN 0917358139) for permitting me to incorporate his concepts of Grail Geometry and The Tilted Square into my manuscript; Dr. Timothy W. Foresman, President of Earth 911 (formerly of NASA, US EPA and UNEP), for his esteemed contribution to this book; Donald E. Ingber, M.D., Ph.D. for allowing me to cite his name and work; Kabal Barak Negby for his spiritual guidance and for affording me his story, 'River Pebbles' as inspiration for Assaf Goren's tale; my new friends and professional colleagues at Pendium for all they have done to turn my raw manuscript into a polished work of which I am proud; Jo Levitt, my sister and most dedicated reader, without whose critical input, patience and constant belief in me this book would never have seen the light of day; the members of my writers' circle and the Webhaven creative writing forum; my husband, Ze'ev, for understanding the road and never complaining about the bumps along the way.

Foreword

Science fact has frequently overshadowed science fiction. For example, Jules Verne and subsequent fiction writers predicted the arrival of humans on the surface of the moon. However, no writer foresaw that millions of people would watch the Apollo moon landing on television from the privacy of their living rooms. Notwithstanding this historical anecdote, science fiction and novel writers have provided a key factor to the human condition that science and scientists often ignore: Passion. Author, Deborah Gelbard, provides this unique, human attribute in her engaging exploration of a world where realism is interwoven with the dreams, designs and beliefs of the creators of the Global Dawn project.

Central to this delightful novel is the Digital Earth idea as first articulated by former Vice President Al Gore, in 1998. The Digital Earth is a visionary technical collaboration concept for development of a virtual, spatially referenced Earth model linked to the planet's entire digital archive of scientific, natural and cultural information. Al Gore foresaw a future in which a young girl would stand before a "virtual three-dimensional Earth" and gain instant access to all the knowledge of history, art, science, music and entertainment contained in the world's libraries. His vision inspired the U.S. Government's Digital Earth program, which I had the honor to lead at the National Aeronautics and Space Administration (NASA) Headquarters. The idea has continued to evolve on a national and a global scale with the formation of Digital Earth activist groups in the US, Canada, New Zealand, Europe and the Far East.

I recall one of the more memorable approaches I received while I was at NASA. An enterprising group contacted me about their ambition to build a regional information network that would grow to serve all of humanity. This group was from Israel. I fondly remember reflecting upon what a wonderful thing it was that in a land torn by

political and religious tensions there existed a group of visionaries fired
by the Digital Earth ideal – a group dedicated to making the world a
better place for our collective futures. Gelbard's prose has revived those
memories.

In the guise of Global Dawn, Gelbard captures the hitherto
unwritten passion of the Digital Earth community – a passion more
often dismissed or denied by the sober and staid scientists and business
leaders involved with unfolding our future. Through the creativity and
unresolved inner-child issues of Reuven, her protagonist, Gelbard
cleverly connects us with the wonder and awe of Global Dawn (alias
Digital Earth), captured in the souls of adults and reflected in the
glowing faces of children. She accurately credits Buckminster Fuller with
the Spaceship Earth metaphor that directly links an important heritage
component to the evolutionary path of the Digital Earth. She also cites
the majestic geodesic dome at Disney's Epcot in Florida as another
reference to Fuller's influence, attesting to the glorious and useful
discoveries awaiting those who are closely attuned to the laws of nature.
Her insightful use of the natural design secrets of the universe in the
structuring of Global Dawn is in harmony with contemporary thought
among those who contemplate a sustainable future for humanity.

Gelbard's portrayal of Reuven's emotional roller coaster and the
dynamic tensions among Global Dawn's Inner Circle generates an
interesting cast of characters. At many points in this visionary and
spiritual adventure, I had the eerie sensation that Gelbard had somehow
taken note of my own experiences with Digital Earth in tethering the
loose strings of an international confederation. By developing Global
Dawn on the foundation of the Digital Earth, Gelbard has achieved an
innovative concept in her novel. She weaves science, art, mysticism and
spiritual growth into an enticing drama that combines the joy and the
angst of embracing a common destiny for humankind amid grim,
present-day realities. Hopefully, this novel will inspire cadres of
thoughtful people, when looking towards the future, to say, "Why not?"
and "Why not now?"

Dr. Timothy W. Foresman, Digital Earth
pioneer and founding member of the
International Society for Digital Earth.

GLOBAL
DAWN

Chapter 1

*"Those who dream by night in the dusty recesses of their minds wake in
the day to find that all was vanity; but the dreamers of the day are dangerous
men, for they may act their dream with open eyes, and make it possible."*
T. E. Lawrence (Lawrence of Arabia)

In his study corner off the terrace, Reuven leaned back, clenched his
fists and stretched. The air was sultry. He furrowed a mass of tousled
hair away from his face and twisted a pen between his lips. He
picked up his desk diary and pulled on the satin marker. August 3rd,
1999. "Just a week till the memorial meeting," he thought.

Yoni's death had reconnected him with Jeanine for the first time
since college. She was well into her forties, now, and still without a
partner in life. Her passions were private, long liaisons not her style. She
even kept the identity of Yoni's father under wraps. Reuven wondered if
her continued celibacy was a matter of choice or whether her arrogance
kept suitors at bay.

Yoni was killed in a mortar attack near the Lebanese border
alongside two other young Israeli soldiers. He had a formal, military
funeral. Reuven recalled Jeanine's disturbing beauty at the graveside
with her ginger hair swept high above her sombre mourning clothes. An
unknown figure stood beside her, head inclined. Reuven observed the
intimate moment when she pressed a comforting hand into his palm.

Now, Reuven smoothed the pages of his diary and wrote,

"A year ago, Yoni's soul was reborn into the universal spiral of
life. We should be celebrating, not crying."

He put the pen down again. To most people, he realised, the
uncertain hope of progression of the soul beyond death was scant
consolation for the loss of a loved one. They needed the ritual of grief.

He would be expected to attend the meeting. It was a matter of loyalty.

Excited barking and clatter in the hallway interrupted his reverie. A teenage girl tore into the living room, a golden retriever at her heels.

She skidded across the polished tiles onto the terrace, flung both arms around his neck and laughed,

"Hey, where were you, just now?"

"Easy, easy, Shahar, you're strangling me," he protested happily. He looked down proudly at his daughter and fondled her braids. Her thickset eyebrows added a touch of gravity to her lively dark eyes and full-lipped smile, and there was a confident air about her that hinted at emerging womanhood.

They had named her Shahar, Tamar and he. It was the Hebrew word for 'dawn', and so she had been since her birth – the dawning light of his soul.

"So, you're back from the training course?"

"Yes. You should've seen Muki, Abba. He's great! He learns quicker than any of the others."

Shahar relaxed her hold on the dog, and he bounded into the garden almost knocking Tamar over as she came up the path.

"Shahar. Thank God you're back safe and sound, dear," she said with relief.

The tension in her smile did not escape her daughter.

"You weren't really worried were you, Ima?"

"I can't help it. You know that road from the kibbutz isn't safe. It's always deserted, and people have been attacked around there ..."

"Oh, Ima, you fuss so much!" said Shahar, dismissing her mother's smothering with a carefree wave of her hand.

"Anyway, Muki was with me."

"And I suppose some magic charm was protecting you, too!"

"Exactly!" laughed Reuven, truly convinced she had the untouchable aura of an angel.

"Well, go and clean up, now. I want a word with Abba," said Tamar.

Shahar disappeared into her bedroom at the back of the house leaving her parents alone on the terrace.

"Reuven ..." Tamar began, "do you really have to go to that memorial meeting next week?"

"Yes," he answered warily.

"Do I have to come, too?" she asked, wrinkling her nose in distaste at the idea.

He looked at her diminished figure, casually clothed with little regard to fashion; her fair, manufactured curls framing a once pretty face.

"You don't need to drag yourself there. I'm only going for Jeanine's sake."

She seemed content with this answer. He sat a while longer watching her go about her household chores. Tamar had scarcely known Jeanine, after all. For him, it was different. The prospect of seeing her again revived poignant memories. She understood his life's mission and recognized the singular burden it placed on him. She also knew about his collapse ...

It was during that dark period of his life that he first met Tamar. She came to his rescue like an 'angel of mercy', and so the story of their love began. The setting up of their home together marked a fresh page in his life. In the years that followed, the miracle of Shahar's birth sealed their joy. All that was twenty years ago and, as time passed, Tamar's love began to mellow into servile devotion, her fire crushed by mundane reality. She was entirely unaware of the throne to which destiny had appointed her.

In recent months, Reuven felt a renewed sense of urgency. His inner voice told him that a revelation of his mission was imminent. According to his word, a small group of followers would begin to construct a magnificent project for the benefit of future generations. A second entry in his diary read as follows,

"I carry a lonely burden not of my choosing. The present-day custodians of the Holy Grail* have open wounds in their hearts; they have no knowledge of their allotted roles in the cosmic scheme of things."

Reuven's starry night awaited the white blossom that would succeed the thorns.

Explanatory note:
* The legendary Holy Grail was believed, in Christian tradition, to be kept in a mysterious castle surrounded by a wasteland and guarded by a custodian who suffered from a wound that would not heal. His cure and the renewal of the blighted lands depended upon the successful recovery of the Grail.

The following morning, Reuven set out at 6 a.m. for a typical day's work in the field. Some forty kilometres south of Tel-Aviv towards Ashkelon, he manoeuvred the red Mini to a halt. He stepped out of the car, rummaged in the back to retrieve his surveying instruments and a map, and then walked briskly across the road. Rising to its mid-morning height, the sun caught the upward tilt of his wide oval face and the outline of his broad shoulders, slightly hunched over a generous physique. He cut a commanding figure, even dressed as he was in scruffy work clothes – crudely cut denim shorts, ragged T-shirt and boyish cotton socks tucked into the tops of field-worn sneakers.

As he climbed across a scanty verge, he noted angles and distances, and cross-checked them against indications on his map. He skirted a planted cotton field where the saline irrigation water had left a whitish residue on the sandy topsoil and a rank saltiness lingered in the air. Verifying existing measurements and calculating new ones, he moved ahead. The results of each of his surveys had to be entered with meticulous care into a computerised geographic information system or GIS. In it, each area's defining features and boundaries, natural and man-made, were precisely referenced.

While striving for objective accuracy in his work, its political significance did not elude him. Struggles over land ownership were at the root of so many of the world's wars, not least in the little country of Israel. He approached his work with a conviction of individual purpose. Master of borders and boundaries, he had the freedom to mark new territory and to re-divide the land according to his judgment. His chosen lines became accepted facts in the street and in the courtroom. He believed himself to be a designated agent of change.

*   *   *

As he had expected, the memorial meeting was a solemn affair. Near the entrance to the kibbutz was an exhibit of photographs and mementos – a tribute to the boys who died. Guests were queuing to express their condolences to the bereaved. Reuven took his place in line, watching Jeanine as she courteously received and thanked each one. Now it was his turn, and looking into her eyes, he saw the courageous spirit he had hoped to find there.

"Nice of you to come all this way, Reuven," she said, pressing his hand softly between both of hers.

"Yoni was your blessing in the years that were given to you together, Jeanine," he answered with the formality that was typical of him in such circumstances.

She lowered her eyes, breathed deeply for a moment, and still holding his hand, she lifted her face towards him.

"I thank God for that," she answered. "I believe Yoni's passing was written in the Master Plan. Remember how we used to talk about the Master Plan, long ago?"

"Of course I remember," he answered softly.

Then, he gently kissed her hand, wished her well, and moved along. He followed the stream of guests to the memorial wall and for a brief moment he thought he noticed a familiar face on the far side. But what on earth could have brought Ora Porath to this event?

Before he had a chance to find out, he heard someone calling his name.

"*Pardon*, please."

He returned a puzzled look towards a comely olive-skinned woman whose large grey-green eyes sought his. She wore a soft, black wrap edged with traditional Moroccan embroidery that afforded her an allure of gently shrouded femininity.

"I saw you speaking with Jeanine, just now," she hastened to explain. "She told me you know 'er, hmm, many years."

Her speech had a lightly accented quality – the occasional dropped 'h' and guttural 'r'. Then, clutching her hands melodramatically to her heart, she added,

"It's a terrible, terrible *tragédie*, isn't it?"

"Yes," Reuven answered distractedly. "I'm sorry, I didn't catch your name?"

"Oh yes, of course. I'm Shira Argov."

Reuven shook her hand.

"Reuven, Reuven Sofer. Glad to meet you, Shira," he said, courteously hiding his irritation at having lost track of Ora in the crowd.

Suddenly, he spotted her again and, hastily excused himself before making off in her direction.

"Hey, surprised to see you here!" he exclaimed breathlessly as he caught up with her.

"Yup. Sad business, isn't it? Brings home what a fragile existence we lead."

She was of average height, but Reuven dwarfed her. There was a classic correctness about her well-fitting trousers and coordinated cotton top.

She was flushed as she spoke to him. He heard she had married
...

"Did you come with your family?" he asked discreetly.

"Nope. Left Gadi at home with the kids. It's my side of the

family and distant, at that."

"So, you're here because of Yoni?"

"Yoni? Oh, no. One of the other soldiers – son of an English couple. It's a remote connection on my father's side. You know, they haven't got much family in Israel, and I thought I ought to come."

Reuven smiled to himself as she spoke. This was the Ora he remembered, imbued with an estimable social conscience.

"And you? Yoni? Was he family?" she asked.

"No. His mother's an old friend of mine."

"Have you spoken to her?"

"Only very briefly."

"How's she holding up?"

"It's hard to know how she's really feeling. She's putting on such a strong public front."

"There's something terribly impersonal about this meeting, don't you think?"

"Yes, well, I really came out of a sense of duty," said Reuven not choosing to comment further on the complexity of his decision to attend.

They browsed the exhibit for ten minutes or so. It was a sentimental display that wooed the pain of the bereaved. Three bright faces; three lives cut short in their prime – Yoni, just nineteen, handsome and ambitious; his two friends, equally passionate, talented and young. Little recognition of the ongoing spirit of the fallen, thought Reuven and, turning away from the grim wall of death, he said to Ora,

"I need some air. How would you like to ride out to the coast with me for a while?"

She seemed relieved to be able to escape the oppressive atmosphere. So, they slipped away from the kibbutz in the direction of Achziv.

She exuded a charming radiance and there was a coy femininity about her. Her chestnut hair fell in loose waves just short of her shoulders, and a warm glow flattered her cheeks in the afternoon breeze. He slid a glance at her pleasantly proportioned physique, taking in its understated sensuality accentuated by the gentle curve of her stomach, her girlish breasts and teasingly prominent nipples. The variegated tones of her hazel eyes reflected her essential ambiguity. None of it escaped him.

They left the car at the edge of the narrow strip of beach and walked out onto the sand. There was an aromatic sweetness to the air.

The surf curled forward above gentle waves in a postcard blue sea. They stood side by side where the water licked the sand.

*   *   *

Ora felt Reuven's eyes assessing her, and the straight-laced woman in her struggled to suppress her wanton side already under his spell. They grew up in the same community back in England, went to the same schools, ate the same *heimishe* Jewish food and absorbed similar ethics. A few years his junior, she was not one of his peer group, but they shared, you might say, a common idiom. She played with a few strands of hair, twisting them between finger and thumb then flicking them nervously away from her face.

"So, tell me more about Jeanine."

"Oh, we were college buddies, you know. I felt pretty close to her at one time, but our lives have rolled along different tracks since then. Actually, she foresaw quite accurately the way things are turning out for each of us right now."

Ora laughed,

"Is she some kind of a seer, then?"

"Maybe so. She has insight."

Ora felt the blood rise to her cheeks, embarrassed by her glib dismissal of something he obviously treated seriously.

"What kind of thing did she predict, then?"

"She told me of the turmoil ahead, of the obstacles in my way and of the roles those close to me would eventually assume."

"What kind of roles do you mean? Professional, personal?" she asked, a little intimidated by his bombastic manner.

"Both. She sensed they would evolve to some preordained stature."

Dissatisfied with this enigmatic answer, Ora persisted in her questioning.

"How did she claim to come by such knowledge?"

"She drew my astrological chart. It was the one and only time I ever indulged in astrology."

"And you're really into all that?"

She was beginning to feel ill at ease.

"Astrology's a fascinating subject," he replied. "Especially its assumptions about the way universal patterns and forces affect our lives," he said, hastening to add that he did not necessarily accept all the conclusions of the astrologers. She shifted her weight nervously from foot to foot.

"Oh? You don't?"

"How can I trust theories rooted in the wrong calendar?"

The way in which he laid his ideas on her seemed somehow

calculated to test her, Ora thought. This time, however, he volunteered an explanation.

"I live by the Jewish calendar. It's lunar-based, and I think it's much closer to the real truth."

"Maybe so," she pressed stubbornly, "but you still let Jeanine prepare a chart for you, and how do you explain the impact her conclusions had on you?"

He was smiling now, delighting in her animated persistence.

"Ora, there are those who find truths in coffee grains or read them in the palm of your hand. The medium's not important; it's the message itself. Jeanine showed me who I am to become and what's required of me. No one before or since has clarified my path as she did. That's why I hold her in such high esteem."

Again, Ora wondered at his references to messages and paths.

His wide brow tensed as his gaze fixed on the water. He crouched down and picked up a sharp-edged piece of flint from among the strewn debris along the tide line. He began to draw shapes in the sand with it – a triangle with concentric circles around it, framed first with a pentagon, then with a square. There was nothing casual about the precision with which he worked. He offered no explanation; however, for the strangeness of his act and left Ora to look on perplexed. Here and there, he scratched a name in the space between the circles – Shahar, Tamar, Michaela ... Nathan, Rikki ... He stopped and looked up at her.

"Does this have something to do with the roles you talked about before, Reuven?" she asked.

He smiled without answering, then stood up, and walked back from his sand drawing as if to admire it from a distance. There was an undeniable mystique about the man. Turning, he beckoned and curiosity carried her captive in his wake.

They walked some way along the beach line that extended northward beyond Rosh Hanikra all the way into Lebanon. She followed in his determined stride over rock pools and scrub. In a courtyard to their right, in the shade of a low stone wall, a boy was kicking a ball. Reuven called to him.

"*Shu ismek?*" – "What's your name?"

Straight away, the answer came back,

"*Ismi Ahmed*".

The boy's ageless Arab guardian offered them a pitcher of water and gestured towards a shaded bench onto which Reuven slung his blue canvas shoulder bag. They sat down and, as they drank together, Ahmed danced circles around Reuven. The ease of his connection with the boy fascinated Ora. It was as though all his worldly cares were erased by the young lad's lively and unconditional laughter. He picked up the ball and tossed it light-heartedly back to Ahmed. She felt glad she had agreed to accompany him.

Ten minutes later, they returned the water pitcher and began to walk back along the beach. From the bar terrace above them wafted the sound of the Army Radio playing the popular song, 'Ah, God is Good'. Reuven eagerly scaled the stone steps winding up to the terrace where he began to dance in private communion with the music. Ora hesitated briefly before joining him.

It was late afternoon when they sat down to eat. Served on a large ceramic platter were tabbouleh and labane sprinkled with mountain thyme, pita bread hot from the wood-fired oven, small local olives and mugs of *limonana* – a cool drink of lemon and fresh spearmint.

"Hmm. This all looks delicious," delighted Ora, "I love the smell of the fresh pita! Now tell me more about Jeanine's insights. Who are the people close to you and what roles are they destined to play? What did she really mean about your path and its obstacles?"

As if by way of reply, he reached into his bag and took out a folded chart. Ora wrinkled her nose at its mustiness as he spread it out over the table. It was a family tree. Fascinated, she watched him earnestly tracing and retracing in it the landmarks of his lineage. He pointed to three names in the centre and said,

"Three women hold the keys to my destiny. In each of them is vested the power of redemption, Shahar, my daughter and dawning light of my soul; Michaela, my sister, protector of my spirit and giver of God's strength; Tamar, my wife, born of the house of Ruth, our revered matriarch by whose leap of faith the Earth's Redeemer is to descend."

The reverence with which he spoke of these women, connected to him by the intimacies of marriage and birth, struck a strangely prophetic note. Ora poured hungrily over the chart, seeking some explanation of Reuven's grandiose statements. The most obvious pointers were the numerous nameless spaces, particularly in the generation of his grandparents. Her suspicions as to the reason for these were quickly confirmed.

"My mother and father were separated from their parents as young children and despatched from Austria to England by Kindertransport to escape the Nazis at the onset of World War II. We can only presume all those unnamed siblings, cousins, uncles and aunts subsequently fell as victims of the Holocaust. They were, at any rate, never heard of again."

His pompous manner did not intimidate her. It was clearly an emotional shield. He described the damaging effect his mother's early life trauma had upon her relationship with him. As Ora listened to the acrimony with which he spoke of his alienation from his mother, she realised how totally different her own childhood had been from his. A welling sadness filled the pit of her stomach.

"I'm sure, deep down, your mother cared for you," she insisted.

"I felt her only as an obsessive domination of my life and denial of the essence of my being."

"And your father?" she asked.

"Oh, we used to be quite close, but he's old and frail now, and there's no real dialogue between us any more."

As he spoke, his face muscles convulsed with the pain of his admission. His eyes glazed over half-crazed as he began to stab the charted ancestral line frenetically with his index finger.

"My soul cries out to them in their blindness!" came the strangulated cry of the orphan child.

Then, suddenly aware of Ora's perplexity, he exclaimed,

"Look at the direct line of their descent from the House of David and the stock of Moses!"

Wounded child of a wounded mother, he sought justification of his present purpose in the shrouded heritage of his past. Ora was determined to find a better explanation of his obsessive drive. She scanned the Sofer family tree again. Reuven, meanwhile, goaded her curiosity even more by expounding on the significance of names.

"You asked about the roles of those close to me. You'll find all your answers in names. Look at our own, for example— By mine I'm connected in spirit with the firstborn of Jacob, patriarch of Israel. Ora, you're a woman of light in Hebrew, and in Latin you're the seashore. In this place of our meeting, our names unite us with our history and our land."

"And what about the future, Reuven?"

"To know the land is my calling. Daily, I plot dimensions and survey frontiers. My vision exceeds the reach of the common eye. I see the merging of earth and sky with the pan-architecture of the cosmos."

He looked up at her and focused on her gaze.

"All the sources known to us predict our chaotic times as an inevitable phase in the cycle of cosmic change."

"And the Holocaust? – Just a discordant phase?"

"Yes, even that," he said adding, with an almost devilish smile, "I **know** what will be, Ora." Then, lowering his voice to a near whisper, "You'll understand in time, but first I must tell you about my dream."

He paused and drew several audible breaths before the nakedness of the moment.

"You can tell me, Reuven. I'm listening. Go on," she urged, trembling as his intensity drove into her consciousness.

"I want to bring planetary awareness into the lives of people all over the world," he declared. "My vision involves the building of a huge project. It will be a live information network aligned with universal patterns. It will give people a total 'hands-on' experience of Planet Earth as never before. Ultimately, it will be their vehicle into new dimensions of existence."

"Sounds like the challenge of a lifetime," Ora gently replied.

In the same instant, the sunlight illuminated the half-buried edifices and signs of former travellers in the Galilee sands.

Flattered by Reuven's unexpected readiness to confide in her, Ora wanted to respond supportively. Instead, she found herself struggling to make sense of a tantalizing puzzle.

"How did the idea come to you?"

"By my working so closely with the land, I guess."

"But you seem to be driven so obsessively."

"Ah, Ora. You're looking for too many answers too fast," he replied, evasively. Then added, "The idea was locked in my belly for years until you ..."

Aghast, she looked straight up at him.

"You surely don't mean I'm the first person you've told any of this to?"

He smiled at her affectionately and nodded. Again she sensed a little boy's craving for love behind the resolute façade.

"But what about Jeanine?" she asked.

"Jeanine has an instinctive understanding of many things. Her knowledge of my mission is on a different level entirely. You see, she senses my spiritual connection with our planet and its destiny. She shares my belief that human consciousness will eventually transcend space and time. The project I'm going to build will serve as a stepping-stone. My dream is an indivisible part of the time-old Master Plan. We're all of us pawns in a much larger game, Ora."

"You make us sound like puppets."

"We're not controlled as puppets are. We have choices."

"Still, we're just players in a plot that's precast?"

"No, it's not like that. Every choice we make affects the basic fabric of the planet."

"That certainly sounds like a recipe for chaos!"

"Planet Earth is tremendously resilient. As long as our actions are in harmony with the Master Plan, it can maintain its natural balance."

"And all the violence and poverty we see around us is what happens when we're out of sync with the Master Plan? Is that your theory?"

"That's what Jeanine taught me."

"So, she doesn't know anything about your idea for global networking?"

"Global networking?"

"Isn't that what you're really talking about? A way of empowering people's choices with global knowledge?"

"I guess that's not a bad way of putting it," said Reuven with a look of sudden amusement.

"And the names?" asked Ora. "The ones you etched in the sand ..."

"Family, friends, co-project workers – a nucleus that's already starting to come together."

"So, tell me. Where are you thinking of building your project?"

"On the highest ground overlooking Jerusalem."

"Mmm. Jerusalem," she repeated. "I see."

*   *   *

"One sits down on a desert sand dune, sees nothing, hears nothing. Yet through the silence something throbs and gleams." "I was astonished by a sudden understanding of that mysterious radiation of the sands."
                                        A. de St. Exupery.

On the early evening horizon, a couple of pelicans veered gracefully from their southerly path into the sundown sea. As the darkness clothed their meeting, Reuven and Ora did not think of moving from their resting-place. Now he was recounting his days, some twenty-three years before, as an army reservist in the Negev desert.

She was so entranced that she no longer distinguished between the stroking of her right cheek by the soft evening breeze and the tender touch of his finger on her left.

The particular desert night of his recall was a chill one in late November. The high-risen moon had thrown its elongated shadow across the granite hollow ahead of the camp. The interlocking limbs of the foothills beneath the ridge were almost obliterated against an ashen sky. In this place, cradled by the raw elements of the Earth, Reuven stood silent guard.

Another joined the watch and Reuven, though aware of his proximity, maintained a meditative stance. After some immeasurable time, the other turned towards him. Softly as a rustle on the wind, he simply said ...

"It's **You**"...

There was no further exchange between the two, Reuven's companion departed without revealing his identity.

In the profound silence that followed, Reuven experienced the radiant expansion of his spirit vibrating in unity with the land and echoing patriarchal visions in just such a desert place. He understood that his had been no commonplace messenger.

A gerbil scampered under the loose tent flap and, from beneath their dry acacia refuge, a pair of ibex darted into the obscurity of the desert trail.

A shooting star fell eastward.

*   *   *

During the short drive back to the kibbutz that evening Reuven said very little to Ora. He had an unusual feeling of calm by her side. When they reached the kibbutz, she left him to rejoin her family group before returning to Tel-Aviv. He wove his way through the marquee where fragmented groups of mourners were still gathered. He saw Jeanine sitting quietly on a bench by the brailed tent flap on the far side. Her head was cupped in her right hand. As he came near she looked up, but seemed to stare blankly through him. He sat down next to her.

"So, you came back," she said vacantly.

"I couldn't talk to you before with all the fuss and ceremony."

"I know."

"How do you feel?"

"Life goes on, and Yoni will always be with me."

"Do you want to talk about him?"

She moved her hand from under her chin and laid it gently over his for a moment.

"You're a kind man, Reuven, but no, I really have no more need for words about Yoni'."

Her manner troubled him. He had never seen her so introspective. Had she broken down in a public drama, he would have coped with it better than this magnificent self-control that preserved her emotional distance from him.

"Where are you living nowadays?" he asked rather stiffly.

"Oh, in a little town near Beersheva."

"Do you have a full tour-guiding schedule?"

"Actually, I'm not guiding much any more. I'm writing a thesis and doing a bit of lecturing, as well."

"So you're back on our old familiar territory, then?"

"Yes, I'm back at Ben Gurion. Feels good."

He looked up and was relieved to catch a fleeting glimmer of her old dynamism. She smiled.

"Give me your hand again, Reuven."

He laid his hand over hers.

"No, let me see your palm, will you?"

He breathed deeply in anticipation as she examined his upturned palm.

"What can you see there, Jeanine?"

"There are two dark clouds over your mission; one hangs over Jerusalem – it will be dispersed when the time is right; the other is masking your soul – the only way to remove it is by faith, balance and clarity in everything you do."

He did not question her reading. He trusted her instincts implicitly.

He found his allotted space in a volunteer's hut, and spread out his sleeping bag on the bed – a simple steel frame and board with a thin foam mattress. The atmosphere was stuffy. There were gaping holes in the mosquito nets at the windows and the walls were insect-ridden. However, the spartan environment and the mosquitoes were not the reasons for his restlessness that night. He turned Jeanine's comments over repeatedly in his mind – her poignant allusions to his personal life and to the future of Jerusalem. He had felt elated by the sharing of his dream with Ora earlier that day. Her readiness to accept his ideas was evidence, he thought, that the timing was right, and he had even begun to visualise setting the whole idea in motion. But, now he was nervous. The blockages of which Jeanine had spoken were very real. Something was holding him back – a subconscious fear of turning his dream into reality, perhaps? And what did Jeanine mean by balance and clarity? By the time he finally fell asleep, the raucous crickets were announcing a new day.

It was still early when, kit bag in hand, he went looking for Jeanine to say goodbye. He found her in the exact same spot where she had been sitting the night before, Had she slept at all? He held her gaze as he stooped down to softly take her face in his two hands and kiss her gently on the cheek. They were startled by the sound of footsteps nearby. It was Shira coming down the path that skirted the lawn. A little dog was scampering after her, yapping at her heels, but she hardly seemed to notice it. When she reached them, Jeanine formally introduced Shira as her close friend and teaching companion at the university. There was a frailty about her and a childlike earnestness about those exceptionally green eyes, tinged with grey.

"I'm sorry I left you so abruptly yesterday."

"You should not apologise," came her reply with a charming emphasis on an over-soft 'g'.

She knelt down to embrace Jeanine. Reuven watched as she tenderly soothed the aching spirit of her friend and, at last, the long-withheld tears flowed freely down Jeanine's cheeks.

"Come, Jeanine. We should go home now."

*   *   *

On the direct Nahariya – Tel-Aviv line, the journey time was about two hours. Travelling south on the coastal route, the early stretches closely followed the edge of the sea. Strange the juxtaposition of this steely sleek locomotive with the pre-State tracks it pounded at high speed. Some multi-national planners hoped for a modern Orient Express to revive the old through-connection from Egypt to Damascus and even to extend it to Europe. Others proposed a route, which would run east/west from Haifa to the Persian Gulf. Pre-supposing peace, it was claimed this line would carry Israelis to Tehran in twenty-four hours. Ora questioned whether peace had necessarily to precede borderless travel. Perhaps the contrary was true?

She spent the journey trying to logically process the varied memories and images of the previous day. At Bat Galim, she hardly noticed the boarding passengers, oblivious of their baggage, noise and turmoil. Her mind was in its own private spin.

Her impressions of Reuven swam against contrary tides in her head. His familiar image had transformed overnight into one of prophet and dreamer. He had challenged her intellect with bewildering new possibilities and had aroused desires in her, both physical and spiritual, that she was quite terrified to acknowledge. Her every instinct told her that in his vision lay untold secrets. As he spoke of it, his brown eyes seemed to take on a haziness that rippled deep as a cosmic ocean. His talk of alignment with universal energies sent her mind reeling into the realms of patterns, plans and signs that New Age marketeers pushed cheaply on the spirit-thirsty of our techno-era. She squinted at the

evasive auras of her travel companions and wondered if the true
distances between people could ever be mapped or quantified?

I need to find out more about Reuven's sources, she thought.
Who first recorded land boundaries? Where and by whom were the first
maps created?

She gave in to her fatigue and her forehead was nodding against
the carriage window as the train entered the small station at Binyamina.

*   *   *

Reuven was on the point of leaving Western Galilee when he
got a call from Tamar about a small surveying project that would detain
him a few days longer. He phoned into the contractor's office to confirm
it and set about planning a route.

His work led him down rarely trodden trails. Every cornerstone
of every site left its imprint in the phenomenal archive that was his
memory. Each new point precisely recorded; each old one checked
before being entered into the computer. The professional equipment he
carried was rudimentary and his energy indefatigable.

Along the way, he was welcomed into homes in the Muslim,
Jewish, Druze and Christian towns and villages he was contracted to
survey. His encounters were often colourful. He heard regional legends
of simple folk living off the fruits of the orchards and the hills, stories of
ghosts in vacated homes and land, and sentimental poems thinly veiling
nationalistic themes. Superstition and taboos were woven into the fibre
of life. Doors were painted heavenly blue, and magical *chamsah* hands
were worn or hung to avert the evil eye. As their guest, Reuven passed
no judgement on the people's beliefs. He went his way offering a
sympathetic ear and a helping hand. An old Arab woman taught him to
heal a sick child by rolling salt in paper, stabbing the paper roll and
burning it to keep evil spirits at bay. In a village close to Nazareth, he
was treated as a divine messenger because of the extraordinary wisdom
and kindness he showed them.

The quietly independent spirit of a Yemenite Jewess captured his
heart in unexpected ways. Her grey stone cottage was set deep in the
pine-forested hillside. A canopy of fruit-laden vines sheltered its southern
façade. There in the shade, she sat on a high wooden stool and stepped
with a slow, measured rhythm on the treadle of her potter's wheel. A
vessel of singular beauty and simplicity was emerging under her slender
clay-caressing hand. Through the natural trellis, a soft, gold pattern of
dusky sunlight was dancing onto the upward spiralling contours of the
reddish-brown clay.

Reuven stood in awe of womankind in whose womb was cradled the continuity of the planet. In women's arms he sought a Madonna to heal the scars of his childhood. He believed in the divine spirit of women as symbolised in antiquity by Gaia, the Earth Mother and in kabbalistic sources by Shechina. Intimate connoisseur of the feminine soul, its frequent sublimation angered him. The object of many women's love, he refused their pedestals and opposed their obsessive adorations.

The woman beckoned to him and introduced herself as Levana.

"What a wonderfully feminine name," he commented as he watched an open smile light her face.

"Well, thank you."

"And yours is?"

"Reuven," he answered, and the name drifted softly towards her on the balmy summer air. She eased the warm clay off the wheel and went to rinse her fingers under a rusted outdoor tap.

"Come on in," she said. "There's some sweet tea in the urn."

He followed her inside.

"So, how did you get your name, Levana?"

"I was born at the time of *kiddush levana* (the blessing of the new moon)."

"In which month?"

"*Nissan* –I'm a child of the spring."

"That, Levana, is as clear as moonshine!"

She flashed another warm smile at her guest. While they were thus engaged in trivial conversation, there was unspoken communication between them on a parallel plane.

The cottage had its own magic, impregnated with the textures, colours and aromas of Levana's art. As she bathed his senses in oils and incense, opening, clarifying and healing his spirit, the presence of this moon woman overpowered Reuven. Their lovemaking was free of questions and history. Intoxicated, he let out a primal cry. They showered, drank a little dark wine, then he slipped back out into the shadows of the late summer night.

As he lay under the stars, he thought of the White Moon Festival when pagans cleansed their spirits under the rising moon. Then he dreamed of the White Moon Goddess, symbol of rebirth, and of Isis, magical goddess of the moon.

Chapter 2

"And you, son of man, take a brick and lay it before you, and trace upon it a city, Jerusalem." Ezekiel 4:1

Ora slammed her bag down on the tiles outside the door of her apartment, opened the door, and announced her return.

"Hey kids! Miss me?"

Omer and Shai sat eyes glued to a video game and all she got in return were a couple of grunts of acknowledgment.

"Hi. Nobody missed you," confirmed Gadi smiling facetiously. Then he gave her a quick, reassuring kiss. He had never been one for great shows of affection, but he was a good, honest guy and a devoted father.

"You'll never guess who I ran into at the memorial meeting."

"I don't need to guess because you're about to tell me, aren't you?"

She humpfed and turned to pick up her bag, but he stopped her.

"Nu? So who did you meet?"

"Are you sure you're interested?"

"Yes. Come on."

"Reuven."

"Sofer?" asked Gadi relapsing into a tone of bored indifference.

"Yup. One and the same."

"What's his connection with your family?"

"None. He was there as a friend of one of the other families."

"Oh."

"Gadi, you're not listening!"

He had the infuriating habit of paying lip service to a conversation.

"I am, I am," he said. "So how was it? I don't suppose you had much chance to speak to him, did you?"

"Well, yes, actually we kind of gravitated towards each other in that oppressive atmosphere."

"Hmm. I can imagine. Hope he behaved himself."

Ora laughed.

"Don't worry. We didn't cross any lines. But listen, he got kind of weird on me."

"Doesn't surprise me. In character, isn't it?"

"That's not a very nice thing to say," shrugged Ora indignantly. "What I meant was that he got rather emotional. He seemed desperate for a sympathetic ear."

Gadi seemed to half tune out again, but she continued, "Did you know he's a second generation Holocaust survivor, just like you?"

"Not exactly," countered Gadi dryly. "As far as I know, his parents got out before the real horrors began."

"Mmm. That may be, but he still has a very problematic relationship with his parents. He attributes it to everything they went through."

"I don't doubt that. After all, his parents lost most of their family. Still, he doesn't have to live with the repercussions every day as I do."

Since Gadi's arrival in Israel from Poland together with his newly widowed mother, he had devoted unending energies to caring for her. In Gadi's book, it was a matter of filial duty.

She cut the conversation short and went into the bedroom, pulling the door to. It would be a waste of time for her to tell Gadi about Reuven's project. He would only scoff and say it was 'over the edge'. Instead, she called her cousin, Michael.

Michael was in his mid-thirties and newly married. Although temporarily out of work, he had ambitious career plans and a generally optimistic attitude towards life.

"Hallo, gorgeous. I was wondering when I'd be hearing from you."

"It's good to hear your voice, too, but when you've finished telling me about your undying passion for me, I want to talk to you."

"Please don't mock my affliction. You know I really miss you."

"Anything you say, Michael. Now will you listen, please?"

"OK, sweetheart. You have my undivided attention."

"You know I went to the memorial meeting for the soldiers who were killed in the Lebanese border incident last year?"

"Oh, right. Say, I bet you ran into Reuven there, didn't you?"

Michael knew Reuven well. In his undergraduate days, he was Reuven's bright and enthusiastic protégé in GIS fieldwork. Reuven appreciated Michael's quick grasp of the job, and, through their work together, a special relationship grew up between them.

"How did you know I met Reuven there?" she shouted in amazement.

"I didn't. I knew he was planning to attend. That's all."

"Anyway, we started to talk, and he told me some pretty heavy stuff about his personal life."

"About that mission of his, you mean?"

Her jaw dropped open

"But, he said no one else knew!"

"Well, I know he has a wild idea to build some kind of global project, but he's never really told me any details. Anyway, I take those kind of Reuvenisms with a pinch of salt."

She felt let down. She had hoped to find a more receptive ear in Michael than in Gadi. Although she realised Reuven's ideas sounded bizarre, she felt they were moving and challenging. They awakened a sense of purpose in her that had been lacking since her teenage days.

"He's very convincing, you know," she stubbornly persisted, "and he's got a way of encouraging me to probe into really interesting questions."

"Like?"

"Well, for example, he's got me delving into cartographic history and its connection with Jerusalem, as well as all sorts of other stuff about the future and how each of us has a role in shaping it."

"Sounds as if he's really fired you up."

Ora blushed, and she was glad the colour of her complexion was not visible over the phone. She wished Michael goodnight, hung up and continued to lounge on the bed for a while, trying to set reason above emotion in the order of her thoughts.

                    *   *   *

In the days that followed, she dedicated her every free moment to surfing the World Wide Web. The shrunken globe that was the Internet enchanted her, as did that wondrous tool's ability to feed her insatiable appetite for answers to questions on every possible topic. Her family, on the other hand, coveted the endless computer hours that stole her presence from them.

When her two boys, Shai and Omer, vented their resentment, she fended them off and plugged herself out of earshot.

Sometimes Gadi would complain, too.

"Ora, you're so glued to that machine I might as well be

invisible!"

"I'm sorry. I promise I'll make it up to you," she would plead, guilt written in scarlet across her temples and cheeks.

At other times, however, he would mellow and even ask about the subject of her research.

One evening, she queried her favourite search engine, and within a few seconds, exclaimed,

"That's it!"

Shai came rushing to her side, closely followed by Omer, both curious to know what she was so excited about.

"Look, Shai. Look at this map."

"What map, Mum?" shouted Omer, elbowing his brother out of the way. "Shai, can't you move? I want to see it, too!"

"It's an ancient map of Jerusalem," she explained, delighted at their sudden interest.

"... and?"

"Haven't either of you seen this anywhere before? Omer?"

He shrugged his shoulders.

"Shai?"

"On greetings cards, perhaps?"

"For sure!" she shouted.

"So?"

"Well, the thing is it's very, very old, but it still gives a realistic view of all the streets and the houses."

Gadi turned around to take a quick look.

"Hmm. Mum's right. Actually, they say it's the first proper map ever made. That is interesting, you know."

However, the kids' attention span for such things was limited, and they had gone back to their various activities.

She bookmarked the Internet address, and returned later that evening to read more. Large pieces of her puzzle were falling into place. The following commentary situated the map in its historical context.

"This beautiful 6th century CE mosaic map found at Madaba in Jordan is the best-preserved example dating back to antiquity. Strictly speaking, it is not the first map ever produced. Most of the earlier examples, however, provide rather scanty and imprecise geographic information.

The Madaba Mosaic contains the earliest known survey of Jerusalem and is of significant accuracy even by today's standards. It extends from the Mediterranean Sea to the Arabian Desert and from the northern cities of Tyre and Sidon as far as the Nile Delta in the South ..."

The house had fallen quiet. Ora had lost all track of time but
sensed it was late. The rest of the family must already be in bed.

She thought about how Reuven wanted to make Jerusalem the
home of his project. Now, she knew his plan was in line with old
cartographic tradition.

The night was almost giving way to morning when she finally
shut down the computer and prepared to catch a little sleep. Through the
wide-open, second-floor window, she glimpsed the pale, white moon like
a phantom in the dawning sky.

*   *   *

Late in the afternoon, on the first Tuesday after his return from
Galilee, Reuven made his way to a carefully chosen meeting-place a few
kilometres southwest of Tel-Aviv. He had invited a select number of
friends to meet him there. Ora, punctual as always, was the first on the
scene having followed his instructions down to the last detail. She
homed in on a small farm and stood waiting at its roadside entrance in
the sparse shade of a ragged eucalyptus.

One by one, three others arrived map in hand at the appointed
spot. The first was Michael. He sauntered up to her, eyes shining with
that glint of superiority that often sets kibbutzniks like him apart from
their city-dwelling counterparts. He was tall, with classic good looks and
a healthy clean-cut appearance in plain T-shirt, blue jeans and sandals.

"How's my favourite cousin?" he asked, but before she could
reply, the next arrival jauntily interrupted them.

"Name's Rikki," she said. "Reuven's group, I take it?"

"Hi. Nice to meet you," said Ora, thinking immediately of
Reuven's sand drawing on the beach at Achziv. Rikki was one of the
names he had written there.

"Reuven mentioned your name to me," she said. "Have you
known him long?"

"Oh, yes, at least seven years," she replied in a self-assured tone,
then, without elaborating any further, appeared to withdraw into some
private meditation.

The last to arrive was a debonair young man of medium height,
bushy eyebrows and a full head of thick, black hair. He took advantage
of the pause in conversation to announce himself.

"Shalom, Nathan's the name. You're Reuven's friends, I take it?"

He wore a cotton sports shirt tucked neatly into well-fitting
slacks. His large, flat feet turned outwards in moccasins apparently
chosen for comfort rather than style. Like Rikki's, his name struck a

familiar chord in Ora's memory.

"Hi, Nathan. Michael." he said, extending a welcoming hand to the fourth member of the group. "And these are Ora and Rikki."

"Tell me, did you all get odd calls from Reuven?" he asked.

"I got a call from him. What was odd about it?" asked Michael.

"The way he spoke. It was as if he was commanding me to be here."

"Yes, I know what you mean. That's exactly how he spoke to me, too, and it's not as if this is your everyday kind of meeting-place, is it?" chipped in Rikki.

"Well, I'd say that's pretty typical of Reuven," answered Ora.

"What's typical of me? Am I being maligned by you, my trusted friends?"

Reuven had approached them unnoticed from behind. He was grinning from cheek to cheek.

"Come, now. Let's find ourselves a table at Rafi's place over there, shall we?"

Just across the road from the farm, Rafi's place turned out to be a cosy, low-lit café. An arm around each of the women, Reuven escorted them inside.

They picked a table away from the kitchen and the fumes of its open grill, and they ordered a round of Maccabi beers. Reuven sat drink in hand observing his friends without saying very much. To steady his nerves, he inhaled deeply then exhaled heavily. As he did so, he stole a glance in Ora's direction as if seeking reassurance from her. She seemed to be the only one who noticed his nervousness, however.

Rikki was busy all the while acquainting herself with the two younger men. Her long black hair was pulled back severely from her forehead into a thick braid, the length of which challenged the age lines on her brow. Michael was already making great play of her readily advertised divorcee status while Nathan assessed her more discreetly. She opened a pack of cigarettes and began to offer them around, much to the disgust of Ora who staunchly opposed smoking. Finding herself a lone smoker in the group, however, she quickly put the pack away again and ordered another beer, instead.

After about ten minutes of mental and liquid preparation, Reuven cautiously broached his chosen audience. He presented his project on a technical level attuned to the palates of logical men like Michael and Nathan, steering as clear as possible of the ethereal concepts he had shared with Ora. At first, the idea was received with a mixture of incredulity and guarded admiration. Ora listened to the ensuing dialogue as it quickly gained momentum,

"... multi-dimensional encounters in cyberspace," he was saying.

"Like a video-conference?"

"Yes, but you'll actually feel as if all the participants are sitting right next to you."

"Does the technology exist for such a thing?"

"In theory, yes. Part of our initial aim will be to involve relevant experts. We'll be needing your Web research skills, too, Ora."

She noticed his use of the plural and smiled to herself. It was a subtle yet effective ploy to create the illusion of an established team.

Nathan leaned into the conversation with both elbows on the table and scratched the back of his head with one hand.

"And then, if I understand you correctly, the project is to be fed by a gigantic data resource. Who's going to create that?" he asked.

One after another, questions were fired at Reuven, and his adept handling of them all amazed Ora.

"It's going to be a lengthy process. The heavy data files of the kind I work with professionally will need to be integrated and converted to a global format."

At this, Michael sat up straight and declared dismissively,

"Sorry, can't see it. I don't think it's feasible. Too many incompatible technologies."

"That's the great stumbling-block of the Internet, right now, but it'll change!" Reuven confidently assured him.

Next, Nathan folded his hands on the table in front of him as if preparing to offer them all a dose of reality.

"OK," he said, "so let's suppose we manage to complete this mammoth task. What exactly do you intend to do with the mountain of accumulated data?"

Reuven was ready with a snap reply.

"I want to set up a massive data flow system at the project centre in Jerusalem."

"Oh, it's going to be based in Jerusalem?"

"Sure is. On the crest of the city as its new pearl."

"Wow! Reuven, you don't go in for modest dreams, do you?"

This was Rikki's first comment since Reuven had begun to speak. There was a false twang in her voice that irritated Ora immensely as did her utter lack of subtlety in trying to win him over. She was intrigued to know what exactly was Reuven's purpose in inviting her along.

"So, you're really dreaming about a new landmark?" she asked.

"Drawing on Jerusalem's natural well-spring of energies, it will become, I believe, the most splendid of all global landmarks."

Ora noted the transfixed expression on his face and the oratory manner creeping into his speech. She looked across at Michael. Familiar as he was with Reuven's tendency towards the esoteric, he would have to be the least affected by this latest discourse. Of course, the technological challenge would appeal to him as would the possibility of working alongside Reuven again – a stimulating experience by any measure. She glanced again at Rikki, who was looking completely mesmerised; once more she wondered about her history with Reuven. Nathan, meanwhile, was giving vent to a stream of objections. He appeared to be quite agitated and even angry at the implications of Reuven's words. He got up from the table, bottle in hand, and began alternately swigging beer and throwing his arms up dramatically in the air.

"I'm telling you, man, my head's reeling with all of this," he was saying. "What about our jobs? Please don't say you think we're all suddenly going to quit our jobs? Hey, and our families? How do they fit into the picture? Some of us do have lives, you know!"

"Watch out, Nathan, that beer's going to be all over you and the rest of us, pretty soon!" warned Rikki.

Ora, was marvelling meanwhile at Reuven's power to fill the room with such heat, passion and confusion. One way or another, she thought excitedly, he had got them all involved in his ideas not just intellectually but emotionally, too.

"Easy, Nathan. No one's asking you to revolutionise your life just yet. We have to work out a long-term plan and organise ourselves gradually. I'm going to set up an 'Inner Circle' of project members who will be asked to volunteer some time to get things off the ground. To begin with, it will be a question of joining in a few planning meetings. That's all. As things develop, we'll see who can take on more. No pressure. Are you with me so far?"

"Where do you want to begin?"

"With the project centre in Jerusalem."

"And what exactly will it contain?"

"Ah, well in the first stage it'll be just the technology core. But eventually I want to build a whole theme park around it."

"A theme park? Oh man!" cried Nathan, jumping out of his seat again. "You're out of your mind, I'm telling you!"

Nathan's hysteria was reinforced by Michael's patronising sarcasm.

"Is that all, Reuven?"

Rikki, on the other hand, was awestruck at this point and asked Reuven how he could even imagine this little group could create such an ambitious project. Actually agreeing with her for once, Michael said,

"She's right, Reuven. We're modest people of humble means."

"Be that as it may, it's going to happen," was Reuven's confident reply and the trigger for Michael and Nathan to start exchanging whispers –

"He's sounding like an off-the-wall prophet, isn't he?"

However, Rikki overheard them and loudly affirmed her faith in Reuven.

"Well, I think it's really great to know that idealism and positive thinking are still alive," she said.

Ora gritted her teeth at this grovelling for Reuven's favour. Perhaps the unsubtle availability of Rikki's admiration answered some unaccountable need in him, she thought.

The arrival of a large party of teenagers was the cue for the four to leave. No specific plans had been made to follow up their discussion, but it was understood Reuven would call them once the Inner Circle had been formed.

*　　　*　　　*

As occurs not infrequently in a small country, such as Israel, whether by coincidence or by fate according to one's viewpoint, Ora bumped into Rikki just a few days later in Tel-Aviv's new Azrielli mall. She did not recall what Rikki's line of work was that allowed her such freedom in the middle of a working day. Obviously not a nine-to-fiver, she thought.

"Got time for coffee, Orush?" she asked, engineering familiarity by using a diminutive of her name.

They sat down in a dairy restaurant and each selected her portion of sweet self-indulgence from the cake cabinet.

"So, how come you're cruising the mall in the middle of the day?" Ora asked.

"Simple," replied Rikki. "Work's spasmodic. We actors, you know, are more out of work than in it, and waitressing for extra cash is not exactly my style."

So that was it. Presumably, Rikki had connections in the entertainment world. That would certainly be an asset for Reuven in his project.

"So, how do you manage?" she asked, feigning concern.

"I've got resources and contacts. I get by, you know. The thing is, when the work starts to flow, there's bags of lovely money to be made in cinema."

She sounds so keen to impress, thought Ora. She must be desperately insecure underneath all that pretence.

"You're divorced, aren't you?" she asked.

"Thank God, yes. Last time I get myself hitched to scum like that, I can tell you!"

Avoiding the dangled bait of Rikki's sordid marital history, Ora enquired,

"Any kids?"

"Actually, I've got a grown-up daughter. Off doing her own thing in the States. I expect when she makes me a grandma one of these days she'll be knocking on my door. Meantime, we don't see much of one another."

Ora actually caught herself feeling sorry for Rikki and thanking Heaven for the closeness of her own family.

"By the way, I have to say I admire your courage, Ora."

Ora looked up in surprise.

"For what?" she asked.

"I mean you're going out on a limb to work for Reuven ..."

"Did Reuven say I was working for him?" snapped Ora defensively.

"Oh, pl-ease!" came Rikki's immediate reply, the pl enunciated as a separate syllable and the e elongated for emphasis. "It's so obvious! The way he relies on you. You two are a team."

With the best poker face she could muster, Ora quickly changed the subject,

"Sweetener for your coffee?"

"Oh no, thanks."

Rikki polished off the remains of her cake and proceeded to lick some sticky confectioner's cream from her fingers. Then, she gave Ora a provocative little dig and asked,

"So, what's the deal between you and Reuven?"

Ora was flabbergasted. Was there no limit to the woman's impertinence?

"No deal," she replied coldly. "And by the way, in answer to your previous question, I'm not working for him. I'm my own boss."

"Sure you are, Ora. Hmm, good coffee."

Stifling a more primitive impulse, Ora challenged,

"So, while we're on the subject. What's your story with Reuven?"

Rikki showed no trace of inhibition in her reply to which she managed to add a twist that grated on Ora's nerves even more,

"I used to be wild about him, but then just about every woman who gets close to him falls in love with him. He affects us that way, doesn't he?"

Ora stiffened at these insinuations. She wasn't about to indulge in such cheap banter. Rikki, on the other hand, was relentless.

"Oh, pl-ease. Don't tell me you haven't seen it?" she pressed, mercilessly relishing the impact of her loose tongue on Ora. "They surrender to his charm like flies to a honey pot."

Subtlety was most certainly not Rikki's middle name. Ora opted to cut the discussion short before it got out of hand. She called for the bill and prepared to leave.

*   *   *

Rosa Levene checked her desk diary, patted the cushion on the low upholstered chair and placed a fresh glass of water on the coffee table beside it. She repositioned the chair at just the right distance opposite her own to encourage relaxed conversation without intrusion on her client's personal space.

Rosa was a demure American lady in her sixties. Her expertise was in clinical psychology, which she practiced both privately and as personal advisor to students on the university campus. Her smallish, perfectly ordered apartment was furnished in traditional european style, unaffected by the middle-eastern character of its location.

The conservative femininity of her modest, floral dress made it difficult to visualise her active youth in Hashomer Hatzair, a Jewish youth movement of the ultra-left.

At the appointed hour, there was a ring at the intercom and a few moments later, after basic introductions, Ora stood in the consultancy room. An impressive collection of books on history, trauma therapy and psychoanalytical methodology lined the walls from floor to ceiling.

"Please sit down," Rosa began, seating herself opposite Ora's designated chair.

"I believe you were referred to me by Reuven Sofer?"

"Yes, that's right"

"When you called me, a few days ago, you didn't really explain why you wanted to see me," she continued.

Ora stiffened and an awkward pause followed.

To break the ice, Rosa suggested,

"Why don't you tell me a little about yourself?"

Ora shifted her back uneasily against the over-soft cushion.

"I'm approaching forty-six, married, mother of two, stable home, bored, frustrated, considering a career change – seems like I'm heading for an early mid-life crisis."

This was a new and unnerving experience. Whatever she said would bounce back at her like a homing boomerang. She studiously avoided the subject of Reuven and his project.

The interview continued for an hour or so during which time she began to loosen up a little and even to develop a measure of empathy with Rosa. The discussion ranged over her family background, her expectations, achievements and disappointments over the years.

She was actually surprised when Rosa announced her time was up. However, as she booked a second session for the following week, the prospect of another introspective afternoon with Rosa seemed about as sexy as tea and cucumber sandwiches on a vicarage lawn.

After leaving the low apartment block, Ora turned right and headed uphill in the direction of Reuven's home. From the palm of her hand, she inhaled the scent of a little jasmine, plucked from a nearby tree along the way. She was anxious to hear if there had been any new developments since the meeting at Rafi's.

Reuven's wife, Tamar, motioned her onto the garden terrace.

"Help yourself to some loquats. They're fresh from our tree. I'll be out in just a moment," she called.

Ora tried to reconcile Tamar's unassuming figure with the label of '*High Priestess*' Reuven attached to her. She wondered what kind of a relationship there really was between them and whether his wife knew anything at all about the awesome extent of his dream.

Freshly showered, Reuven came out to sit with them. He glanced at Tamar, and Ora tried to guess what he might be thinking. She glimpsed his study area at the end of the terrace. The top shelf was full of gramophone records.

"What about some music, Reuven?" she suggested. "Didn't you tell me there was always music in your house?"

"Now, there's a girl after my heart!" — And with that, he vanished into the house to re-emerge a split second later, guitar in hand. Unwittingly, he chose a song that Ora had loved as a teenager. He began to sing and taken by sudden nostalgia she joined in.

"To everything there is a season,
and a time to every purpose under heaven."

She sensed he was watching her now. The new closeness that had evolved between them in the short time since Achziv afforded her the role of both confidante and protégée. This was not something they openly discussed, but she was aware of this change in his attitude towards her. Where Reuven was concerned, however, nothing was ever simple. She thought back uncomfortably to the telephone call she received from him quite out of the blue, two days previously. He had launched into an attack on her emotional vulnerability towards him despite her vehement protests that he had it all wrong.

"Don't put me on a pedestal," he warned her. "I don't want to be adored, I don't want to play centre field. I don't place myself above you. I'm fallible and far from perfect."

She was dumbfounded and embarrassed by her apparent transparency. The project was highly stimulating for her, intellectually. Nothing more, she assured him. None of his admonishments were necessary.

"I respect you and your project," she told him, but again he protested,

"You don't just respect me, you treat me as if I'm some kind of prophet! I'm not! The days of gurus and prophets are long gone. All I am is a messenger, nothing more.

Eventually, I'm going to disappear – I'm just a tiny element in the whole Master Plan."

She was quite adamant that she did not need him – or anyone else, for that matter – as a personal guru, but still he pressed her to seek professional guidance from Rosa. Now, he seemed to be observing her with a critical eye and she was surprised he had not asked her yet about the therapy session.

His next comment, however, was on their music-making.

"We make a good duo, don't you think? Next time we'll get Shahar to join in."

"I hear she's very talented."

"Yes, we're really proud of her," replied Tamar. "She seems to have the makings of a professional, depending on how hard she works at it, of course."

Ora responded with polite interest.

"Are you going to send her to the academy, then?"

"Oh, it's much too soon to say. Anyway, when the time comes, it'll be her choice not ours."

Reuven nodded in agreement and continued to strum in the background.

"You should hear her sing, too," he added.

"I'd love to hear the two of you singing together, Reuven."

"I'm sure that can be arranged," he smiled.

Ora glanced at her wristwatch.

"Mmm. But right now, I should be making tracks for home."

It had been a long day on insufficient sleep, and she still had a lengthy bus journey ahead of her. Reuven seemed disappointed she was leaving so early.

"Don't rush off," he said. "Stay and have dinner with us; then I'll run you home."

"Are you really sure you want to drive all the way across Tel-Aviv to where I live?"

"My God, just listen to the woman! So bloody diplomatic, you'd think she'd never left England! Yes, I'm sure!"

The invitation was confirmed by a friendly lick from Muki whose doleful brown eyes won her over right away.

The meal was in hand and her offers of help politely rejected, she rested in the string hammock under the loquat tree. Her lazy outstretched figure caught Reuven's eye and he smiled contentedly. Then, taking advantage of the brief moment they had alone, he confided in her.

"I worry about Tamar, you know. She's lost all sense of purpose. She doesn't seem to care about anything other than material things any more."

"I guess she's been through a rough patch."

"She has. That's true. She's suffered badly from our family being out-of-pocket all the time. A lot of it's my fault, I know."

"It'll blow over in time."

"Possibly, but what really bothers me, in the meantime, is the wedge this is all driving between us."

Privately, Ora thought Tamar's total dependence on Reuven quite insufferable. However, she kept her opinion to herself and replied tactfully,

"The two of you still look pretty cosy to me."

"Well, I do still love her, of course. After all, she gave me the most blessed gift a woman can give to a man – our beautiful daughter."

His every reference to the women in his life seemed so artificial. The very idolisation he had criticised in Ora seemed to her to characterise all his descriptions of his wife and daughter. It was no wonder his relationship with Tamar failed to ring true.

Tamar called them to the table.

"Reuven, bring some extra drinks out and there's another salad in the fridge. Thanks my love."

"OK, my love," he replied.

Ora winced. His words to Tamar sounded so affected.

"Ora, what about you?" he asked. "Something to drink?"

"Some of that fresh juice with a hunk of lemon, please. Tamar, quite a spread you've produced at a moment's notice," she called out.

She was good at posing as the correct and courteous guest but beneath her show of etiquette was the uncomfortable knowledge that a sophisticated game of charades was being played for her benefit.

"Oh, do quit the speech-making!" laughed Reuven and her blush immediately deepened. She finished her meal without further comment. Then, after a quick word of thanks to Tamar, she signalled to Reuven she was ready to leave.

During the drive home, she remained quiet. She turned over in her mind the increasing embarrassment she had felt as the evening progressed. She thought it partly due to Reuven's tactlessness and her own tiredness, but there was another reason, too. She was uncomfortably aware of all the subcurrents beneath her host and hostess's 'happy couple' façade. Noticing her change of mood, Reuven commented,

"You know, you're going to have to develop a much thicker skin if you want to work with me."

There it was again, she thought, his presumption she was going to work with him. She let it go, however, and replied,

"Oh, it's nothing. It's just everything that's happened in the past few weeks – It's a lot to process, that's all."

"Speaking of which," he said, "how was it chez Rosa?"

Glad he remembered to ask, she said,

"She seemed professional. But we didn't really get into anything very deep, today. Anyway, I've fixed to see her again next week."

"Good. That's good."

They were turning into her driveway, and she hunted in her handbag for the house keys.

"Ora, what're you doing tomorrow evening? D'you think I could stop by your place to talk some more about the project?"

"Yup," she said, "Should be OK."

"Time?"

"Any time after eight ought to be alright."

*   *   *

He arrived promptly at eight the following evening to find her all fired up about her latest Internet discoveries.

"Didn't I tell you about all the leads I've been tracking?" she asked, brimming with enthusiasm.

"No. Good for you. You're really getting into this, aren't you?"

The adrenaline was coursing merrily through her veins again. She loved the sense of partnership developing between them.

"So, what did you come up with?" he asked.

"The fact that ancient cartographers were drawn to Jerusalem, just like you."

"What makes you think that?"

"It's at the centre of all the old mapping sources."

"Aha. And that surprised you?"

"Well, no, but it's interesting. And then, yesterday, when I was at your house I saw the confirmation that you think so, too."

"Don't follow you. Now you're talking riddles."

"It's easy enough to understand," she said, brimming with satisfaction. "On your living room wall you've got the exact same map I found on the Internet!"

He flashed his splendid white teeth in an amused smile.

"The Mabada Mosaic," he said.

Gadi walked in. His self-diminishing stoop was accentuated alongside Reuven's imposing stature.

The two men shook hands.

"Interesting stuff, that mapping history you've got Ora into."

He was making polite motions, but seemed a bit put out by Reuven's appearance.

"I got so excited about the map, I told the whole family about it," she blushed.

"Hmm. So you did," agreed Gadi snidely.

"You don't mind that I invited Reuven over to talk about the project, do you?" asked Ora hesitantly.

Of course, the question was rhetorical. If he did mind, he was not going to say so in front of Reuven. Anyway, now was not the time to smooth things over so, with a pleading look, she shunted him into the next room where the kids were watching TV.

Reuven, meanwhile, seemed self-absorbed and unaware that he might be causing any friction.

"So, what conclusions did you come to?" he wanted to know.

"About what?" asked Ora vaguely.

"The map?"

"Oh, the map, of course. Just the fact of Jerusalem's centrality in your project and in cartographic history."

"You're right, but there's more to it."

"What do you mean?" she asked, excited again.

"Cartography didn't spring up in a vacuum," he began. "The people who drew those early maps knew far more than we do now about the Earth's patterns and forces."

She quickly guessed where he was heading with this.

"And you want to help people recover all that forgotten knowledge?" she asked.

He nodded.

"But, however are you going to do that?" she asked, puzzled.

Again, no direct answer.

"I think we're getting ahead of ourselves," he said. "You'll understand far more once we're working together on the project and you can feel its energy."

In other words, it was a skilfully weighted choice – only by working on the project could she expect to understand its energy.

"I'm sure that's true, but the big question is what magic are you going to use to put the tools of change into peoples' hands?" she asked, her readiness to believe still censured by practicality.

He gave her a penetrating look and said,

"Not magic. We'll tap into the most ancient energy source of all – Planet Earth, herself."

He was artfully edging her towards a leap of faith, and she was taking the bait.

"I hear you," she replied, enchanted.

"Once we rediscover our planet's formidable powers, we will be released into a new era of knowledge and harmony."

"Sounds like the Age of Aquarius!"

"Or, as the song says, its dawning."

"Meaning?"

"Come and take a look outside."

They walked over to the window.

"Watch the birds, the animals and the sky. The planet is never really at rest. On the quietest of nights, you can sense the orbit of the Earth."

He stood protectively behind her. She felt the reassuring pressure of his body against hers and the warmth of his breath on the back of her neck.

"The birds and the animals see and hear things our senses aren't sharp enough to pick up. Pay attention now."

They stood quietly looking out at the scene, where the shadows of young saplings spread across a high wall close to the building.

"Wait," whispered Reuven. "See there ..."

The tiny head of a yellow lizard emerged onto the warm window ledge, followed by two spindly forearms. Head uptilted, it rolled its chestnut eyes at them and froze.

"Its movement into our line of vision is a sign of the synergy of our paths. If it were not so, we'd be unaware of its echo in the air right now. Listen ..."

As if responding to an unspoken order, the voice of another dreamer floated towards them on the evening breeze.

"Imagine all the people
Living life in peace.
You may say I'm a dreamer
But I'm not the only one.
I hope someday you'll join us
And the world will be one."
John Lennon.

*   *   *

By mid-September, Ora's daily routine in a low-reward marketing job began to slip into monotony, and she tendered her resignation. Her web management studies had been progressing well, she thought. It was time to put them to the test. The liberating feeling of imminent change carried her swiftly through the remaining fortnight of her employment.

When she told Reuven of her decision, he immediately presumed she was going to come and work with him on his project. She, on the other hand, was wary of rushing into such a commitment. There had already been signs of the strain it might cause within her family. She did come up with a neat compromise, however. She could use the project as a test bed for her web skills. Immediately, she applied herself to designing a website for the project, and within a week she had a concept ready to run by Reuven. When she invited him over to view her work, however, she was shocked by his aloof response. He gave the pages she had so painstakingly prepared no more than a cursory look before dismissing them as a 'nice effort'. Then, he announced,

"Soon we'll meet the real experts."

It was like a whip cracked across her pride. She swallowed hard and rushed out to the kitchen to make some strong coffee.

Meanwhile, apparently oblivious to the effect his words had on her, he sat at the computer absorbed in his own train of thought. After a bit, he called out to her,

"I have to go soon. D'you think we can finish off a couple of things before I go?"

Furious at his presumptuousness, Ora charged in from the kitchen, slammed her coffee cup onto the table and countered,

"I really don't think I'm up to that right now."

She did not recall having agreed to be at his beck and call.

His face stiffened.

"Alright. Call me when you're ready to work," he shouted and, with that, he threw his bag onto one shoulder and headed straight for the front door.

Ora watched from the doorway as he navigated his Mini out of its tight parking space and onto the access road. He could be really cruel, sometimes, she thought resentfully and slammed the door after him.

She sat down on the sofa and hugged a couple of comfort cushions to her stomach. A few minutes later, she noticed the white edge of a visiting card on the side table. Her first inclination was to shove it angrily away, then curiosity got the better of her and she aggressively snatched it up to have a closer look. The logo was intriguing – a globe inside an eye set in a blue triangle. Immediately, she connected it with the geometric shapes she had seen Reuven trace in the sand. She tried to work out what it was meant to symbolise. She had heard about the use of triangulation in mapping – it made sense for him to put a triangle in his professional logo. She tried visualizing the logo in three dimensions instead of two so that the triangle became a pyramid. Still, she was convinced there was more to it. Then there was the eye. An 'all-seeing eye', perhaps? By association, she linked the image of the pyramid with its ancient archetypes in Egypt and South America giving it a fourth dimension – that of time. In this way, simple deduction led her through four dimensions of Reuven's logo. Yet, she sensed its ultimate essence eluded her.

*　　　*　　　*

Meanwhile, Reuven was driving by the old port of North Tel-Aviv past the fashionable pubs that filled that quarter of town. He was seething over Ora's behaviour. He had expected a more mature approach from her. How can I possibly rely on her, he thought, when she's capable of such childishness?

With a screech of the brakes, he veered to the right by the power station, then onto the flyover. From there, he accessed the Tel-Aviv-Haifa highway and got ready to step on the gas. Much to his annoyance, however, the thickening mid-day traffic forced him to slow down. He banged his fists in frustration on the steering wheel and loudly cursed a driver snaking from the parallel lane into his. He tightened his grip on the wheel to steady the vehicle against a blustery coastal wind. It was the Hebrew month of Heshvan that marked the beginning of Israel's rainy season. The autumn showers now spraying his windscreen were blurring his vision, as was the blackness of his mood.

As Ora had begun to discover, his temperament admitted little compromise between ecstatic heights and disconsolate lows. Jeanine's warning about the cloud over his soul flashed across his mind, and he knew he should moderate his behaviour. It was no longer the squabble with Ora but his own bad judgment that was annoying him. He knew such outbursts would work against him in the long run. He was foolish to lash out so harshly at Ora – the one person who had shown real faith in him. Damn it, he really needed her on his side. How stupid of him to toy with her goodwill after nurturing it so carefully. He yawned and reached for a rag to wipe the condensation off the windscreen. There was no alternative but to patch up their disagreement at the first opportunity. A little more delicacy in his relations with her, and the natural synergy between them would surely prevail. Calmed by these thoughts, he began to regain his composure and the traffic cleared ahead.

*   *   *

Early the following morning, Ora's phone rang. It was Reuven.

"So, did the night soften your bristles? Can we get on with our work, now?"

"As long as we're partners and not dictators," she replied, silently congratulating herself on finally taking an assertive stance towards him.

"Alright. I'm sorry for my tactlessness, yesterday."

"Apology accepted."

"How soon can you be ready to go out?"

"Five minutes."

"I'll be there in two."

In less time than it took her to question him, Reuven was outside her building, looking spry in a crisp blue shirt. She ran downstairs and jumped into the red Fiat.

"Hi. I think it's time for you to meet Ariella," he said.

Chapter 3

There is a segment of Israeli society whose members are bonded by a special spirit, vivaciousness and tradition. This is the bohemian community of creative artists. Among them are painters, actors, musicians, sculptors, storytellers, visionaries and mystics. This was the company in which Reuven felt most at ease – a way of life unbounded by social pretence and rules. These were people of courage, directness, humour and a thirst for life. To live among the artists was to be in touch with the vital vibrations of the land.

At ten o'clock on a Tuesday morning, Tel-Aviv's *midrahov*, the Nahalat Binyamin arts and crafts street market, is the passionately beating pulse of the city. A few paces away from the Carmel Market, where cheap food, garish clothing and bargain-priced household products are loudly traded, the *midrahov* parades its decorative artistic wares. Street entertainers range from a parrot-on-shoulder quick photographer to glass blowers, Tarot readers and portrait-while-you-wait commercial artists. There are bronze kaleidoscopes, silk scarves and hand crafted wooden toys. There is even a Bedouin tent where freshly prepared pita bread is served with soft goat's cheese and locally grown herbs.

Reuven directed Ora with the assertiveness of familiarity straight into the bustle of the adjacent Carmel market, weaving with agility between the densely milling crowds around fruit stalls, vendors' carts, strewn boxes and garbage. They cut through an alley by lettuces, flowers and leftover yarns, where pirate music stands blasted levantine rhythms into the sultry, aromatic middle-eastern air. They continued past a shoe repair stand hung with assorted laces of various colours, textures and lengths. Then, they crossed into the diverging stream of pedestrian traffic. Reuven strode on while Ora struggled to keep up with him. Despite his recent words of apology on this very issue, he was again demonstrating his need to set both pace and direction for them both.

However, on this occasion she voiced no complaint, apparently content to meet the challenges he fed her.

They turned seaward from the main street into a side alley. A slender young artist was displaying filigree jewellery on a Persian rug on the ground outside her studio. Through the half-open door, they glimpsed the studio walls covered in a blue and purple fresco. It was a celestial fantasy populated by birds, butterflies, sun, moons and stars. Inside, hand-woven textiles and rugs covered an improvised table and some rough wicker chairs. As they ambled past, she raised a baby to her shoulder, and slipped him gently into the wrap-around cloth carrier she was wearing. She continued to occupy herself with the sale of her craft. Beautiful and unassuming, her child and her art completed her natural grace.

Reuven and Ora cut away from the crowds through another alley leading directly to the central intersection of the *midrahov*. It joined the thin path running along the back of the stalls between the seated merchants and the shop fronts behind them. In this way, they approached Ariella's stall from behind.

It surprised Ora to discover that Ariella did not look at all like the dauntingly divine being Reuven led her to expect. She was actually a vibrant woman in her early sixties, with a down-to-earth attitude, a direct manner of speaking and a shock of orange dyed hair to complement the striking green of her eyes. She was exhibiting her latest commercial venture in the shade of a magnificent wooden-framed umbrella – heavy, ornamented bracelets, pendants, and rings from twisted forks and spoons of quality metal. Local and foreign shoppers and visitors congregated at this central point in the *midrahov* pedestrian walkway. Many of them sought her out as much for her wide and open smile as for their intended purchases.

Reuven encircled Ariella's shoulders affectionately with one arm. Mildly startled, she turned around, whereupon he presented Ora to her.

"Pull up a couple of stools. A pleasure to meet you, Ora."

"Same here – Reuven's already told me so much about you."

"Really," she said, raising both eyebrows in a meaningful glance towards him. He was revelling in this encounter and laughed out loud in response.

Ariella took out a cigarette, and Ora instinctively shuffled her stool away from the smoke.

"We market folk tend to smoke rather a lot, I'm afraid."

"Where smoking's concerned, our Ora's a purist."

A little surprised, Ariella shifted the offensive article to the other side of the table. Then, she turned to Reuven.

"So, how're things at home?"

"Shahar's the light of her Daddy's eye, as always."

"I bet she's quite an independent young lady by now?"

"Oh, absolutely. Unfortunately, her mother and I don't always see eye to eye about how much freedom she should be allowed."

"So, there's still a lot of tension between the two of you?"

"Yes. It's not really surprising, though, given our very different ideas about what's best for Shahar."

"Are you sure that's the real problem, Reuven?"

He got up and paced to and fro. Then, he sat down again facing her, legs astride the stool, shoulders thrust forward as if intent on saying something, but instead he just listened.

Perhaps Tamar needs a little pampering?" she continued. "There's nothing like it for mollifying a woman, you know."

Ora began to feel uncomfortable with the direction of the conversation. She picked up a bracelet from Ariella's display, tried it on her wrist, put it back, tried another. However, her attempt to appear preoccupied elsewhere was over-obvious. From the corner of her eye, she saw Ariella give Reuven a pointed nudge before changing the subject.

"So, Reuven. What about the project you and Ora were working on? Is that a gleam of satisfaction I detect in your eye?"

He gingerly whipped a copy of a newly drafted project summary out of his bag and handed it to her.

All the while, Ora had the feeling Ariella was assessing her. She tugged at the straps of her knitted cotton top, adjusting it to hide a little more cleavage, and pulled her stomach in self-consciously.

"Here. This is the latest thing we've prepared. Take a look."

Ariella took the paper eagerly.

"This is beginning to look serious," she said with exaggerated gravity. "It's too technical for me, but I'd like to show it to one or two of my friends. Would that be alright?"

"That would be wonderful. The more feedback we get the better."

"So, how do you plan to take things from here?"

"We think it's time to give the project a name and open it up to a wider forum."

"Good idea."

"Can you keep Saturday night free for a meeting?"

Ariella seemed hesitant about participating.

"I'm not sure I can contribute very much to such a meeting," she

said.
But Reuven was insistent.
"Do me a favour. Stop being so modest. You know I need your positive spirit there," he said.
"Well, OK. Don't worry. If you put it like that, I'll be there."
Ora, meanwhile, was put out at hearing about the meeting in such a by-the-way fashion. When had Reuven planned to let her in on the secret?

*   *   *

Nathan stomped the sand off his shoes onto the thick rope doormat. Reuven had left the door ajar, so he nudged it open and went straight into the living room.
"Hey, Nate. Nice to see you, man!"
Reuven greeted him with a friendly slap across the shoulders.
Then, just as the phone began to ring, a corpulent figure appeared in the doorway.
"Come on in. It's open!" called Reuven, picking up the receiver at the same time. "Glad you could make it, Menashe," he said covering the mouthpiece with his palm.
"Hmm. Thanks to Michael. Traffic's terrible. Road blocks everywhere."
He tossed his jacket onto the coat stand. His broad forehead was beaded with perspiration. His lank, brown hair was combed tightly across a balding scalp and held back in a small ponytail by a plain rubber band. Playing hostess, Ora stepped forward to introduce herself and held out a welcoming hand. Immediately, she felt herself under the scrutiny of enquiring eyes.
"Nice to meet you," he answered with a grin.
"Did I hear you say you were with Michael?"
"Oh, he's just parking."
"Hmm. I hear the roads're chaotic tonight."
"Yes. There's a whole *balagan* with the police on the look-out for infiltrators after that bomb scare in Netanya."
"All this stuff's getting to be a regular part of our lives, isn't it?" commented Nathan.
Menashe answered him with a cursory nod before cutting over to the drinks table. Oblivious to any implied slight, Nathan turned to Ora and continued,
"... as soon as there's a lull and we return to some kind of normality, another attack comes to keep us on our toes, doesn't it?"

"That does seem to be the pattern," agreed Ora, "although it was only last week they rooted out a whole terrorist cell and arrested them."

"Those arrests don't help at all, though. As fast as one lot are put away others are released."

"What do you mean?"

"Surely you've heard about the promises the new Government's been making to release hundreds of jailed terrorists?"

"Not those with blood on their hands."

"So, they've got blood on their lips and in their minds. What difference does it make?"

"You're not over-optimistic, then, despite the latest peace moves? What about a little faith and positive thinking, Nathan?"

"One thing's for sure. We're not the ones in the driving-seat of Israeli politics. It's all a White House pawn-pushing game isn't it?"

"I bet if Rikki were here she'd say it was all predicted in ancient kabbalistic sources." chipped in Michael who had just joined them.

"Speaking of whom, Reuven, isn't Rikki coming tonight?" asked Ora.

"Actually, that was her on the phone just now. She's delayed in traffic, but she should be here soon."

Nathan latched onto Michael next.

"So, you're hopeful the new government will help the peace process?" he asked.

"Maybe, if Arafat doesn't make any *faux pas* first."

"You mean, like announcing Palestinian statehood unilaterally?"

"For example, yes."

Mercifully, however, the evening was saved from an overdose of politics by another ring at the doorbell. It was Ariella. Reuven showed her into the living room.

Rikki flew in a few minutes later huffing and puffing an exaggerated apology. Her arrival completed the designated number for the first meeting of The Circle.

Reuven opened the discussion by handing out copies of a summary of the project.

"Some of you have known about my project for a while. One or two of you heard about it from me only a couple of days ago, and I'm sure you're still trying to make sense of it. As we begin to accept it, I predict it will empower us. We'll all be feeling the changes it brings to our lives quite soon. I can't begin to tell you how much your being here today means to me. I thank every one of you from the bottom of my heart."

He paused as if to gather strength for what was to come next. There was an atmosphere of uncertain expectation in the room, and questioning looks were being exchanged.

"The first matter of significance to be dealt with by The Circle is the naming of the project. Great care must be taken in our selection of the name. By it we will define the very essence of everything we plan to achieve together in the future."

And so, the search for a name began.

Nathan, a systems engineer, wanted to adopt a methodological approach:

"Language is really just a logical system of symbols," he pointed out. "I'm sure our search could be computerised."

This prompted a facetious retort from Michael.

"Right, so all we have to do is feed some letters into a computer, add a rule or two, and, hey presto, it's going to come up with the right name for us!"

A general chuckle spread across the room, effectively dismissing computerised name hunting as a serious possibility.

However, Rikki was taken with the idea of systematic analysis. She suggested they use the Kabbalah to analyse their choice of name. At this, Reuven turned to Ariella.

"Ariella, you're quite an expert in *Gematria*, aren't you?"

He had already told Ora about Ariella's knowledge of *Gematria* – the kabbalistic science of names, and Ariella's opinion was obviously important to him. She listened carefully to what Ariella had to say,

"In *Sefer Yetzira* – 'The Book of The Creation', the ancient Kabbalists laid out a method of analyzing a name by its mathematical value."

"Do you really believe in those mystical theories about the meanings of names, Ariella?" enquired Nathan reticently.

"Personally, I do. But you're sceptical, I see?"

"Afraid so. I suppose it's my scientific background."

"It's not just you, Nathan. You're part of a whole generation that has been blinded to universal signs as sources of knowledge."

"So, how did you come to believe in *Gematria*, Ariella?" asked Ora.

"I started going to a discussion group."

"And that convinced you?"

"Not just that. To begin with, the subject was quite daunting, but I immersed myself in it and after a while it all started to make sense."

"I'm afraid I don't really understand how *Gematria* is supposed to work," said Nathan, scratching his chin as he had a habit of doing when perplexed.

"According to the Kabbalah, the numerical equivalence of letters, words, or phrases isn't coincidental. If we calculate and compare the numerical values of two words, we can discover the creative elements in them and the creative potential between them."

"So, you think we can use *Gematria* to learn about the creative potential of whatever name we choose for the project?"

Ariella was reluctant, however, to promise any magic recipes.

"At this stage, I think we should just go by our intuition. I've a hunch that when the right name's pronounced we're all going to agree on it, anyway."

A brainstorming session began, and names spilled forth in rapid succession.

"Land Light", suggested Ora brightly.

"No, that's no good. It has nationalistic and religious connotations," said Nathan.

"Planet Ray"

"Sounds like a killer fish!" retorted Rikki.

"Planet Mine or Earth Mine"

"No, no," laughed Michael. "Next you'll want to call it Land Mine!"

"Well, what about Geoplanet?" asked Nathan.

"No, Nathan. I'm pretty sure there's already a Geoplanet somewhere. Isn't it the name of some mapping technology? Anyway, we need a name with a more musical ring to it," said Reuven.

More names were offered – Eye of the Planet, Earth Eye, One Planet, Planet All, Cosmic Light, the list was endless. Some were already in use, some lacked music or rhythm and many failed to capture the real meaning of the project.

For a while, no one spoke and Reuven began to look despondent. Rikki was twirling a cheap-looking bracelet around her wrist in apparent boredom, and Ora thought she caught a hint of resentment in her eye as she watched the more mature and self-assured Ariella who had stolen the floor from her.

Then, quietly from a corner of the room came another suggestion,

"Global Dawn!"

Suddenly, all eyes were on Menashe.

"Global Dawn." repeated Reuven. "Global Dawn. That's it! It says it all."

Ora waited a few minutes for some further reaction, then, when none was forthcoming, she asked,

"Are we agreed, then? Is the project to be called Global Dawn?"

She was utterly amazed the name had been found so easily.

"It seems Global Dawn has our unanimous vote," said Nathan, sounding rather as if he were summing up a company board meeting.

"It does, doesn't it?" said Ora, eyes fixed on Ariella.

It had happened exactly in the way Ariella had predicted – without any dissension.

A stunned silence followed. Then, eyeing the untouched bottles of wine on the refreshment table, Nathan asked,

"Shall we raise a glass to mark this historic occasion?"

"Pass the glasses around, Nate, my man, and I'll open some of this new Golan white," Reuven happily agreed.

Nathan made a toast to the successful implementation of Global Dawn.

"Do you want to fix a date for another meeting, Reuven?" he asked with an air of practicality.

"Yes. About a month from now?"

"We can meet at my place in Ein Karem, if that suits everyone," Menashe volunteered.

"OK everyone? Next time at Menashe's, then."

*   *   *

Tempestuous days were upon Reuven. The battle to keep afloat financially was becoming ever more oppressive. Furthermore, he felt himself caught under the controlling yoke of an avaricious and corrupt employer. He conducted protracted negotiations for minimal improvements in his working conditions, but to no avail.

His day-to-day working reality stood in stark contrast with the stuff of his ideologies and dreams. He found himself drawn into the middle of land and property disputes in which his position as a sub-contractor frequently placed him on what he perceived to be the wrong side of the moral fence. He witnessed situations where political wrangling and municipal corruption endangered the homes and livelihoods of simple folk, and not only did he stand powerless to help them, but they looked upon him as the threatening tool of their oppressors. He suffered brutal personal attacks while working in the field, ranging from verbal outbursts to sabotage of his vehicle or instruments, and even on occasion to physical violence.

Although such unpleasant confrontations with land and property owners were the exception and not the rule, they strengthened his resolve to see fair play in such matters. He began to frequent the regional courts and tribunals where he spoke on behalf of the abused meek. These worthy endeavours, however, led him only to deeper disenchantment with the system that allowed such shameful exploitation and its victims whose faint-heartedness perpetuated their own vulnerability.

Meanwhile, the Annual Conference of the Cartographers Association of Israel was looming on the horizon, and Reuven, a registered member, was ready for battle. Like any meeting of such a council of elders, the conference would be conducted according to formal ritual. Opening speeches would afford a promotional platform for each self-congratulatory speaker in turn. The main morning session would be given over to an erudite examination of the Association's standard policy and future strategy in which the aim would be to safeguard the proponents' interests. A magnificent luncheon would be the highlight of the day – justification for the exorbitant conference participation fee.

This was the 'Comedy of Experts' Reuven had chosen to address and, despite the size of the challenge, he was determined to shock at least a few of them into the twentieth century. In the weeks preceding the conference, he diligently compiled his paper. Its title was 'The Democratization of Cartography'. Against this backdrop, he would gently introduce his ideas for geographic information interchange. In this way, he hoped to give them some insight into his vision. He knew it would not be easy to gain the attention of the loyal guards of the status quo whose primary concerns were Protocol, Property, Privilege and Prestige.

*   *   *

A couple of days after the naming of Global Dawn, Michael paid the Sofers an impromptu visit. Tamar came to the door.

"Hi! This is a surprise! Come on in. Reuven's out walking the dog. Should be back ..." she began, but before she could finish her sentence, he was there, slapping Michael heartily on the back. As he did so, an exuberant Muki raced passed them into the garden, leash trailing behind him.

"Hey, Man, how's it going?" asked Reuven, his familiar baritone resounding throughout the house.

He made for the kitchen and Michael followed.

"Watermelon?"

"Mmm. Sounds good."

Reuven grabbed the weighty fruit from the fridge and divided it into generous chunks that the two attacked enthusiastically, fingers oozing with the sticky pink juice. Michael laughed boyishly. Then, looking around and seeing Tamar had left them alone, he asked,

"Where's Tamar vanished to, again?"

"Again?" queried Reuven.

"Yes. I missed her at the meeting of The Circle, too, you know."

The smile froze on Reuven's face as he made a weak attempt to gloss over his feelings.

"Global Dawn's not Tamar's thing, right now. She'll come around in time."

"That's what he'd like to believe," she called out from the adjacent room. "He's had this crazy fantasy for more years than I care to remember," she added, joining them in the kitchen just in time to catch the embarrassed expression on Reuven's face.

"Now, he's found himself an audience, and I'm supposed to be delighted for him."

Michael gave her a questioning look.

"No, don't look at me like that, Michael. I'm not enamoured with it at all, I can tell you!"

"Isn't that rather harsh?" asked Michael.

"Not when we're struggling to make ends meet, and he's flittering away valuable time on that nonsense. Perhaps it would be different if you were to take charge of things, Michael?"

"Well, now there's an idea, indeed," agreed Reuven enthusiastically. "How about it, Michael?"

"I don't think so. I'd love to work with you again, but I need some serious cash right now and soon!"

"Well, listen. You play your cards right and Global Dawn could be your answer."

At this, Tamar threw her hands up in despair, and Michael's response was no less dismissive.

"Get real, Reuven! You really think I'm going to rake in the gold with your dream? It's going to take some pretty high-powered investment to even begin building such a huge scheme!"

"It's all a matter of being in the right company at the right time, Michael."

"Meaning?"

"How'd you like to help me get some power-players on our side?"

"Who're you talking about?"

"The Cartographers' Association."

"What, that lot of self-satisfied ..."

"They've issued a call for conference papers, and I reckon it's a chance to win over some of our biggest data hoarders."

"OK. I'm with you. So, you're thinking of presenting a paper about Global Dawn?"

"Well, I don't think I'll go so far as to name the project there, but I can present the general concept – 'Global Networking', as Ora likes to call it."

"And where do I fit in?"

"Come along to the conference with me."

"No, no, Reuven. It's really not my scene."

"Well, couldn't you at least help me prepare the paper?"

Tamar interrupted them to ask if Reuven could pick Shahar up from a rehearsal.

"That's me," he grinned. "Family taxi service. Michael, think about it, will you?"

"OK. Good to see you both."

As Michael made his way home that evening, he wondered what he had actually agreed to and why it was so difficult to refuse Reuven. He connected the speaker attachment to his cell phone so he could use it legally while driving. The sound quality was usually poor and irritating, so he avoided using the mobile in the car as a rule, but he needed to sound out someone else about this latest conversation with Reuven. He loaded Ora's number and waited for a dial tone. If he really were to take on the management of Global Dawn, would Reuven ever be able to release the reins of his cherished dream, he wondered?

Ora's voice came drowsily over the speaker.

"Michael? That you?"

"Hi there, angel," he replied with the play of gallantry he reserved for her.

"Why so late?" she asked, yawning into the phone.

"I missed those dulcet tones and just had to ring you."

"Sure, Michael. So, what's going on that couldn't wait 'till morning?"

"Global Dawn. Is it for real?"

"It will be if you want it to be, Michael."

"Oh, no. You're sounding more and more like Reuven! You know I'm beginning to get drawn into this against my better instincts. How does he manage to make it so damned impossible to say no?"

"Probably, by letting you know how much he needs you. You're the one person who could really put the project on a sound footing, I reckon."

"But I need an income, Ora. It's not going to drop out of the sky! My wife's pretty keen to know where it's going to come from, too."

"Why don't you have an honest discussion with Reuven and see what the two of you can come up with?"

"I've just tried that!"

"And?"

"He wants me to prepare some paper for him."

"And you agreed? That's good."

"I didn't say I'd agreed!"

"Listen, he needs your input. You've got first-hand experience of the subject and of his ways of thinking."

"Without getting paid for my efforts?"

"That's the way all projects are in the beginning."

"Ora, you're becoming just like his echo, these days."

Her tired voice had become indistinct, so he wished her goodnight and rang off.

When the day of the conference arrived, Reuven reached the banquet hall with time to spare. He wondered how his message would be received. Glancing down the agenda, he saw he was listed as the final speaker of the day – not a favourable position for one who was seeking to awaken dormant souls. He reminded himself of the need to approach this audience with discretion. He had to present everything in a simple, factual way, making the benefits to these veteran cartographers crystal clear. Such stalwarts of the mapping establishment would not want their positions usurped or their work methods labelled antiquated.

He sat patiently through all the morning sessions of self-congratulatory splendour. Lunch was the elaborate centrepiece he had expected, thanks to which the first afternoon lecture was conducted to the tune and rhythms of slumbering satisfaction. At last, the final session was announced and Reuven, closing speaker of the day, took his turn at the lectern. Like Abraham before Sodom and Gomorrah, he prayed that at least ten, five or even one solitary person would show an enlightened attitude.

Taking one look at the passivity of his audience, he threw his carefully planned, logical presentation to the winds and launched dramatically into a challenging impromptu discourse. After about fifteen minutes, he was practically heckled off the rostrum, and the chairman saw fit to cut the session short with a muttered apology.

He flew out of the conference hall in a rage and took straight off across the beach towards Jaffa, kicking at sand and stones in his frustration.   The bitter taste of stolid establishment was lodged like a stubborn fishbone in his throat.   He soon reached the clock tower at the entrance to the old town and flung himself into the first vacant chair of a street café, where a huddle of elderly men were absorbed in a game of backgammon.   The café owner, recognizing at once Reuven's agitated state, brought him a revival potion of Turkish coffee with *hel*, a sweet Mediterranean spice, together with a honey-soaked baklava filled with almonds and pistachios.

Reuven began to take an interest in the game and to take note of his surroundings.   A street away in one direction was the old opera house, and up the hill, the flea market towards which he now wandered. Ariella's home was not far from there – through the park and across Kedumim Square, the central plaza of the old city. He gave her a quick call and invited himself over for some sympathy at dusk in her one-roomed studio overlooking the port.

As he slumped into the largest armchair she possessed, she enquired whether he felt like talking about the reason for his gloom.

Her mass of orange hair was pulled back severely into a tight bun, and there was an unusually stern look in her eye as she folded her arms in front of him.

"Ariella, you always know how to put the right perspective on things. How do you view the impossible challenge I set myself, today?"

"Your attempt to slay the giant of institutional cartography?"

"Was I naïve to think that in that enormous conference hall there might have been at least one pioneering heart ready to listen?"

"I wouldn't have thought so."

"Well, there wasn't a single, positive reaction to my much abbreviated words."

"Why abbreviated?"

"Because they put me right at the end of the day in the calculated hope they'd be running short of time by the time I was called upon to speak!"

"Reuven, you're sounding paranoid. If that were the case, you wouldn't have been asked to speak in the first place."

"With all due respect, Ariella, I don't think you understand their twisted politics. It's all to do with being seen to be correct."

"Maybe you're right. I do understand how you feel, but I think you're jumping to conclusions far too soon. A few months from now some of those who seemed so deaf to your speech today are going to show you just how wrong you were."

"Ariella, as they say in Arabic, *sadak allah la'azin* – from your mouth to God's ears!

*   *   *

Soon after the fiasco of the Cartographers' Conference, fatigued from channelling so much energy into a false direction, Reuven finally decided to abandon the slavery of salaried employment and to become his own master. By becoming self-employed, he was able to combine his GIS fieldwork with project development activities. He planned to officially register Global Dawn as a new company on the first of January to serve this unified role.

His new independent working status, however, would not be devoid of pressures. He still had to earn the family bread, and land surveying projects were not in copious supply in the aggressive local market. He now stood in direct and uneasy competition with his former employers and similar companies of long-standing reputation in the GIS industry. While he was confident of his eventual success, he was less convinced of the patience of his bankers and creditors. In this game of survival, noble perseverance counted for little and time was of the essence.

*   *   *

The project trail soon returned Reuven and Ora to the alleys and passageways between the Carmel Market and the sea. Their purpose was to meet with a graphic artist by the name of Sam who had made his home and part-time massage parlour in that area. The mission to be conferred on Sam was the conversion of Reuven's logo to suitable graphic format for the Global Dawn website.

As they came up to his turquoise painted door, a peep corner of the window drape was lifted to reveal a pair of bespectacled beady eyes. He came to the door and let them in. There were scented candles, meditation music, herbal teas, a healer's couch – all the elements of a relaxed and spiritual environment. Yet, Ora sensed something disturbing to her psyche the moment she stepped into this well-ordered abode.

Sam treated Reuven like an intimate friend, and while the two of them enthused about the spiritual understanding between them, Ora battled with her instinctive dislike of the man.

His main professional tool, she quickly discovered, was a Macintosh computer that was completely incompatible with her own PC. As they began to examine the image painstakingly drawn in Freehand on the screen, two youths came into the room.

"Ah, I see our Web experts have arrived," said Reuven to Ora's surprise.

Although she was getting used to his way of springing unexpected situations on her, she still could not fathom why he did so. Perhaps seeing her disarmed, in this case by the age of her prospective associates, gave him some perverse pleasure? Anyway, it was not, she thought, one of his more pleasing habits.

The boys were both around fourteen. One of them claimed to be Sam's son although he bore no visible resemblance to his father. The negotiations conducted by this bright pair of electronic generation kids were as mature as they were mercenary. They promised a slick web design for what had to be the most advantageous rate in town on condition that they also provide site management services at an appropriate fee. They were ready to talk terms for content, hosting, graphics, publicity, and would come up with a first draft within a couple of weeks. The contrast between their pace and Sam's was quite amazing, and their power of persuasion left Reuven and Ora nodding in breathless agreement.

"OK, lads. We'll give you this chance to make some good cash and a name for yourselves in the market. We'll be in touch a week from now to check on your progress!"

"Reuven, you know where to find me." said Sam. "I reckon I'll have the logo ready for you within a couple of weeks. I can't vouch for a shorter timescale than that, I'm afraid. Ora, here's my card," he volunteered, "in case you feel like sampling my range of therapies some time."

Taking the card, she barely succeeded in controlling an all-too-transparent wince.

"Thank you, Sam. This meeting with you and the boys has been quite fascinating," she replied dryly. "Reuven, shall we go?"

"Yup. I'm ready when you are. You'll be wanting a lift home, I take it?"

"Yes, thanks."

As they drove off, he asked,

"Tell me, did you enjoy meeting Sam or was he just too freaky for you?"

Ora found herself lost for words. She was piqued at his utter blindness to the phoney transparency of the man!

*   *   *

When Reuven arrived home, Tamar handed him a letter.

"I opened it by mistake," she said. "I didn't realise it was from Jeanine. She's sent you a copy of a newspaper article all about her occult activities. Did you know they call her the 'Tarot Queen of the South'?"

Reuven took the letter from her rather brusquely, irritated by her invasion of his privacy. The rather sensationalist press cutting read as follows,

"In southern Israel, spiritualists, sorcerers and soothsayers abound, and in equal measure, popular credence in their wisdom and healing powers. Riding high on the easy profit waves of this subculture is one Jeanine Danan, also known as the 'Tarot Queen of the South'. Jeanine has employed great talent and ingenuity to earn a reputation for clear and balanced revelations. She claims she's a mere medium, and her extraordinary insight is of divine emanation.

Outside the world of Tarot, however, Ms. Danan sports a very different image. A woman of great charisma and influence, she is known on the Ben Gurion University campus as a ringleader among women's rights activists. Quite a schizophrenic existence, Ms. Danan!"

Scrawled erratically in red ink across the bottom edge of the press cutting were some comments. They read roughly as follows,

"The cursed media seek me out. They satisfy their craving for scandal with never a care for the person upon whose reputation or sensitivities they feed. This, Reuven Dear, is the toll of success."

He fell to wondering what had possessed Jeanine to send him such a strange message. It was entirely out of character for her to bow to gossipmongers such as these. He found her portrayal as the modern suffragette quite amusing and wondered if the gentle Shira also wore feminist colours at the university. Remembering his brief encounter with Shira, he regretted not having taken the time to get to know her a little better.

He folded the letter back into its envelope and carefully copied Jeanine's address into his diary. He would answer her missive with a personal visit in due course.

Chapter 4

Between the main road and the sea,
Where narrow streets whisper lost names,
And half-perished palaces
Seek new light for their broken balconies and faded façades,
There is a blue-gated courtyard.

Unlocked, the gate swings easily open.
A cat lurks watchfully on the path.
Along the far wall are displayed the textures and tools of transience;
Rugs, mattresses and craft-woven draperies by earthenware pots
Outside a vacant shack;

Turning through a half-moon the seaward door is visible,
And its feline attendant steps aside.
A warm blend of incense, tobacco and fresh mint, clean white walls,
Low-slung, soft-covered seating offer themselves to the visitor's senses,
As he is gently appraised by enigmatic eyes
And the smile of secrets yet to be revealed.

Rikki, Autumn 1999

Inspired by Ariella's explanations of *Gematria* and kabbalistic philosophy, Reuven decided to seek out her source – one Assaf Goren. Best known for his sculpture, he was also a respected philosopher and spiritual guide. He lived towards the sea on the edge of Tel-Aviv's commercial hub. On summer evenings, when he held study circles in his courtyard, the smoke tails of illumination wafted into the after-dark sky above the neighbouring Carmel Market. Now, the creeping chill of autumn had ushered his intimate following inside his stark and humble abode.

Reuven found the front door propped wide open. A black cat lay warming the brush mat next to it. She was curled into a velveteen ball that rose and fell with the rhythm of her breathing. Inside was a narrow anteroom. A drape hung from the lintel, at the far end, to screen off the living room during Assaf's consultations.

Ariella arrived for her study meeting and, seeing Reuven, immediately offered to introduce him to Assaf.

"You won't get much conversation out of him now, though," she explained. "He never talks to anyone before his lessons."

"That's alright," said Reuven. "I don't mind waiting a while."

"Instead of just standing around waiting, why don't you sit in on the lesson?"

A tall, dark-skinned emaciated figure drifted through the entrance. He kissed Ariella theatrically on both cheeks then scolded her for having made herself a stranger in recent weeks.

"Oh, Antoine, what a fuss. I've just been busy doing some good business for a change!"

Antoine turned with a grin towards Reuven. He touched his side-cocked beret in salutation, and Reuven rather stiffly volunteered his name.

"Reuven Sofer," Antoine repeated as if savouring the name. "*Mais oui*! You're Ariella's idealist with the *grand projet* to make us ready for the new millennium!

"I see Ariella's been spreading the word, but the project's really no more than an embryo as yet," he replied in surprise.

"*Pas d'importance*. This idea is magnificent. I wish you success with it."

"Thank you."

At this unexpected gesture of interest, Reuven whipped a project summary out of his bag and handed it to Antoine. Folding the document carefully into his breast pocket, Antoine went over to the other side of the anteroom. A two-ringed hob stood on a counter by the wall. Coffee was bubbling there, sweet and spicy, through the tapered spout of a decorated brass *finjan*. Antoine poured some of the fresh brew into the tiny porcelain cups on the tray beside it.

Meanwhile, some other members of the group arrived. Among them, Reuven was surprised to spot Rikki who had apparently managed to persuade a reluctant Ariella into inviting her along. Seeing her standing apart from the regulars, the gallant Antoine swept up to her,

"Mademoiselle, welcome. You must share a *petit café* with us before the *leçon*. Please."

Rikki smiled apologetically at Reuven then followed Antoine to the coffee corner.

There were two others in the group; one was an elegant woman, the oriental slant of whose eyes echoed the angularity of her cheekbones. Moving towards Reuven with pointed care, she introduced herself in an artificially satin voice as a Bach Flower therapist. The other was a roughly dressed and pot-bellied man with a lingering odour of stale tobacco about him. His unkempt appearance contrasted with the radiance of his eyes.

Assaf acknowledged the small group with a nod and they entered the study room. They seated themselves around a table laden with heavy, bound tomes of *Sefer Yetzira*. – 'The Book of the Creation'. On the main wall, a sombre self-portrait was the only visible remnant of a lifestyle abandoned for one more pious. Only Assaf remained standing. Elderly and wild-bearded, he spoke with quiet authority.

"Today, we'll take another look at the interpretation of signs and letters," he began.

The large tomes of *Sefer Yetzira* were distributed and opened at a page where all possible pairs of letters were arranged systematically inside a reference grid. Each letter was paired first with itself, then with its neighbour, and then the next in sequence through the alphabet: *aleph-aleph, aleph-bet, aleph-gimmel*, and so on.

"These pairs," explained Assaf, "are the basis of our understanding of the entire world and its creation. Their union is like that of a man and his wife."

"Why do you pair each with itself?" asked the Bach Flower lady.

"This pairing with the self symbolises the initial challenge of every human being entering the world. Self-awareness and self-knowledge are the necessary foundation for any successful union."

"And *Sefer Yetzira* gives us guidelines for studying these pairs?" asked Ariella.

"That's right. The totality of this knowledge is presented to us in *Sefer Yetzira*. There are, however, many levels of meaning, some of which are hidden. Kabbalistic study is our key to the hidden and the magical."

He continued to expound on the meanings of specific paired letters as parts of words or names.

"Do you put these interpretations forward as universal?" ventured Reuven.

"These are my conclusions based upon years of study. Obviously, there are many other viewpoints."

"So then, how can you know which interpretation is correct?" asked Rikki.

Ariella stiffened and coolly interjected,

"I think you should trust Assaf's integrity, for now."

Rikki persisted, however, undeterred.

"I've studied Kabbalah with another teacher, too, you know, and he gave us a clear set of rules for finding the exact meanings of all the letters and numbers. Your approach seems confusing."

Her words were met by a censorious silence that continued until Antoine came to her rescue once again.

"Hey, it's okay to be confused. Many scholars have studied all their lives to understand these things."

With dignity, Assaf continued his explanation.

"Every letter in the alphabet has four faces. The pairs of letters we are analysing each have a masculine and feminine aspect, too. Just think how many combinations of meaning and interpretation are possible for whole words and phrases. Our studies open up channels to new ways of thinking that can enrich our lives."

Then, he turned towards Rikki who was still looking rather sullen and suggested,

"Try to clear your mind of fixed ideas, my dear."

The discussion returned to its original course, and the group began to experiment with analysis of various names. Finally, Assaf cleared his throat and summed up the lesson.

"And so, we see that rigidity of analysis reflects only the limited perception of the analyst, as for each sign and letter there are endless possibilities of interpretation. The Kabbalah is our entry gate into a secret world that encompasses all possible nuances and levels of meaning."

*   *   *

"All you have to do is contemplate a simple grain of sand, and you will see in it all the marvels of creation." Paulo Coelho, The Alchemist.

The lesson was over and Assaf came over to speak with Reuven.

"So, what did you want to talk to me about?"

"I'm intrigued by the Kabbalah."

"Yes, Ariella has spoken to me about you. She told me about your project."

"I understand you've given a lot of thought to its name. Is that right?"

"Yes. A group of my friends helped me to pick the name."

"And the chosen name is ...?"

"Global Dawn."

He patted his bearded chin thoughtfully. He got up and walked around the room, then came back to where Reuven was sitting. He gave Reuven's shoulder a reassuring squeeze before sitting down again.

"I like it. It has strength and glorious potential."

"What else can you tell me about the path I've chosen? Can you offer me any advice?"

Assaf sat down again. He stared into Reuven's face as if to uncover the essence of the man. Then, he sank back in his chair,

"Hmm. I have a story for you, Reuven. Come, come closer," he beckoned, pointing to an empty chair beside him. Reuven came and sat down right next to him.

"It's a story about a dreamer like you."

"One morning, long ago, I'm sipping a coffee in the yard and watching my neighbours going about their daily business. They have no time for me, oh no. To them a dreamer like me is a lazy good-for-nothing parasite."

His weathered complexion creased into a smile and his keen blue eyes reflected an incrongruously mischievous sparkle.

"Well, I carry on sitting there, watching it all and sipping my drink, you know. Then, out of the blue, an angel of a creature appears in one of the doorways."

With exaggerated strokes, he drew her voluptuous silhouette in the air.

"She starts to walk straight as a sunbeam across my line of vision, gliding by me, hardly noticing me at all."

His expressive storytelling gripped Reuven's attention, and the levantine mannerisms with which he embellished it added colour to the tale.

"Our eyes only meet for a second. Then I stand up and confront her. I catch hold of her like this," he said, seizing Reuven's hand and closing his fist tightly around it, "and I press some stones into her palm."

He stopped and sighed for a moment as if recapturing the memory. Then, releasing Reuven's hand, he threw his head back and thrust his open palms upwards in an exaggerated gesture as if to say, "What in Heaven could I do?"

"She takes a quick look at the stones then drops them straight onto the ground. I protest that they aren't common pebbles to be discarded like that, but she just shrugs and snaps that, for sure, they aren't diamonds either. She goes on her way leaving me standing there staring at the stones on the ground in front of me. I see them shining like gems. I want to run after her.   I want to show her what a treasure they are. If only she would stop, pick one up, look at it closely. She could find in it the soul of the planet!"

Again, he paused for effect.

"But she just continues along her straight and lonely path, cold and untouchable."

Then he channelled a penetrating look at Reuven.

"Artists and dreamers are alchemists," he said. "Their souls can turn the commonplace into treasure. Their worlds reach to the edges of the universe. You're a dreamer, Reuven. Tell me, are you also an alchemist?"

Reuven did not reply, straight away. He seemed absorbed in silent contemplation. After a while, he said,

"Your story is extremely moving, Assaf. Those of us who follow an unbending course through life remain ignorant of the planet's magical treasure trove. One thing puzzles me; alchemy, art and dreams – aren't these the antithesis of Kabbalism?"

Assaf pulled at his beard thoughtfully before answering.

"The kabbalistic viewpoint is that everything emanates from everything, and all sources are our teachers. By the way, the kabbalists knew all about the alchemy of stones, too."

"Oh? Now, I'm intrigued. Go on."

"According to the Kabbalah, there are sparks of the Creation everywhere."

"And stones have special powers?"

"Only in the right hands. Look at the famous example of the *hoshen*."

"What's that?"

"It was part of the special garb of the High Priest in days of the Temple."

"And it had precious stones on it?"

"The *hoshen* was the priest's breastplate, and it was set with three rows by four of gemstones, each of which represented one of the sons of Jacob."

"And they were supposed to have divine powers?"

"In the hands of the righteous, they were gateways into divine dimensions."

"And in other hands?"

"Just dull stones like those my cold-eyed angel disdained."

"The transformational energy that shines from the alchemist's stone is the same spark of the creation that pervades all things according to the Kabbalists. To glimpse that energy is to perceive the contantly flowing, cosmic reality that parallels our linear lives."

As he stepped out of Assaf's place, Reuven knew Assaf was right. His gift of seeing beyond the linear dimensions of the everyday world was a unique privilege. With renewed conviction of his purpose, he resolved that the Global Dawn project would become a bridge between the common world of finite vision and the elusive treasury of the absolute.

*   *   *

These were pre-millennium days. The world's technical support system was about to undergo the ultimate test. Panic was rife before the threat of a global shutdown on the 1st of January, 2000. Religious predictions of a first coming or second coming of the Messiah were accompanied by declarations of doomsday and the apocalyptic events that would be its forerunners. Even the die-hard sceptics were positing new hypotheses and a paradigm shift. Jerusalem, meanwhile, was preparing for an onslaught of pilgrims to greet the third millennium.

At this critical time, a nagging inner voice kept urging Reuven to clear his life of every obstacle to his higher purpose. However, master visionary though he might be in his soul, the demands of material reality were clouding his perception and straitjacketing his ability to act. Moreover, there lay rooted in his subconscious a profound fear of failure – a characteristic sickness of dreamers.

On the morning of the 20th of *Heshvan*, which fell that year at the end of October by the Gregorian calendar, he marked his fiftieth birthday with the following entry in his diary.

"I'm afraid my path forward is being barred like that of the cursed seekers of the Holy Grail. This is just as Jeanine warned it would be."

A further entry in his diary read,

"I know in my heart that Global Dawn is part of the universal Master Plan, and it will come into its own when the time is right. In the meantime, however, my own wife treats my mission as an unreasonable fantasy, and the very thing that should be our mutual inspiration is driving us apart."

Thus confounded by inner conflict, he prepared to hit the road in search of some peace of mind. He rolled a few maps into his kitbag and set out. He drove up the coast road for about twenty kilometres. With the windows rolled down, he felt the exhilarating drive of the sea wind across his face and through his hair. He sped up the highway drumming on the wheel to the rhythms of his favourite music tuned up to full volume. Some way after Netanya, he swerved inland onto a meandering side-road flanked by orchards and cotton fields.

He turned onto a dirt track and left the car beneath a gnarled and aging fig tree. Then, with the aid of his survey map, he followed an overgrown and barely distinguishable footpath leading to a reed-camouflaged reservoir and birdwatchers' paradise. A kingfisher was perched on an overhead wire displaying its brilliant turquoise back in the morning sun; it turned around to offer the splendid whiteness of its breast to him as he approached. The chorus of warblers grew persistently louder on all sides as he made his way through the undergrowth and out at the water's edge. There he rested, feet above head, on a piece of rough, dry ground beneath some tamarisk.

He looked up through its spindly branches at a party of gulls circling above him. The sweet, musty smell of this waterside refuge lulled him into an easy sleep. He dreamed he was lifted into the air by a hundred gulls that carried him to a flattened Jerusalem hilltop. There, where no international force or 'peacemaking politicians' had yet laid claim to the land, he beheld the foundations of a glorious futuristic city. Above it already towered a great crystal dome. It was a dazzling image.

An ardent rush of excitement swept through him, and he awoke to discover the noonday sun striking hot overhead. He took a long drink from his water bottle, stretched and yawned, consulted his map again and glanced across the water. He identified the continuation of the path on the far side of the reservoir. He jumped up, shouldered his pack and picked up the trail with renewed energy. Now, he entered an area of denser vegetation, some of which he had to cut aside with his pocket-knife. Some fifty metres into this bushy undergrowth, he caught sight of a shape that made him stop in his tracks in wonder. Was he still dreaming, he asked himself, or perhaps what he saw in front of him was some kind of mirage? As if conjured out of the vagaries of his mind, unabashedly facing him in the middle of the open field ahead stood a dome!

As he came nearer to it, he could make out a hemisphere of lightweight metal. Its frame was filled with triangular panels of wood, alternated in places with Perspex glass to form windows. Dumbfounded, he walked around the scene several times as if he had just discovered a landed UFO. Then, judging the place to be deserted, he ventured a glimpse inside. The interior of the dome was neatly fitted with the basic necessities of a nomadic existence. When someone addressed him in English from close behind his shoulder, he was quite startled.

"Er ..., I see we're the subject of interest."

A fair-haired man in khaki shorts with pocket telescope strapped across his lean chest stepped forward and courteously offered him his hand.

"I do apologise for intruding ..."

"That's alright."

"I'm Reuven."

"Reuven, this is my wife, Rachel and er ... I'm Lawrence."

He spoke with the unhurried cadence of a West Countryman, and rolled his 'r's with the gentlest quiver off the tip of his tongue.

Rachel was as dark as he was blond. She was obviously locally born, as was their engaging little daughter who, finding herself the sudden centre of attention, raced over to bury her head in the folds of her mother's baggy white harem pants.

"And this is er ... young Ilanit," he said. "There, then, Princess. No need to be bashful, now."

She responded by cautiously peaking out of her safe place with a comically inquisitive expression, then darting back again in shrieks of laughter.

"She takes a while ..." began Rachel, but she left her sentence hanging incomplete in amazement as little Ilanit ventured towards Reuven, tugged mischievously at his trouser-leg, then scampered off again with a yelp of glee.

"Well, it didn't take her long to warm to you, that's for sure!" she laughed in surprise.

Rachel was slight with the natural poise and delicately pointed features of a dancer. She wore rope sandals, and her thick black hair was plaited in micro-braids decorated with girlish butterfly clips. The little girl ran barefoot.

"Kids seem to like me," acknowledged Reuven. Then, digressing, he commented,

"Unusual way of life you've chosen."

"The closeness to Nature suits us," said Rachel with a smile.

"I can understand that. But this kind of warm-weather igloo you're living in is unlike anything I've ever seen."

"Er ... come and sit down," said Lawrence. "I'll tell you all about it."

"I hope you're not planning to rush off," grinned Rachel. "Once he starts on his pet topic, you'll not stop him!"

Lawrence heaved a couple of giant bean bags into a corner and left Reuven to sink comfortably into one of them while he went off to fetch something cool for his guest to drink. Then, he settled himself down and began pointing out the structure of the dome's inner wall.

"It's a geodesic dome, you know. Er ... built on the principle of tensegrity."

"What's that?" asked Reuven.

"It's the way Mother Nature keeps her architecture perfectly balanced."

Ilanit was darting to and fro, quite delighted by Reuven's fortuitous arrival and intent on attracting more of his attention.

"Run along, then, Ilanit, and leave us be a while, will you?" said her father with an indulgent smile.

"Er ... Quite a handful, that little one, sometimes."

"She's adorable. How old is she?"

"Just three."

Lawrence's conversation was a little terse and awkward. There was a striking discordance between his ungainly colonial style and the easy rapport of his wife and daughter with their surroundings.

"Er ... I can give you a good article on the subject, if you like" said Lawrence and immediately began rummaging in an old paper rack for the relevant magazine. Reuven watched in disbelief as he brought out a whole hoard of dog-eared copies of 'Scientific American', and proceeded with surprising alacrity to locate the relevant issue.   The article was the work of a certain Donald E. Ingber and was titled 'The Architecture of Life.' He began to read and found the whole concept enthralling. It explained that Nature's inherent resilience comes from a "tuning" of its elements to a common vibration."

He looked up at Lawrence and asked,

"So, a building constructed on these principles should be able to withstand just about anything?"

"That's right."

"Storms? Earthquakes?"

"Er ... that's the theory."

"Man, you're a genius!"

"No, no, not me," he laughed. "It's Bucky who's the genius!"

"And who might Bucky be?"

"Richard Buckminster Fuller."

"Ah yes, I see his name's quoted here. Isn't he the one who designed Disney's Epcot dome?"

"Yes. Built a dome home like this one for himself, too."

Reuven read on.

"This is amazing," he said excitedly. "He sees the whole planet as a single geometric system and tensegrity as a kind of energetic glue holding it all together, right?"

Universal synergy, just as he had described it to Ora – scientific proof of the inherent energy of the planet. There was no doubt now in Reuven's mind his meeting with Lawrence was no simple coincidence.

"Er ... there's more tensegrity stuff in here. I can show you, if you'd like ..."

Lawrence had opened the lid of a wooden crate and was pulling out various large files and folios from it. He took one out and closed the crate quickly.

"Those documents," Reuven said pointing to the crate," are they your work?"

"Yes. I do a bit of mapping. Er ... historical landmarks, mostly," Lawrence explained.

"Would you mind if I take a look?"

He lifted the lid again and slipped his hand inside one of the folios at random. He withdrew a single map and spread it across the table. It seemed to show various holy sites in and around the Mediterranean.

"What are all those geometric shapes pencilled over it? Following in Bucky's footsteps?"

"Er ... it's my own theory. I've found that each of those sites is positioned to correspond with patterns in the sky."

"You and Pythagoras?"

"Right. He knew all about earth-sky harmony."

"Of course, there are masses of theories about it."

"Hmm."

"So, what about your findings around here?"

"Er ... There's some stuff I'm working on right now on the big table over there."

Reuven held his breath as he looked at the work in process on Lawrence's table. Its focus was plainly the city of Jerusalem, and a whole mesh of geometric shapes was superimposed on it.

"Go ahead. Have a look. Only please er ... don't breathe a word of what you've seen here to anyone. I want to publish it, but until I do ... I'm sure you understand."

"Yes, particularly at this time. I'm sure it's best not to attract all sorts of millennium theorists who'll misinterpret your work."

"Reuven, er ... can I ask you something personal?"

"Sure. Go ahead"

"You seem to know a lot about mapping, am I right?"

"Actually, I'm a land surveyor by profession."

"Ah. So that's it."

Before he could say any more, Rachel interrupted their discussion with a mid-day meal. Her oriental allure might easily be mistaken for servile submission, he thought, and yet there was a contradictory free-spirited air about her. She smiled discreetly at him as if to reassure him she was indeed the mistress of her station. She opened out a folding table on which she laid some hot pita and salad. After gratefully washing this down with rough red wine, Reuven and Lawrence laid back on a threadbare couch, nibbling sunflower seeds from their salted husks.

He accepted their invitation to stay for a few days. It was ideal – well distanced from the pressures of the city. Little Ilanit proved truly delightful company, and her initial timidity was soon replaced by relentless angling for attention from her new friend. She dragged him outside to see the brilliant colours of the butterflies and out-of-season anemones. She played hide-and-seek, racing in and out of the rushes and tall grasses. She had a thousand questions about his home, his family, the scar on his leg and his sprouting beard. She filled his days with her laughter and pure love of life. Meanwhile, her mother remained watchful but did not intrude. She asked only after his daily welfare without prying into the personal reasons that brought him, an unexpected stranger, into her home.

On the morning when he prepared to return home, Lawrence presented him with a rolled document – a token of their common interest. He embraced Reuven, and Rachel uttered a brief prayer for the strength of his spirit in the challenges that lay ahead.

Chapter 5

In Reuven's absence, Ora had been pursuing the concept of global networking across the World Wide Web. She was delighted to discover among its proponents none other than Al Gore, Vice-President of the United States, whose own vision, called 'A Digital Earth', involved the creation of a 3-D global model embedded with geo-referenced data. NASA was already testing a prototype in museums and science theme parks. She was thrilled to find this validation of Reuven's idea, and was impatient to share her discovery with someone. She wandered over to the window-seat rubbing her palms indecisively against her thighs. Then, she stooped to pick up the phone and called Michael.

"Hey, listen, listen. I think I've made a real breakthrough!"

Michael began his usual flirtatious banter, but she stopped him short.

"Michael, listen to me, please!"

"OK, love. I'm all ears."

"It's about Reuven's project."

"Of course. What did we decide to call it? Something spiritual, wasn't it? Ah yes, Morning Glory."

"Michael! You're driving me crazy!"

"Ah, success at last. In desperation, the lady succumbs."

Her irritation was mounting.

"Did I ever tell you how sexy you are when you're angry?"

She smiled, in spite of herself.

"It's about Reuven's Global Networking idea. I've discovered the White House is its natural supporter."

"Clinton's joining Global Dawn?"

"No, Michael, but Al Gore has his own global networking project by another name."

"Ah, you've stumbled upon the Digital Earth."

Her smile sagged instantly.

"You know about it?"

"Sure I do. Al Gore even spoke about it here in Israel a few years back."

"Then you think it's worth approaching him?"

"Can't hurt to try. We need to work out a convincing line of approach, though."

"When Reuven comes back ..."

"Right. Where is he?"

"He's off on one of his trips, you know. I don't exactly know where, but I'm pretty sure he'll be back in a day or two."

"And when he comes back ...?"

"We'll draft our letter to the White House. What about getting them to link the two projects – Global Dawn and the Digital Earth. What do you think?"

"We won't know until we try, will we?"

With these ambitions in mind, she waited for word from Reuven.

Later the same day, Ora's doorbell rang unexpectedly. It was Reuven's sister, Michaela. She strode into the living room, and launched into a tirade about the state of her brother's misfortunes.

"Did you know, Ora, he actually had the audacity to come begging us for more money, the other week? Does he think we have a cash tree flourishing in our garden?"

Ora was flustered by this confrontation, and at a loss to understand what Michaela expected from her. After all, it was certainly not her place to meddle in Reuven's private affairs and still less in his financial mismanagement. Yet, Michaela apparently judged her a fitting target and, illogical though it may have been, she felt a slight sense of guilt as she sprang to his defence.

"Michaela, I know it's hard for you, but we have to help him as best we can. He's going through a very difficult patch. Building a project from scratch is no easy challenge, particularly in the current state of the market, and he really needs the support of his close family and friends."

"I don't understand you. The state of the market is precisely the reason no one in his right mind would try to start up a new enterprise right now. It's pure folly, in my opinion. He's heading for a big downfall, him and his dreams."

"Did you never have any dreams, Michaela?"

"Maybe, but I don't base my life on fantasy. The Jews in Germany made that mistake. They thought they could build a good life in Europe, and what happened? The Nazis butchered all their hopes and dreams."

"They were victims of a reality so cruel it's impossible to contemplate. But that's exactly why Global Dawn is so important to Reuven. Can't you understand that?"

Michaela scoffed again.

"It's a pipe-dream! People who can't cope with the real world love to fantasise. I'm sorry, I can't afford to subsidise my brother's every caprice."

"Have you told him that?"

She was quiet for a moment. She glanced at the NASA photos on the computer screen and the various printouts littering Ora's living room table. Then, looking her directly in the eyes, she said,

"Not in so many words. Look, I'm his sister. I'm his only relative here in Israel. I know he needs me."

"Yes, he does."

"But I don't understand what your connection with him is, Ora?"

She blushed in embarrassment again.

"I'm just a friend trying to help him, too."

"I think there's more to it than that. Are you having an affair with my brother?"

Ora froze at this effrontery. She gasped, mustering all her powers to control her anger before answering icily,

"I'm a woman of family and conscience. Apparently, the bond of mutual respect between your brother and me is something that's beyond your understanding. Now, please Michaela, let me show you out of my home before I say or do something I may regret."

Michaela shrugged her shoulders indignantly and walked out. Shaking with rage, Ora slammed the door firmly after her. She walked back into the living room and felt for the arm of the sofa behind her to steady her balance. She was quite profoundly troubled by the hostility of this encounter. Michaela, the same sister on whom Reuven conferred the title of 'guardian angel', was adamantly opposed to the project and so reproachful of her liaison with him.

Meanwhile, there was no news of his arrival, but Ora's intuition told her she would be hearing from him before too long.

*   *   *

Reuven knocked on the door of Shahar's room. She leapt to her feet and dived into his arms. Then, she skipped over to the piano and began to show off all her new pieces. Suddenly in the middle of a rather hard passage, she stopped, swivelled round on the piano stool and flung herself affectionately about her father's waist.

"Missed you, Pumpkin," he said, tenderly squeezing her towards him while fondly smoothing her lush, dark hair.

"Me too, Abba. I didn't get to say goodbye before you went. And I didn't know when you'd be back …"

"Hey, you know your Daddy can't keep away from you for long, don't you?"

"I guess so," she said suddenly pouting and pulling away from him.

"What is it, sweet? What's wrong?"

"There's a ceremony at school tomorrow. I so wanted you to come, but …"

"What ceremony?"

"It's for the local soldiers who died in the Yom Kippur war, and guess what? I'm singing a solo. They said the mayor's gonna be there, too."

"Well, of course I'll come! You surely didn't think I'd miss your solo, did you?"

"Really? Cool!"

Her face lit up.

"Now, what about that Bach piece of yours? The snippet I heard sounded pretty good."

"I can't play it fast enough, though."

"Is that what your teacher thinks?"

"Probably. She's ever so critical."

"Only because she thinks you're very talented."

She shrugged.

"What's that to do with anything? She never lets up!"

"She's right to insist you practise. She shouldn't stop you from being a bit creative with the music, though."

He could see the relief in her face. No one understood how she felt about her music as he did.

"Why don't you play it for me your way?"

She began to play for him, and suddenly the piece took on a new life. As a musician himself, he understood her need for a sensitive audience to make her performance really live.

"Bravo!" he applauded.

"But it was full of mistakes!"

"Oh, that's nothing. You need to practise a bit more, that's all."

"My teacher wouldn't have liked it. That's for sure. She expects everything to be spot on."

"Fine, but that doesn't mean you can't be a bit imaginative. That's what I love about your playing."

"I think it should sound different each time you play. Know what I mean?"

"Of course. What about those pieces you wrote a while ago? Have you finished any of them?"

"What, the ones I put together for the school show? They're not really that interesting. Hey, I'll tell you what I'd really like."

"I know. You'd like us to improvise together."

"Voilà! Come on, get your guitar out!"

He was torn between his pressing curiosity about the document Lawrence had given him and the fact that he could never refuse his daughter.

"It'll have to be a short session. I've got some urgent stuff to see to."

Bach gave way to rock and pop in an instant, and the two soon filled the house with their unique sound.

When Tamar walked in and took in the blissful scene, her initial anger at Reuven's disappearance was dissipated. Over the years, she had learned to accept his way of cutting out when the going got rough. This latest escape was relatively short and seemed to have soothed him. She poured some coffee and sat down to listen to the joyful sound of the two people she loved most making music together. Muki came and lounged contentedly at her feet.

The scene was interrupted ten minutes later by the arrival of Shahar's girlfriend. With a rushed apology, Shahar raced off to change. In a flash, she donned a pair of faded jeans, a skin-tight sun top and a perky crimson felt hat, and the two girls were out of the house with the briefest wave of the hand in farewell.

Reuven lay back on the giant floor cushion and beckoned Tamar to him. She nestled her head against his chest.

"I'm so relieved you're not angry at me this time, my love," he said, stroking the back of her neck gently as he spoke. "Your tolerance means a lot to me, you know."

His fingers reached deftly for the fastening of her shirt as his impatient lips sucked and pulled at her nipples with a hunger that caused her to cry out. She wrestled into freedom from her clothes as his mouth traced the contours of her body. His arousal was full, and he entered her with a passion they had not shared in months. Uninhibited by the brilliant daylight pouring into the room, they banished the world of mundane cares.

It was a blessing to be home. However, Tamar had news for Reuven that would very soon distance him once more,

"There's a message for you on the voice-mail. It's about a new surveying project they need you for in the northern Negev."

"Well, well. Good news! Any idea when it's due to start?"

"Pretty soon, I think. They left a contact number for you to phone for details."

In excellent spirits, he took himself off to his study corner. He was dying to examine the gift he had received from Lawrence. He spread the document out on the table and began to pour over its contents. It was a map of Jerusalem similar to the one Lawrence was working on. In this case, instead of plotting shapes on the map itself, he had marked them on a separate sheet of tracing paper. At the bottom edge of the page were some mathematical calculations, and next to the various traced points were pencilled names. Reuven guessed they were the names of constellations. He manoeuvred the two pages until the plotted shapes coordinated with key points on the map. The striking result was a clear alignment with the Via Dolorosa, the Church of the Holy Sepulchre and large segments of the walls of the Old City. Judging by the equations and formulae scribbled on his tracing, Lawrence's work would challenge the generally accepted location of the Temple Mount. Reuven had a hunch that Earth-Sky symmetry was not the whole story. Lawrence claimed to be a Druid. Druids were known for their skills in geomancy. He went over to the bookshelf and lifted down a large reference book entitled 'The World Grid'*. Then, he thumbed through the index to locate a definition of the Messianic Ley.

Author's Note. This relates to the hypothesis that Planet Earth has a magnetic core to which is linked a network of ley lines and magnetic vortices forming a natural energy system known as the World Grid. The theory extends to the siting of sacred places at carefully calculated high-energy points in the grid. Some proponents of the World Grid concept also claim that the vortices act as gateways to a multi-dimensional level of existence.

The glossary text read as follows,

"The Messianic Ley runs from the Mount of Olives and along the Temple axis, pointing directly to the hill of Golgotha – the purported site of the crucifixion."

Golgotha, Reuven knew, was the strangely shaped mound over which the Crusaders had actually rebuilt the Church of the Holy Sepulchre. The burial and resurrection of Christ is only one of the many legends associated with the spot that got its name from its skull-like form. Other traditions claimed it was the site of the binding of Isaac and even the burial site of Adam.

He turned to a centre-fold grid map spanning a full panorama of the Jerusalem area. Carefully he compared Lawrence's tracing with the grid map. Even though the map was large-scale and had little detail, the correspondence with the Messianic Ley was astoundingly clear. He followed the north/north-western skyline from Scopus to French Hill and into a major convergence of grid lines on the highest peak on the far left of the page. There it was! Nebi Samwil was perfectly aligned at a major intersection of ley lines. According to the World Grid theory, such a vortex was a veritable energy hub, possibly having the power to transport its visitors into other dimensions. What a power source it would be for Global Dawn! He was beside himself with excitement.

"Tamar, my love," he called. "You have to come and see this!"

She did show a little grudging interest in the map, but as soon as he began explaining his theories about the grid, she scoffed and rejected them out of hand.

"Ley lines and power sites. What a bundle of pagan bullshit," she said scathingly.

"Don't you see how ALL the sources are pointing to this one place? The city of Jerusalem. Layer upon layer of human history with so many hidden messages impacted inside it. And here, look at this convergence at the height of Nebi Samwil. This, my love, is where I shall build Global Dawn!"

"Reuven, I know you love the place and feel it's your destiny. What can I say? I can't help the way I feel. You know how I hate Jerusalem and its stifling religiosity. It's just not in my blood the way it's in yours."

"Listen, I've got an idea. What if you were to come with me next time I go to Jerusalem? I've got a gig coming up there and I'm sure you'd enjoy it. I could take you to some of the places on Lawrence's map, too."

"You want me to go to those places so I can feel the special energy you're talking about. The trouble is we've tried this kind of thing before and I never feel anything. You'll only be disappointed by my reaction, and we'll end up having one more thing to quarrel about. Sorry, the idea doesn't appeal to me."

Let down by her negativity, he said nothing more. Her loathing of Jerusalem and anything connected with religion was not news to him. He held on to the conviction that her attitude would change some day. Until then, however, there was no point in stirring up more discord between them. She left the room rather abruptly, and he listened to her receding footsteps until he was sure she was out of earshot. Then, he pulled the door to and picked up the phone to call Ora.

"Hi," he said, "it's me. I'm back and things have taken an amazing turn."

"New Global Dawn developments?" she asked.

"Unbelievable signs and confirmations of our path, Ora!"

She bit her lip and answered him a little dryly,

"More indications of universal synergy in support of your mission?"

Oblivious to her lingering cynicism, Reuven exclaimed,

"Exactly! How did you know?"

"Oh, telepathy, I guess," she said with a wry touch.

"Oh, Ora," he said, sadly. "If only Tamar had a fraction of your faith in me."

"You haven't had another tiff, have you?"

"No, no. Actually, we've never been closer. It's just she still squirms at the least mention of Jerusalem."

"In connection with the project?"

"Well, yes and no. I mean, Global Dawn aside, she refuses to even visit Jerusalem with me! I've got a gig there next week, and she doesn't want to come."

"Couldn't you ask Shahar instead? I'm sure she'd love to hear you on stage."

"Perhaps. I doubt she'd come, though. She's too busy with her own social life."

"So, it's Tamar's apathy that's upset you again, then?"

"Well, it might have if I weren't on such an incredible high, right now."

"But you're not going to tell me what this good mood's about? Do I have to worm it out of you?" she asked, teasingly.

"You can't," he replied in that authoritarian tone of his with which it was impossible to argue. "This is something quite spectacular you have to see for yourself," he said.

"OK. Then, when do I get to see it?"

"The next meeting of The Circle."

"Oh, so you're determined to tantalise me!"

He smirked to himself. How he loved to keep her guessing!

"Well, anyway, I've had my own excitement while you were

away."

"Nu? What?"

"Michael and I have drafted a proposal to the White House. What do you think of that?"

"To Clinton?"

"No, to Al Gore."

"Why Al Gore?"

"He's behind NASA's Digital Earth Project."

"Which is ...?"

"All about global information for the masses. It links up beautifully with Global Dawn, and we're going to offer to be its Israeli reps."

"You and Michael make a sharp team, don't you?"

She was quiet for a moment then, seemingly out of the blue, she asked,

"Reuven, what if I were to accompany you to your Jerusalem gig?"

His reply projected a strange mixture of amusement and wariness.

"Seriously?" he asked.

"Of course."

"Can I get back to you on it later in the week?"

The week drifted on, however, and no call came from Reuven. So, on the evening before the performance, Ora took the initiative to ring him. She found him in a raw temper following a frustrating discussion with Sam. Sam's inept rationalization of his delay in completing the logo was reason enough for him to be annoyed, but all that was exacerbated by his obstruction of the boys' work on the website.

"I can't stand the way he suffocates his son's talents in the name of good parenting."

"I thought his son was a pretty independent-minded lad," replied Ora. "I doubt he'd be that easily put down by his father's meddling."

"You don't understand!" Reuven fumed. "Sam thinks we're in the business of exploiting youth labour and he's forbidden his son from working with us!"

To Ora, this was only confirmation that her antipathy towards the man was well founded from the start.

"Hmm. How I love controlling parents! Did you try to set him straight?"

"I was too bloody outraged to discuss it with him. I feel like taking the logo right out of his hands now. How can we let him do work for Global Dawn when his whole attitude is so out of sync?"

"Mmm. I felt there was something phoney about him from the moment I stepped into his pseudo-spiritual home."

"You've got good instincts about people, Ora. I guess I should have listened to you."

"By the way, you should be hearing from Nathan."

"Oh? Why?"

"He rang me today. He sounds enthusiastic about Global Dawn, but he's got some questions for you."

"Good. I'll call him when I can. To be honest, though, I need to catch a few hours sleep right now. Coming with me tomorrow then, are you?"

"That's the plan ..."

"Till tomorrow, then?"

"Yup. Till tomorrow."

* * *

Reuven and his guitar had travelled the roads of Europe in traditional troubadour fashion during the days of his bohemian youth. Into rock rhythms and love ballads, he poured the totality of his soul in sentiment, satire, humour and sheer volume release. He carried his music to bars, café-theatres and festivals. His publicity was by word of mouth, and the gigs helped to keep him solvent in dry periods of fieldwork.

Ora was delighted to be accompanying him to Jerusalem not only for the music, but also because of the symbolic poignancy of their travelling together to the city of their mutual dream. He picked her up in the early evening, and the little red Fiat shot out of Tel-Aviv onto the Jerusalem highway.

They drove past Sha'ar Hagai and began climbing into the winding approach hills of Jerusalem. Soon, the outlying suburbs came into view, darkly silhouetted against the dying sunset. Reuven pointed across the valley to their left.

"Look. Can you see a minaret over on the ridge?"

"Aha, just about."

"That's Nebi Samwil. It's the highest point in the whole Jerusalem area. The view from the top of the mosque is incredible. Next time, I'll take you there."

Ora glimpsed that familiar otherworldly look in his eyes as he watched the distant shadow of the ridge merge with the night.

They entered the city by the International Convention Centre and then cut along a side road where they slowed to a crawl behind a garbage collection vehicle through the debris of the Mahane Yehuda market.

He tapped impatiently on the wheel.

"Jerusalem's quite a different world from Tel-Aviv, isn't it?" remarked Ora, cheerily.

Some young Arab boys on bikes piled high with pita bread, bagels and discarded fruit were navigating narrow spaces between the chaotically parked trucks.

"Skillful, aren't they?" she carried on.

"If you say so," came his disgruntled answer making her turn towards him in surprise. But before she could say anything, he had stuffed a tape into the machine, turned it up to high volume and resumed his finger-tapping to the beat of the music. With a shrug of incomprehension, she went back to her window-gazing.

When they emerged from the market, they crossed over the congested Jaffa Road and headed towards the Old City. The road narrowed as they approached the Russian Compound, and Reuven parked across from the imposing green-domed cathedral. The floodlighting of its white stone façade gave it an extraordinary luminescence.

"Been here before?" he asked.

"Mmm. Long time ago. Seems different now, somehow."

"They've done a clean-up job on some of the buildings."

"The cathedral's magnificent, isn't it?"

"Certainly is. The Russian Consulate used to be in that building over there. There was originally a hospital here, too – back at the end of the nineteenth century. And over there were kitchens and hospices for Russian pilgrims."

Ora loved to hear all his explanations. He was a fascinating travel companion. At some time or other, he had mapped almost every street in Jerusalem, so he knew the place like the back of his hand and told its history with professional confidence. She latched onto his arm, leaning affectionately towards him as they walked and he talked. She was relieved that he seemed to be over his grouchiness.

The original stone houses of the compound had undergone a facelift recently to suit the cool fashions of a music-seeking, beer-swilling crowd. Bars were installed where waitresses circulated in the aisles taking european-style tips. The café-theatre at which Reuven was due to appear was one of numerous such entertainment centres along the cobbled alleyways of the Compound.

"Look down the passageway by the club over there. What do you see?"

"Nothing much," said Ora. "Just some rather ugly old buildings and a high stone wall."

"That's the courthouse," he said breezily. "You must have seen it a thousand times on TV. The other two buildings are the police headquarters and the detention centre. Grim, aren't they?" he said with apparent satisfaction.

She agreed. Paradoxical, she thought, the proximity of these dour establishments to Jerusalem's most popular young entertainment dive.

"In here," he called, cutting into her thoughts and prodding her stiffly through an open doorway. "This is it. Park yourself where you can. I'm on pretty soon."

With that, he disappeared into the back leaving her to her own devices. She found an empty table towards the stage and ordered a long beer. The loud grating of metal on the stone floor behind her told her tables were filling up. It looked like a full house.

The current set was by a resident musician whose crude renditions of Israeli pop songs encouraged an enthusiastic off-pitch sing-along by the audience. Passable, but no competition for Reuven, Ora thought to herself. The garrulous crowd – soldiers, students, here a tourist, there an ageing hippy – were generous with their applause.

When he went on stage, his black waistcoat open over a fresh white shirt and a wide performer smile stretching to the limits of his cheeks, there was no hint of the nervousness that she had glimpsed earlier. He ruffled his hair back from his brow and launched theatrically into a baudy English ballad. In his inimitable style, he challenged his listeners' inhibitions with the artful movement and explicit gesture that accompanied his music.

Ora watched his gyrating, ecstatic figure enticing listeners and reeling them in. What would it take, she wondered, to satisfy such a voracious appetite for adoration? If the beat was wild, he needed it wilder; if the lyrics were crude, he took bawdiness to its limits – a king on his platform, commanding, manipulating and defying the rules of convention. And his audience followed him from exuberance to trance and from bright hand clapping to blues. His voice needed no amplification in the hollow acoustics of the place. Jacques Brel's sardonic tale of illicit ladies in the Port of Amsterdam, delivered with guttural relish and a rawly declaimed finale, ripped wild cheers from all corners of the room. Then, with saddened eyes he seduced his audience right into the gut of Elton John's evocative eulogy to the light of Diana,

'Candle in the Wind'. Ora, too, was wooed to tears by its tragic beauty. He actually spoke very little on stage, relying on eye contact and body language to convey the messages in his music. The high-spirited response was evidence that he had conquered enough souls to justify this journey to the City of Peace.

At her solitary table, Ora sat sipping beer until her head began to reel. She looked on in wonder as Reuven's thirst for self-endorsement manifested itself on this stage. It was the same passion that drove him to lead Global Dawn. The Circle was just another stage, after all – a clutch of fellow travellers, believers in his elusive self. She thought back to his anger at her hesitation to work with him. He needed to be able to count on her unqualified commitment. His wounded child spirit ever sought affirmation of its self worth in the glances and arms of women in a great circle of project followers and here on stage.

Towards the end of the evening, the audience dwindled and the ambience warmed. The remaining loyal number moved closer and joined in the refrains of better-known tunes until closing time was announced.

Off-stage and awaiting the owner's reaction, Reuven seemed agitated again. Instead of admitting his anxiety to Ora, however, he avoided her glances and made a superficial show of self-confidence by flirting with one of the waitresses. When, at last, the owner came over to exchange a few words, he responded with a contrite smile and a terse handshake. Then he beckoned to Ora and made to leave.

On the way home, she was dying for him to share his feelings with her, but he was incommunicative. She looked up at him, but his eyes were fixed on the road as if oblivious of her. There was a chill in the air, and she reached behind her for a jacket to pull across her shoulders. She rubbed her palms together to warm them. His focus on the road seemed undeterred by her fidgeting.

"You were really fantastic, tonight," she ventured.

"Thanks"

More silence.

"It was so special for me. I felt as if you were aiming some of those songs directly at me. As if there were secret messages there ..."

"Could be."

Still intoxicated, she was coping badly with his stonewalling of her. As they drove on, however, he maintained his detachment. She stared at his rigid profile, searching for ways to soften it into one more amiable.

"Reuven, doesn't it thrill you?" she insisted. "You have such power over the stage!"

"Yeh, I guess so," he replied, poker-faced.

Not knowing how else to react, she snuggled up to him. She felt his shoulder first stiffen then relax. Naïvely misreading his passivity, she let her cheek fall onto his arm.

A half an hour later, the car pulled up outside her home, and she was utterly unprepared for his sealing of the night in anger.

"Your infantile demands for attention are really the last thing I needed, tonight, Ora! I thought you were adult enough to accompany me on a gig without exploiting the opportunity to selfishly dump a whole load of emotional baggage on me!"

"I wasn't," she protested. "I was just trying to be supportive."

"Well, that's not what it felt like. It seemed like an uncalled-for intrusion on my privacy!"

Devastated, she sulked wordlessly out of the car and into the lobby of her building. As she entered the darkened apartment, she was relieved her family were asleep and would not witness her confusion and tears.

*　　*　　*

"A map of the world which doesn't include Utopia isn't even worth glancing at."
Oscar Wilde

Her mood was scarcely any calmer in the morning when she arrived at Rosa's for her scheduled weekly consultation. Rosa's cat with the all-knowing amber eyes escorted her from the doorway into the consulting room. Her nerves were all on edge. Eyeing the low chair she was expected to sit in, she lingered on the couch.

She felt Rosa scanning her face and body language.

"Ora, why don't you take your usual seat?" she asked.

"I'm not sure I'm ready to talk, today. It's been a very confusing time for me."

"Why don't you just tell me what's been happening at home? What's going on with the kids?"

"Oh, they're all fine. Nothing dramatic to report," she said dismissively. Then, as an afterthought, she added,

"Well, I suppose my decision to leave my job is having some affect on them."

She got up from the couch to take a drink of water and sat down again in the regular chair.

"So, the pressure's off. That's good, isn't it?"

Ora shrugged her shoulders.

"Or are there other pressures on you, now?"

"Oh, I don't know. Just the usual me, over-anxious to please everyone. Miss Perfection, know what I mean?"

"Absolutely. I think you're probably your own worst critic. Do you think I'm right?"

"For sure."

"What about your friends. How do you think they see you?"

"It's funny, actually, my closest friends seem to admire me. Apparently, they think I'm a reliable workmate, a good mother and wife, hospitable and very energetic."

"But you don't view yourself so positively, do you?"

"I just feel so mediocre."

"And what about your new project partner? How are the two of you getting along?"

At this, Ora collapsed into a flood of tears. She tugged a great wad of tissues from the Kleenex box beside her and downed a whole glass of water in one gulp.

"I had a really unpleasant row with him yesterday," she sobbed.

"Is it something you can talk about?"

"I don't know," she mumbled. "I thought everything was really great between us; I was only trying to be supportive!"

"And what happened?"

"He lashed out at me; said I was intruding on his privacy!"

"Do you think you were?"

"I don't know. I didn't think so," she said, clenching the compacted tissues in her tight fist. "I thought we'd got really close. After all, he did share his precious dream with me, and I accepted it all in perfect faith, too!"

"Perhaps you had expectations of him he wasn't ready to handle?"

"I guess. And you know, this incredible dream of his – sometimes I wonder if it's even feasible!"

Her confusion and anger suddenly seemed to come to a head.

"My, my. This is really taking a toll on you," said Rosa.

Little by little over the next half hour or so, Rosa succeeded in coaxing out of her the full picture of how intertwined her life had become with Reuven's and the nature of the web he had spun around her.

"On the one hand," she was saying, "I find the project incredibly stimulating. Then again, the sheer size of it frightens me."

"From what you've just told me that's hardly surprising!"

"Still ... this is going to sound crazy, but I find working with him more satisfying than anything I've ever tackled before."

"Even when he behaves as callously as he did yesterday?"

"Oh, it was really my fault ..."

"There you go again! Will you just listen to yourself? Sounds to me as if he's created some kind of utopian fantasy, and he's got you flying up there on his cloud without a safety net!"

Ora felt crushed. This psychotherapy seemed to be developing into an exercise in demolishing her dreams. The aim was to bring her down to Earth, but the truth was she was all too acquainted with the boredom and monotony of a grounded existence. After all, who was to say where the limits of possibility really lay?

She looked up ready to challenge Rosa's judgment, but Rosa was checking her watch.

"Well, dear," she said, "I suggest you think carefully about our conversation, and we'll talk again in a few days."

As she came down into the street and made her way to the bus stop, she went over and over the incident with Reuven in her mind. Was Rosa right? Did he have unfair expectations of her? Her family certainly seemed to think so, and he did seem to take an awful lot for granted. She thought back to his previous angry outburst when she refused to be at his beck and call. Then again, he had been so adamant about not wanting to be looked upon as someone special, like a guru. A call on her cell phone from none other than Reuven interrupted her meditation. She was stunned by the levity of his tone.

"Ora, I'm sorry I was so harsh, yesterday."

She said nothing.

"Ora?" he asked. "You're not still upset with me, are you?"

Had he stood facing her at that moment, she might easily have slapped him in unbridled indignation. As it was, she launched into a vehement verbal outpouring.

"How could you behave like that towards me? I was only trying to be a good friend! I'm sick of playing doormat for your bad moods! You take me for granted, Reuven. Expect me to work like a slave! Not a word of gratitude! And Heaven forbid there should be any feelings between us – oh, no, that's too heavy! You can't cope with it, can you? Must be me who's immature and self-centred! Couldn't possibly be you! Better pack me off to a psychologist! Salve your bad conscience, did it? Well, how convenient!"

She had worked herself up into a state of near hysteria. Reuven was stunned into silence. Eventually, he said in a matter-of-fact tone,

"I guess you're not used to the company of artists."

"What do you mean?" she quipped, pressing her free hand to her forehead. Her head was aching from the stress of it all.

"I need quiet space to rebalance after a performance."

Somehow, this couching of his apology in self-justification irritated her even more. He must have sensed as much when he hurriedly added,

"Look, I think you should get some rest. I promise we'll talk about this properly.

Perhaps I could come round this evening?"

"I'm sorry, but this evening's already booked with my family," came her piqued reply.

"Well, what about tomorrow, then?"

"How about I call you when I'm ready, Reuven?" she asked coolly.

"Fine. Speak to you, then," he answered in an incongruously high-spirited manner.

He rang off, leaving her totally confused by the volatility of his moods.

*   *   *

The week dragged on and Ora put off confronting Reuven. The next meeting of The Circle was due within a few days. She knew they ought to talk, but pride kept her from making the call even after her anger had actually subsided. Eventually, he took the initiative by suggesting they meet in a café – neutral ground to avoid antagonism of either family.

She spotted him immediately standing gazing distractedly through the terrace doors and out across the park. "Hello, Reuven," she said.

He turned towards her but seemed only half aware of her presence beside him. He had that hazy visionary look of his about him.

Then he began to speak in the cautious, formal way he always used to test new ideas on her.

"Ora, I'm thinking of building a great dome at Nebi Samwil. We can house Global Dawn's central information system inside it."

His voice was forceful, and the public display he was making began to embarrass her. As luck would have it, however, the café was almost empty. She relaxed and listened as he spoke about his dream of such a dome and about how its echo had materialized out of nowhere in the shape of Lawrence's home.

His words painted themselves into her imagination. So, Nebi Samwil was his chosen site. She visualised its peak topped by a stunning dome of sparkling crystal. It was an icon of pure beauty to accompany her through all the coming months of her work on the project.

"Perfect," she whispered, thinking there could be no more fitting expression of their dream than to build this crystalline landmark on the Jerusalem skyline. At night, it would appear as luminous as a white moon above the city, and by day, its light would be diffused into a myriad of rainbows across the land.

"I can see it now," she said. "A totally translucent structure casting its splendid aura far and wide."

Reuven seemed deeply moved by her words.

"Your vision is exquisite, Ora," he said, and he leaned over to kiss her in a gesture of promised partnership. At that moment, Ora knew their alliance was far more compelling than any friction between them that might have temporarily clouded her senses.

Totally mellowed and entranced, Ora asked,

"Isn't this a special Global Dawn moment that deserves to be celebrated?"

"I think so. What kind of celebration did you have in mind, Ora?"

His question hung unanswered in the air as he drew her spontaneously into his arms in an ecstatic embrace of extraordinary tenderness and truth that seemed in that moment to be the convergence of all their previous journeys.

Chapter 6

Menashe Ben Eliezer rises daily with the early dawn in his stone cottage, overlooking the southern, forested slopes of Ein Karem's Yemenite Valley. Clothed in white cotton pyjamas, he places an urn of water on the gas and shuffles across the cold bare stone floor, down a few shallow and uneven steps into the bathroom. A large enamel tub stands beside the crudely exposed wall facing him. All is designed for utilitarian purpose – unabashed and unrefined – a sturdy message of silent opposition to lovers of fancy fashion trim. Menashe's home is the product of his own hands. In the foothills of Jerusalem, the local stone graces the architectural landscape in warm shades of cream, red and pink. Menashe's skilled hands have chiselled and formed it into the basic building blocks of his home. He has smoothed and polished the harder dolomite rock to tile the floor. All the window frames and doors are of local wood, and the artistic embellishments of the inner hallway and upper courtyard are worked in rustic iron.

To enter Menashe's pristine home is to distance oneself from the fastidiousness of modernity. He lives with the bare minimum of furniture in symbiotic connection with his environment.

* * *

On the particular day when Reuven first stumbled upon Menashe's homestead, he approached it from the North across the outermost boundary of its domain. As he stepped up towards the olive grove, terrace by terrace, a fox darted across his path and then slowed its pace in stealthy pursuit of a frightened hare. Reuven maintained an unobtrusive distance in order to observe the tracking tactics of the fox. Without warning, curiously, it abandoned the chase and allowed the hare its freedom. A shy kitten nestled all the while deep in a side bush, trembling.

As Reuven proceeded through the grove above the north face

of the house, he spotted the silhouette of a man extended across a reclining branch of a twisted tree, face lifted to the flight of ravens in the morning sunlight. Reuven lay back against a neighbouring tree. For twenty minutes or so the two remained thus side-by-side in silent meditation. Eventually, the man clambered down from the tree and offered Reuven his hand in welcome. As they went through the ritual of exchanging names, each felt in his soul the other was no stranger.

Menashe showed Reuven his pottery shed and the modest exhibition of his artistry inside the house where they lounged over coffee at a low table in the single furnished corner of the living room. Reuven felt extraordinarily relaxed – a fact that might be attributed both to the natural beauty of the place and to the easy, unquestioning hospitality of its owner.

*   *   *

A literal translation of the name Ein Karem is 'Spring of the Vineyard' after the natural spring that originally watered its vine-covered terraces. References to Ein Karem in Christian and Islamic religious sources are extremely obscure, but they have nonetheless marked the place with a spiritual association in the hearts of their believers. The village today is a predominantly Jewish centre of art, music and tourism, attracting international visitors of all religions and cultures.

Menashe welcomed The Circle warmly to his home, which provided a singularly attractive setting for their second meeting. He had arranged an intimate discussion area with casual rugs and floor cushions at the centre of his spacious living room. On the terrace, he had laid out salads, olives, labane, cheeses, herbs and bread, all fresh from the market. A few bottles of rough but potent, local red wine added a festive note to this second meeting of The Circle to which came all those who had attended the previous gathering. Reuven was delighted by the full house.

"So, what have you got planned for us, today? Another brainstorming session?" asked Michael provocatively.

"I think we should talk about the overall design of Global Dawn."

"Architectural or operational?"

"Both. Same principles apply."

"How so?"

"Universal synergy."

"Reuven, you're talking in riddles," protested Ariella.

"Nature basically consists of a huge geometric system, made up of spirals, hexagons, pentagons, triangles and so on."

"Like snowflakes and galaxies and cosmic wheels!" exclaimed Rikki.

"Can someone get the girl a coffee, please? I'm not sure she can handle this esoteric stuff," laughed Michael.

"Go on, Reuven," urged Ora.

"Actually, she's right about the cosmic dimensions of what I'm describing. That's why it's the ideal design for our project."

Nathan began to twiddle his thumbs restlessly, then got up and wandered out onto the terrace.

"You're saying we can model our project on Nature itself?" asked Ariella.

"Exactly. There's no more flexible or resilient design in the world."

A faint smile indicated Menashe's concurrence with Reuven's words. His inflated physique was extended across a scarlet floor cushion that almost competed with his dimensions and rotundity. He rolled over into less of a slump and more of a semi-recline, pensive chin on crooked wrist, to add his perspective on how Global Dawn would evolve.

"The project's going to take on different forms at different times," he said.

"And we will be the constant feeders of its fire," asserted Michael with sudden enthusiasm.

"Mmm. Yes and no."

"What do you mean, Menashe?" asked Reuven, half-distracted.

"As the project changes and grows, there'll be a natural inflow and outflow of people."

"I'm not sure I follow you."

"You, for example. You're Global Dawn's leader now but, like Moses in the Bible, you're not guaranteed the job of carrying it into the Promised Land."

"That's true," Reuven agreed. "I'm not the project's creator. It's my task and privilege to lead it through this stage of its journey. It existed in essence long before me; it has its own life and purpose."

He glanced around the room anxiously. Menashe had a tendency to draw the discussion onto a philosophical plane, and he had thus already managed to alienate several members of the group. Nathan had just returned to his place, but now Ariella and Ora had withdrawn to the window-seat where they were chatting in subdued tones just out of earshot.

"Let's take a little break, shall we?" he suggested.

"So soon? We've scarcely begun," objected Michael, but

Reuven was already heading for the terrace. He helped himself to a drink and stood looking across the valley as the dusk crept over it. As the rest of the group filtered out to join him, softly, at first, came the sound of drumming and Rikki's shrill soprano voice. The drumbeat faded. Someone handed Reuven a guitar. The music was actually Reuven's own composition based on an old Arab melody. He chose it to convey in words and rhythm the imprint of the former inhabitants of Ein Karem. A hearty round of applause lifted his spirits. It had been a well-timed interlude, after all.

"OK, now let's get back to work," he said cheerily. "I want you all to pull up your chairs and cushions so you can see what I'm about to show you."

As they organised themselves, he unrolled Lawrence's map and laid it out ceremoniously on the low table.

"Is this your work, Reuven?" asked Nathan.

"This, my friend, is a vital piece of the Master Plan!

"How so?"

"Like the Kabbalah, Rikki, this map has different levels of meaning – some evident, some obscure."

"This map shows Jerusalem through the eyes of a sacred sites researcher.

He took out the page of tracings and carefully positioned it over the map.

"And these are his tracings of their prototypes in the sky."

"So, he's matched the layout of Jerusalem with various constellations of stars?"

"Yes, that much he told me, but Lawrence is very secretive about his discoveries."

Ora was captivated by the geometric shapes before her. They reminded her of the shapes Reuven had drawn in the sand at Achziv – a pattern of triangles, a pentagon, an oddly slanted rectangle ...

Clearly relishing the suspense he had created, Reuven brandished the World Grid Atlas in front of the group and whipped it open at the Jerusalem page.

"I guessed my Druid friend wasn't telling me everything about his work. But then I had a brainwave. The key's in here!" he said triumphantly.

Nathan peered blankly at the open book.

"This is a visualisation of nature's energy patterns. It's every modern Druid's handy guide."

"So, your new friend, Lawrence claims to be a Druid, Reuven?"

"And he goes out dowsing for ley lines?"

"I'm pretty sure that's what he's up to, yes."

"I see it, now!" exclaimed Ariella in sudden realisation.

"What, Ariella?"

"Have you found Reuven's magic key?"

Ariella's eyes were laughing, now.

Obviously still utterly in the dark, Nathan was looking impatiently over her shoulder.

"Ariella, come on, girl. Give us a clue?" entreated Michael.

"You're all missing Reuven's point, here. Forget about the Old City. Look at the far left of the page. See how that mass of lines converges over there?"

"As if all roads lead to Nebi Samwil!" shrieked Ora in a rush of excitement.

"Exactly. See how easily it fits into the pattern?"

"Yes," she answered in quiet disbelief. "It gives a most uncanny feeling of ancient design, as if Nebi Samwil's just waiting for us."

Reuven looked at her elatedly. So, at last, even the sceptical Ora had accepted the existence of a higher design. Her eyes met his in unspoken acknowledgement. Michael and Nathan, meanwhile, were exchanging looks of concern.

"So that's where you plan to build Global Dawn? But, won't it cost an awful lot of money to buy all that land?" asked Rikki.

"Maybe so, but all in good time. Just remember that our intended location is chosen."

Reuven folded away the map and the tracing, and firmly closed the book.

"And now," he said, "Ora and I have some more ideas to run by you all."

"Oh, right," said Ora, suddenly leaping into action. "Disney and all that!"

Nathan began to look disgruntled again. He began scratching his chin and tensing his face muscles.

"Nathan, what's wrong?"

"First, all this talk of magic energy sources and now we're back to your grandiose theme park idea. Aren't we bouncing around rather merrily in Fantasyland?"

"Steady on, Nathan. Walt Disney's vision of Epcot was pretty radical too, you know," replied Reuven.

"Yes, and his real vision was never actually built because it was too impractical," said Michael.

"What do you mean?"

"Epcot was originally intended to be the 'Experimental

Prototype Community of Tomorrow'. He wanted it to be a whole town that would be a continual showcase of modern living. Disney believed, like you do Reuven, that the special energy of the place would magically generate solutions to all the technical problems as they occurred."

"And look at the wonderful success of Epcot!"

"Yes, but it's nothing like his original dream!"

It was Menashe's turn to put things in perspective.

"This is just proving the point I made at the beginning. We can't set a rigid format for our project because it will inevitably change along with the people involved in it. Michael, what you're saying doesn't detract from Disney's idea. He was its visionary, not its creator."

"OK, so where do we go from here?" asked Michael with a sudden urge to get things moving on a practical level.

"Well, what we need now is to organise ourselves to approach investors, isn't it?" asked Nathan.

"Right. That's what Ora and I wanted to tell you about."

Ora explained about the Digital Earth and the possibility of an alliance between the two projects.

"Okay, but how are we going to persuade NASA or an investor to take us seriously?" Rikki wanted to know.

"That part's right up your alley, Rikki. You can use all those hot Hollywood contacts of yours, can't you?"

"But we have to have something to show them."

"Disney produced a whole film about Epcot. That's how he did it."

"I vote we do the same," she said, her voice squeaking with excitement.

"Don't forget we have no budget for anything glamorous," cautioned Ariella.

"OK, guys, here's my suggestion," said Reuven. "Rikki, I want you to get a promotional team together, and Michael, you and Nathan can handle the technical side of things. Menashe, Ora, Ariella and myself will, of course, support you, but you should also be thinking about getting some new blood involved in the action. Ora's computer is, for now, our central Global Dawn contact point, by the way."

"We should arrange another review and planning meeting of The Circle before the end of the year, Reuven."

"OK. Any volunteers to host it?"

"You can probably have it at my place," said Rikki, "but I'll need to get back to you on it."

"OK. Sounds good."

Nathan slipped out onto the terrace and came straight back

swinging a bottle and corkscrew.

"How about a parting toast to the success of Global Dawn?"

"Good guy!" agreed Michael as the glasses clinked.

*   *   *

The next day Ora was due to visit Rosa again. She decided to put the visit off and, telephone receiver already in hand, she searched for a feasible pretext. After conveying her brief message, she could tell from Rosa's tone her excuse was transparent. No doubt, she would question her about it at their next meeting. Meanwhile, she felt too relaxed and free of pressure to have a therapist knock her off her new cloud.

Reuven's work contract in the northern Negev was due to start the following week. He picked up the phone to Ora and arranged to meet her in a café near his home.

No sooner did they sit down than his cell interrupted them. It was the long-awaited call from Nathan.

"Nate, my man. What's on your mind?"

"Reuven, I listened carefully to everything at the last meeting, and I'm afraid the project doesn't work for me. At least, not as I see it, right now."

Reuven stiffened at this belated negativity.

"Why didn't you mention this earlier?"

"I wanted to, but the thing is my whole approach is so different from yours."

"What do you mean?"

"I don't feel the project has enough spunk to grab potential investors. Your philosophy is inspiring, but, as a project basis, it just doesn't do it for me."

Reuven did some quick thinking.

"Listen, Nate. What if we give you a chance to turn our image into dynamite? Something you can do from home without it impinging on your work schedule?"

"Try me."

"How would you like to design the Global Dawn website? You can get help from Ora – she's already put some ideas together. Michael can give you a hand, too, I'm sure. But this would be your baby."

"Do you think you'll like my ideas?"

"Can't promise anything till I see them. What do you say?"

"Yeh, why not," said Nathan. "I'll give it my best shot."

"Keep me posted then! Bye for now," said Reuven, tucking his phone back into his pocket and flashing a look of satisfaction at Ora.

"That was clever of you."

"Hmm. So, on the subject of psychological manoeuvrings, what's happening with you and Rosa? Been to see her lately?"

"I wanted to talk to you about that. I think I'm going to stop going to her."

"Isn't that a bit soon? Are the sessions stressful?"

"That's just it. I don't feel she really tackles the sensitive things."

"Isn't that up to you?"

"To some extent, yes, but a professional therapist shouldn't let me gloss over stuff. It's almost as if she's letting her own emotions get in the way of her professional judgement."

"I'm surprised. Perhaps you really have outgrown her, already. So, when are you going to tell her?"

"On my next visit, I think, – at the beginning of next week. What about your problem with Sam? Is it resolved?"

"Not really. I'm meeting him later this week to collect the logo. I'm presuming the boys' effort on the website is dead."

"Pity. Guess it's a good thing you put it to Nathan, then."

Reuven signalled the waiter for the bill.

"Where are you rushing off to?"

"Ariella suggested I meet her in the *midrahov*. D'you want to come?"

"Not this time, Reuven. I've got plenty to keep me busy for the next day or two!"

"Let's be in touch later, then."

"Okay. Say hello to Ariella for me."

*   *   *

Reuven found the *midrahov* brimming with its characteristic life, vivid colours and sounds. He took in the scene hurriedly as he wound his way past the multitude of merchant stands displaying what seemed to be a greater preponderance of kitsch than he recalled from previous visits.

Ariella spotted him in the high tide of the approaching crowd, and called out brightly,

"Reuven, it's good to see you."

He embraced her warmly and joined her behind her familiar umbrella. They sat observing the ebb and flow. She lit a cigarette as he sipped thick Turkish coffee from a brown-stained, paper cup.

"Business good, today?" he asked.

"Moderately so."

"So, what's up?"

"I remembered how fascinated you were by Assaf's story."

"Yes, I was. I've thought about it a lot since we met, but what does that have to do with your inviting me here today?"

"I came across a book that gives the all-time definitive word on Assaf's pet subject."

"Which is?"

"Perceptions of time."

"The all-time definitive word, you say?"

"I reckon so. It's quite heavy reading, though, based on the ideas of an ancient civilization."

"You're talking about something far-eastern, maybe Tibetan?"

"No, American. I'm talking about the Maya. They created what's said to be the most accurate calendar ever known.

"Sounds pretty interesting. They were supposed to have been amazingly knowledgeable about the cycles of Nature."

"I can lend you my copy of Arguelles' book, 'The Mayan Factor' to read, if you like?"

"That's the book you're talking about? I've heard about it."

"It's quite incredible. Not only did the Maya understand the cycles of time, but they knew about universal rhythms."

"What do you mean?"

"According to the book, they kept close track of changing patterns in the sky and used complex mathematical calculations to predict the movements of the planets."

"What kind of predictions did they make?"

"They could tell in what season and what year there would be an eclipse, for example."

"How accurate were they?"

"Very – to the extent that they've left modern scientists baffled by their sophistication."

"And what exactly is the 'Mayan Factor'?"

"You'll have to read the book to understand it properly. It involves the use of their unique calendar to forecast events thousands of years ahead."

Without a doubt, she had Reuven's attention now. He moved his stool closer to hers and placed his blue bag on the ground close beside him.

"So what did they predict?"

"They saw world history as the unfolding of a great cosmic plan … Excuse me a moment, Reuven."

An attractive young Scandinavian woman had approached the table and was holding one of Ariella's most elegant double bracelets over her slender sun-bronzed wrist.

"The card says 'Ariella'. Is that you?"

"Yes, that's me," she responded with her habitual fresh, bright tone.

"Your jewellery is exquisite."

"Well, thank you. Can I help you at all?"

"It's a difficult choice."

"Take your time. Would you like me to pick out a necklace to match that bracelet, perhaps?"

"No. I'm really just interested in a bracelet. I like this one, but it seems a little large for me."

"I can adjust it for you and, of course, I'll put a fastening on it."

Ariella reached into a canvas bag pinned to the side of the table and, as she fumbled inside it for the right weight and style of fastening, she apologised to Reuven for the interruption.

"Don't worry. Why don't I go and get us both some drinks from the kiosk while you give this lovely lady the undivided attention she deserves?"

Meanwhile, Ariella offered his seat to her customer and worked with her skilled, nimble fingers to fit the bracelet comfortably to the woman's satisfaction.

"How's that, now?"

"It's lovely. Thank you, so much. How much does it cost?"

"It's a hundred and sixty shequels."

"You don't happen to know how much that would be in dollars, do you?"

"I can calculate it for you, if you like. It's roughly forty dollars, and I'll give you a special ten percent discount on it if you promise to come and visit me again on your next trip."

"Thank you so much."

"Goodbye and have a good holiday in Israel."

Reuven returned with the drinks and began pressing Ariella to tell him more about the 'Mayan Factor'.

"According to the famous Mayan Prophesy, the great cycle of the Mayan calendar which lasted almost five thousand years, will be over very soon. Its final day will be the 23rd of December, 2012. Of course, there's a lot of controversy about the specific date."

"So what exactly is supposed to happen after the calendar finishes?"

"The Mayans believed the world as they knew it would end.

Their vision was that Earth would enter the fourth dimension in 2013.

"Weren't the Mayans said to be cosmic time travellers?"

"Yes. Their writings predict their return to Earth in 2012."

"Sounds intriguing."

"It's actually a difficult book to understand. Arguelles' sources are very obscure, and they involve interpretations of Mayan hieroglyphics and symbols."

"How widely are his theories accepted?"

"Scientists, archaeologists and other experts continue to debate them. In the end it comes down to whether or not you can make a giant leap of faith to accept his extraordinary viewpoint."

"I'm sure I'll enjoy the challenge, and I look forward to discussing it all with you when I've finished reading."

Ariella straightened the tablecloth and anchored its corners against the wind. She pinned her hair back from her face and stretched her legs under the table. She enjoyed Reuven's visits, their cultural and philosophical exchanges, and occasional gossip. Reuven took the book from her and began to read it with great curiosity the same day.

During the following week, he spent almost every evening engrossed in studying the book. He entered the following thoughts and comments in his diary.

"Trying to fathom the meanings of the Mayan glyphs is like tackling a whole new computer language. I'm amazed to find my favourite theme of linear and non-linear time as a *leitmotif* in the story of this ancient civilisation.

By tracking the movements of the Moon, Venus, and other heavenly bodies, the ancient Maya became aware of the cosmic cycle of time and foresaw the eventual transition of humanity to a multi-dimensional future. Just like Assaf Goren, the author points to art and the artist as the keys to this change."

He put down his pen and picked up a photograph of Shahar at nearly four, half-naked and delightfully uninhibited, balancing an inflated plastic globe above her head. Already, as a toddler, thought Reuven, she held the world at her command. The photograph was mounted alongside a framed reproduction of the Global Dawn logo. The globe at its centre also formed the pupil of an eye – the fifth dimensional mirror of the human spirit. He resumed writing.

"The lines are clearly drawn. As to whether the Maya will indeed return in their spaceships in 2012, or whether the world will see messianic revelations preceded by an apocalypse, any comment I might enter here would be presumptuous. I'm convinced, however, Planet Earth is now moving into a new cosmic plane and towards new dimensions, as foretold by our distant ancestors and ill understood by modern science.

During the period of transition, we're going to see an evolving drama of confusion, disbelief and intellectual chaos. As these developments intensify, it will be vitally important for Global Dawn's information network to be ready to disseminate knowledge and enlightenment. This is the challenge I accept as my personal mission."

Chapter 7

*"Who is this that comes up out of the desert like pillars of smoke,
perfumed with myrrh and frankincense, with all the powder of a merchant?"*
                                                          Song of Songs, Chapter 4.

The casual traveller discovers in the desert no greater truth than the evanescence of the sands. To him, the desert is inhospitable, and its mirages reveal illusory promises. To the timid, the desert is intimidating, to the fugitive it offers no refuge, and whoever flees from his own self in the desert will ultimately face a cruel mirror.

The bold may find the desert an exhilarating testing ground. Believers may find here inspiration and salvation, and a man in search of his soul may indeed discover it in the desert.

The desert sands appear unchanging over history as they breeze over the traces of all those who have traversed them. The rocks of the Negev desert and its craters bear testimony to ancient volcanic upheaval, at once a stark memory of prehistory and a forewarning of future Earth dramas. The native inhabitants of the desert are wandering tribes whose features are unaltered over millennia.

Desert faces are shrouded in mystery. They carry an otherworldly aura beyond linear time.

*   *   *

A few kilometres to the south of Beersheva, on a hill above the main highway stood the small town of Kadmon, home of Shira. Born in North Africa, Shira was a woman of the desert, carried to the Negev on a hot dry wind via the southern beaches of France. As she swept the obstinate dust layers again and again from her balcony, she felt no anger at this intrusion of the desert into her home. The rocks and sand had a historic claim on this territory justified by centuries of undisturbed existence before ever she stepped onto them. She accepted them, submitted to their ways, and derived intense pleasure from the gifts they offered her – goat's hair, lambswool, olive wood, dates, a wealth of minerals and the luxury of an oasis, shimmering with the freshness and cool serenity of its palm-circled waters. A pure, angelic spirit, Shira's name in Hebrew means 'song' and 'poetry'. Her synergy with the land was a source of joy for which she simply thanked God in her daily prayers.

In the central plaza of Kadmon were one flower shop, one real estate office, a café and a gift shop. The latter, Shira's private enterprise, became a popular local meeting place. Shira's personal connections in North Africa blossomed into healthy business sources whence she procured a varied stock of original craft items. Aided by her keen artistic eye and love of vivid colour, she designed her shop with the qualities and shades of ethnic authenticity.

On recent trips to Morocco, she gathered artefacts including fine cedarwood sculpted figurines, woven and embroidered textiles, painted ornaments of onyx and marble, and more. These treasures she lovingly displayed on open shelves allowing customers to appreciate the subtlety of their angles and textures. To them, she added scented candles, musical chimes, incense sticks and some hand-sewn, natural dyed garments. Her days were divided between the shop and the university where she taught English to Arab and Bedouin students.

On the day when Reuven arrived in Kadmon, Shira was routinely serving customers in her shop. A black Persian cat scurried out of the doorway as the chimes announced his entry. He browsed around for a few minutes. Then, he noticed a tapestry couch in the far corner and walked over to it. As he sank into it in the semi-darkness, a soft voice at his side said,

"Shalom, Reuven."

The voice caressed his memory as the silken finish of a long skirt brushed against the bare roughness of his knees. Surprised, he looked up into a familiar face.

"Shira?"

"*Mais oui*! How wonderful to see you!"

She kissed him dramatically on both cheeks.

"My God! Fancy running into you here of all places!"

She smiled at him with that mixture of shy sensuality and childlike candour he remembered so clearly from their first encounter.

"But this is my shop."

"Yours! What a turn of fate!"

"You look tired. You need *energie*. Per'aps some cinnamon tea?"

"No, thanks. Not now. Some water from your cooler'll do me fine."

"You 'ave been working in Kadmon? *Comme c'est bizarre.* Visitors, they are usually big news in our little town."

"I only got here this morning. I'll probably be around for a few weeks, though."

He touched her hand gently, encouraging her to sit down next to him.

"So, this is your place?"

"Yes. Do you like it?" she asked with an ambiguous little smile.

"Mmm. It's got a soothing feel about it. Sensed it as soon as I walked in."

"Maybe it's the candles. Also the rose petals – they 'ave a sweet fragrance."

"Could be. Business here good?"

"*Comme-ci, comme-ça.* Some people come in to buy; some just want a nice place to relax."

"And where do you find all these lovely things?"

"North Africa. Actually, most of them are from Morocco."

"You brought them over here yourself?"

"But of course. Now, it's enough about me. What about you? What is the work you are doing here?"

"Mapping."

"Oh, how wonderful. So, you travel a lot?"

"Yes, but it's not so much the places I get to as the people I meet that I care about."

"Ah. I understand this very well. So, you love people more than places."

"Mmm. Especially when they're as beautiful as you."

"Oh," she blushed and laughed a timid little laugh.

"You know, chance meetings such as this often turn out to be more significant than they seem in the beginning."

"What do you mean?"

"They raise questions; offer new choices. They're signs."

"So my life is very full of signs!"

He lifted his brow and directed a penetrating look into her seductive grey-green eyes.

"All our lives are. Only we don't always notice them."

Shira left him to rest on the couch while she attended to some customers. Meanwhile, her young daughter popped in on her way home from school. Reuven overheard her playfully badgering her mother for the local gossip. Then all of a sudden, she looked over in his direction and gasped.

"Ima, there's a strange guy asleep over there!"

"Yes, Nava, be quiet now. I know 'e's there and 'e's very tired."

"Did you talk to him, Ima?"

"Yes, dear. I know 'im. He's a nice man, and you don't 'ave to worry about 'im."

"But he looks all dirty," she whispered loudly. "His clothes are covered in dust."

"That's because 'e's been working outside."

"Can I talk to him when he wakes up?"

"Yes, but don't disturb 'im now, Nava. Oh, Nava ..."

"It's alright. I'm awake," grinned Reuven. "Hello, Nava."

She looked at him suspiciously and pursed her lips. Then, she turned towards Shira and asked,

"Ima, can we go home, now? I'm hungry."

"Well, I can't close up just yet, because ..."

Reuven sat up and interrupted her glance in his direction.

"I've overstayed my welcome."

"Oh, what nonsense!"

He turned over a blue beaded wristband and asked its price.

"Those are just five shequels each or eight for two."

He found a matching band and paid Shira for them. She began to secure the safety lock of the shop front.

"Just one other thing, Shira."

"Of course. How can I 'elp you?"

"I'm looking for cheapish lodgings here in town. Do you happen to know of any?"

"Oh yes. There is a family 'ere. They have a basement studio. I will ask about it for you."

There it was, again, thought Reuven, that charming French intonation that put equal stress on the 'i' and the 'y' in 'family'.

"Reuven, I want to invite you now to my home. We will eat something nice, and after this, we can contact them. Okay?"

"That's a very generous offer."

"Nonsense. Where is your car?"

"Over there. The red mini by the next block. You lead; I'll follow."

Shira's house was in the newest section of the town, some parts of which were still being built. She and her husband, Yoram, had planned their home together and had moved into it only a couple of months previously. It was a split-level construction with one entrance from the street at ground level and a lower level second entrance at the back. The wide concrete arch of the southern façade sheltered the largely glass wall of the living room, providing an expansive panorama of the surrounding hills. The open design of the spacious interior, in which kitchen and living areas merged, was a clear indication of Shira's approach to home life.

On the colour-stained rough wood of her kitchen surfaces stood a collection of stoneware utensils, a few wooden spoons and some spatulas tails down in heavy ceramic jars. Beside them, a variety of preserves, cooking wine, oils, dried herbs and other condiments.

The walls were hung with original artwork by lesser-known Negev painters, mostly portraits of the local Bedouin – dark eyes behind veils of a disappearing world. A pair of traditional Spanish-style commodes displayed a collection of North African artefacts. A variety of tapestries thrown across chairbacks and tabletops added bohemian warmth to the place.

The tumultuous activity generated by Shira's four children and their friends was, she assured Reuven, the norm of the household. She accepted it with measured calm and without even trying to raise her voice above the rabble.

"What can you do?" she said with a fatalistic shrug. "That's the way children should be. Thank God they're 'ealthy and full of energy."

He watched as she juggled an animated dialogue with the children and the preparation of a meal. Soon, the smell of a spicy marinade generously permeated with garlic began to fill the room.

"Mmm. Smells fantastic!" called out Reuven.

She turned some pieces of beef in olive oil. Then, she seasoned them with cloves, onions, coriander and black pepper. Next, she stirred in some vegetable stock and emptied it all into a serving bowl.

At last, Reuven was called to the table. Shira's four children scrambled around it, and Yoram, taking his place at the formal head, nodded in brief acknowledgement of his guest. The adults drank a full-bodied local red wine of which the oldest two children were given a half-glass diluted with water.

"Yoram, your wife's a remarkable lady," remarked Reuven between mouthfuls. "Good in business and at home, too, I see."

Yoram, however, was not over-gratified by Reuven's appreciation of his wife's talents and returned the complement with a scowl. But little Nava piped up,

"And don't forget she's a great teacher, too!"

"Really?"

"Pay no attention – I just teach a few little classes at the university."

"I bet Nava's right. You're obviously wonderful at everything you set your mind to."

Shira blushed very obviously at this generous compliment while her husband continued to look at her strangely as if he suspected there was more to Reuven's presence at his table than he had been told. He turned to Reuven for clarification.

"You seem to have some very definite opinions about Shira considering the two of you only met for the first time a few weeks ago."

Reuven smiled back complacently.

"I'm a very quick judge of character, and Shira's open spirit makes it easy to get to know her."

His answer obviously annoyed Yoram all the more. He got up from the table abruptly and strode out of the room. Reuven gave Shira a questioning look, but she shrugged off his anti-social behaviour, saying,

"Yoram, 'e never trusts new people."

They finished their meal without speaking much. Reuven helped Shira tidy up and, as they were doing so, he asked,

"How often do you teach?"

"Almost every morning. In the afternoon, I'm usually in the shop.'"

"I was lucky to find you there, today, then."

"Yes. Today, I 'ad no classes."

"Ah."

"Reuven, tell me. Your work, it pays well?"

"So, so."

"Then, how do you manage?"

"Oh, I have a few hidden talents."

"Sure," she answered, her eyes with a glint of flirtatiousness in them, now. Then, suddenly switching to an air of gravity,

"But it must be very 'ard for you, isn't it?"

"Well, sometimes I sing for my supper and sometimes I put on my teacher's hat," he said smilingly.

"Oh, you are also a teacher?"

"Used to be. Don't do it much any more."

"The kids in your classes must love you."

"I use a special method with lots of music. It gets results."

"It sounds wonderful. Maybe I could 'elp you get some extra work."

"At the university?"

"Yes. They want to give me so many hours. It's too much for

me. Per'aps you can 'ave these extra hours."

Reuven was stunned. He thought about how generously Shira stepped forward to help him. Less than four hours previously, he had wandered into this town, a perfect stranger seeking temporary rest for his aching limbs. In that short space of time, he had been wined and dined, found a place to stay, and even a possibility of some extra work. This was surely a blessed encounter.

"Shira, this is all quite incredible."

"Of course, Beersheva is very far for you. It could be a problem?"

"I'm a very mobile person. Distance is no barrier. Me, my Mini and the road are inseparable buddies."

"In this case, we only 'ave to persuade the university to take you. You can stay 'ere tonight, and tomorrow we will sort this out."

"What about Yoram? I doubt he'll be happy about my sticking around ..."

"Don't worry. He will not make any problem about it."

After agreeing to her plan, Reuven took his leave of Shira. He wanted to complete a few more hours of fieldwork before nightfall. He turned over in his mind the events of the past few hours. He had the irrepressible feeling of destiny at work, as if the desert itself held him in its power.

While he was setting up his surveying equipment in new terrain, his cell phone rang. He recognised Nathan's number on the display panel.

"Hi Nathan, what's up?"

"I've been going over a few ideas for promoting Global Dawn on the Internet. When you get back, I'll run them by you."

"Great. Let me know if you come up with any problems, will you, man?"

"What was that? Line's fading ... I can hardly hear you. Which planet are you speaking from?"

"A planet called the northern Negev. I'm enjoying being away from so-called civilization."

"You're enjoying making me jealous!"

"On the contrary, you're very welcome to join me. By the way, the reception my end is as clear as can be."

"It's clearer this end, now. Anyway, I really phoned to clarify some aspects of our overall concept. As it stands, I still don't think it's convincing enough."

"The next meeting will help. It'll be a good opportunity to thrash out all the details you need. All being well, we'll have some visuals ready by then, too."

"Who's handling that?"

"I did ask Rikki to look into it. You know what, it's good we spoke. We need to get onto her about it. Perhaps you could give her a call and see how she's doing?"

"Sure. No problem. When did you say the next meeting of The Circle would be?"

"I don't know whether Ora's fixed a date, yet. As you noticed, I'm a bit out of touch with the real world down here. It'll definitely be before the end of the millennium, though!"

"So, how long till we see you back in Tel-Aviv?"

"Probably, a couple of weeks. Gotta go, now. Thanks for filling me in, Nathan."

He began calibrating his tools, but was interrupted again almost immediately. This time it was Ora.

"Reuven? How goes it?"

"Hey, Ora. It's only the first day, but Kadmon's looking pretty good. I'll have a lot to tell you when I get back."

"It sounds as if the desert's inspiring you."

"More than that. It's empowered me. If tomorrow reaps its promised rewards, I'll be travelling here regularly for quite a while."

"Go on, tell me more," begged Ora.

However, he suddenly found himself irritated by her plaintive tone and cut her interrogation short.

"You'll get to hear everything in good time, I swear. Got to ring off now; my phone battery's nearly flat. Let me know when you've fixed things with Rikki, and be in touch with Nathan, too."

"Oh, did he ring you?"

"Yes, we had an excellent conversation. Talk to you again, soon. Take care, Love. Bye."

"Bye, Reuven."

*   *   *

Reuven's nonchalant telephone manner jarred Ora's sensitivities. She felt, at once, suspicious, jealous, offended and exploited without being able to put her finger on tangible reasons for any of those reactions. Reuven was changing. Something new was affecting him, and she felt excluded.

*   *   *

The following morning, Shira's promises were smoothly fulfilled. Reuven was taken on for the Bedouin project, teaching ten hours of English a week. He also met his hosts, the Esheds. This all neatly settled, he was wandering back towards the parking lot when a friendly face stopped him in his tracks.

"Jeanine! I was about to look you up and here, Fate has worked in our favour."

She was exuding that vivacious air of spontaneity that she had always had about her in the past – before her bereavement. Indeed, he thought, she was looking strikingly resilient in a daring orange catsuit, low cut over her tall, trim figure.

"What brings you to Beersheva?"

"Work. What else? Join me for coffee?"

"Sure. I've got a bit of free time now, so you're in luck."

They wandered over to the student café and sat down together at an empty table on the lawn under the awning.

"So, Reuven, are you here with those two lovely ladies of yours?"

"They're both busy and this is purely a working trip for me."

He delved into his wallet, pulled out a small photograph, and flourished it in front of her.

"Here, what d'you think of my baby girl?"

"Shahar?"

He nodded with pride.

"A looker as I would have expected. Apples don't fall far from the tree, do they? So, where is she? And Tamar? Aren't they with you?"

"Tamar's got her own work and Shahar's in school. Anyway, I like to be on my own when I'm working. Now, what about that strange press cutting you sent me? I must say you had me intrigued. You seemed pretty upset about it, at the time."

She shrugged her shoulders.

"I was. I was livid, but it's all faded into history, you know, as these things do."

He studied the controlled detachment in her face and wondered at the dexterity with which she brushed off her anger and pain. He wondered if she was suppressing her grief over the loss of her son and, with the same skill, driving herself resolutely forward. And Yoni's father – her sole partner in the depths of her sorrow – had she had any contact with him since the funeral?

"The press can be awfully callous," he commented sympathetically.

"They're not paid to consider the sensitivities of the people they write about. Then again, I've never been one to stay out of the limelight for long, so I guess I should expect press attacks, now and then."

There was a lot of truth in what she said, he thought. She was almost incapable of doing anything in a quiet, humble way if it could be done with panache. Perhaps that was why she was so good as a tour guide. Travelling in her company was always a scintillating experience.

"So, has the country's best tour guide really given it all up?"

"Not entirely, but you know how seasonal it is. I have to spread myself to survive."

"Hmm. I sympathise. My work's patchy, too. If there's a lull in the market, then the cupboard's bare."

"So, what are you up to, these days?"

"Pushing ahead with my project. We've named it "Global Dawn.""

"We?"

"Aha. I've got a circle of friends working on it with me."

"So, you've really begun work on your part of the Master Plan?"

"We're just laying the groundwork now. I know I have to wait until the right time, just as you warned me."

"Reuven, this is no small challenge ..."

"I never thought it would be easy, but I'm a traveller, like you. When did we ever choose the easy path?"

"Still, you must take care. You're already being pulled in too many directions, aren't you? Project, work, family ..."

"How in Heaven's name can you know all that from the little I've said?"

"I'm not easily fooled, Reuven."

"Ah, the lady dazzles with both body and brain."

"You talk as if you have never a care, but I know you better than that. I can read the tension in that irresistible smile of yours," she said, smiling, too, in spite of herself. "Anyway, there are other information sources we can consult, if you like."

"Wow, now you're really being cryptic! What kind of sources?"

Before she could answer, Shira hurried up to their table and breathlessly exclaimed,

"Reuven, I see you and Jeanine 'ave found each other!"

"Not only that, Shira, but it has taken Jeanine exactly ten minutes to uncover almost all the latest secrets of my life. She even claims to have hidden ways of revealing more."

"Trust 'er, Reuven. She has wonderful insight."

"Well, you two, I have to leave for my lecture, now. Reuven, can I call you this evening?"

"Sure. Shira has fixed for me to stay with friends of hers in Kadmon."

"With the Eshed family. You can reach 'im there."

"Take care, then. Look forward to hearing from you later."

He watched Jeanine striding confidently in the direction of the lecture hall. He took a moment to finish his drink, following her silhouette with his eyes until she disappeared from sight.

The Esheds welcomed him warmly. He retreated early to the privacy of the room they had prepared for him and sank into a sleep of heavy fatigue from the heat of the Negev and the emotions of the day. His sleep was disturbed around ten o'clock by Jeanine's promised call to pursue their earlier discussion. In exhausted relief, he realised she was suggesting they continue their conversation on another day at another location. Her irrepressible dynamism overpowered him in his half-slumbering state, and he muttered a few words of agreement, jotted down the details on a handy scrap of paper and wished her goodnight.

Upon re-examining the scruffy note by his bedside the following morning, he discovered he had actually somewhat gracelessly accepted an invitation to a soirée at Jeanine's apartment that same evening. As he collected his gear for the day's work, he strained to remember more details of her message and resolved to call her a little later for clarification.

He arrived on foot a little after nine, guitar case in one hand and a hastily acquired bottle in the other. Through the half-open door came mingled sounds of the party already under way. He pursued them into the living room where Jeanine was lounging in a floating, white on black hostess gown on a mountain of soft orange and red floor cushions. The feast was laid out on a long low Perspex table top, stylishly balanced on two slabs of rock for table legs.

"Reuven, hi there. Come on over and meet everyone. I was just telling Arik, here, about our surprise encounter." Reuven extended a warm hand to Arik.

A lively drumbeat began, accompanied by rhythmic humming, and Reuven quickly tuned his guitar strings down to a compatible pitch. Jeanine added a deep wailing tone that gradually rose to a continuous high note of wordless angst.

She linked arms with Arik on one side and with Reuven on the other. Arik reached out, in turn, to his other neighbour and so the links spread around the room and eventually back to him completing the circle. Jeanine lowered her voice to a murmur, and someone placed a few candles in the centre of the floor. In the flames and the shadows, Reuven fancied he saw the silhouette of Global Dawn as it would stand one day above Jerusalem. Around its luminescent dome danced faces – so many faces, familiar yet unnamed.

He raised his head. Jeanine had moved across to the opposite side of the circle, and Shira now stood next to her. He had not seen her enter the room. The two women nodded towards him as if in silent conspiracy. Jeanine reached into the deep pocket of her gown, and withdrew a set of cards. Fanning them forward, she cast an enquiring look at Reuven. He understood he was being subtly invited to travel with her into the world of Tarot. As if in a trance, he followed her beckoning finger into an intimate niche, dimly lit by a dripping candle. She pulled a curtain across it and sat down cross-legged on the floor, gesturing to him to do the same.

"I have important messages for you, Reuven. They're here in the cards. Would you like to see them?"

"Maybe, but first I want you to tell me about the Tarot. It's a whole blank page for me."

"There are so many theories about it. I can tell you mine. I believe the twenty-two cards of the Arcana are linked to the Kabbalah, the Hebrew Alphabet, and the biblical symbol of the Tree of Life."

"And how do you go about interpreting them?"

"First of all, it's up to you, Reuven, to choose the cards and position them as you like. Our psychic energies will follow the patterns you choose."

"Patterns?"

"It's a very complex system. With God's help, the cards you select can show me the patterns of your life, and I'll be able to read any signs of disharmony in them."

"What do I have to do?"

"Take the deck and shuffle it really well. Then pick ten cards, and spread them out here on the floor between us."

Reuven followed her instructions with a swift hand. Then, he sat back and watched her concentrate on interpreting the cards he had chosen.

"There's a giant emotional barrier blocking your way to your goals. You've a long struggle still ahead of you."

"Can you see anything more specific?"

"Your charisma is hiding your true persona. You're going to have to face your own self and believe in it if you want to acquire a real following."

"Sounds as if I need a complete character switch."

"Nothing so extreme, Reuven. You've got a lot of work to do on yourself, though, to restore your natural inner balance. "

"Do the cards give you any clues to help me?"

"Certainly. The lovers' card, for example, shows the importance of your family. Be patient. They're going to accept you in the end."

"Is that it?"

"Financial concerns are eroding your spiritual freedom. There's work to do there, too."

"What else?"

"I see a wonderful new influence already present in your life. She will guide you on your journey of self-discovery."

"At last, some good news! Can you tell me more about her?"

"If you look honestly into your soul, you'll recognise her. I see a journey for you in the near future, too."

"And my project? What about Global Dawn?"

"Global Dawn will only happen for you when you've overcome all the obstacles I've described."

Reuven was deeply moved by Jeanine's words. Her quiet and selfless delivery of the Tarot's message contrasted surprisingly with the bold Jeanine he knew. Already she had drawn back the curtain and was circulating among the party players in full hostess performance mode once again. The transformation was quite miraculous. As for him, he felt emotionally drained. He begged his leave of the party and began to walk back to his lodgings. On the way, he mulled over everything that had transpired. Most troubling were Jeanine's words of warning.

Sleep refused to relieve his restlessness that night. He was unable to dispel ominous fears and images from his aching mind.

*   *   *

Work with the Bedouin students was due to begin right away, and Reuven greeted it with enthusiasm. Shira suggested a visit to one of his prospective students. It would be helpful for him, she said, to gain some insight into their way of life before he entered a class. He agreed and was most grateful to her, once again, for her guidance.

They walked just a little way out of Kadmon along the main highway towards Beersheva, and turned off the road onto an open expanse of land. Shira directed Reuven along a barely distinguishable path through an opening in the wire that stretched across it – an improvised territory marker. In front of them stood a collection of corrugated metal shacks and some tents. She led him to a particular shack owned by a leading family of the Nabari tribe. This was where Yusuf Nabari lived – one of Shira's former students. He came out to greet them and immediately invited them inside for coffee. This was the customary way to welcome guests. The repeated emptying and replenishing of their cups was a traditional bonding process designed to induce an atmosphere of trust between them.

Shira had already briefed Reuven on the long-standing land ownership dispute between the residents here and the government. Yusuf had gained notoriety in Kadmon for pressuring the authorities into granting utility permits for his village. The village was not officially recognised. In heavily accented, guttural Hebrew interspersed with Arabic, Yusuf explained,

"Is very important my family stay always on this Bedouin land."

"You see, if it is not seen officially as a permanent settlement, nobody interferes," Shira added.

"Yusuf," said Reuven, "I think I may be able to help you put your village more firmly on the map."

"Reuven is a mapper, Yusuf," Shira explained. "It is 'is profession."

"I'm preparing a new survey of this area, and I intend to include villages such as yours in it."

"I think you will not be allowed to do this, Mr Reuven," he answered solemnly. "Maps, you see, they are like weapons."

"Trust me, Yusuf. I know what I'm saying."

Yusuf listened intently to Reuven.

"The survey is a part of a big project I'm planning. It will give information and services to people everywhere without discrimination."

"Mr Reuven," replied Yusuf, "I think if you do this, you are true friend of Bedouin people."

Then Shira turned to Yusuf and asked,

"Will you be coming to the English classes this term?"

"Indeed. I hope so, *In sh'Allah.*"

"Reuven is going to be your teacher."

"Mr Reuven, you are very busy and talented man! It has been for me great honour to welcome you in my humble home."

"The honour is all mine, Yusuf. You serve excellent coffee and are a fine host. I look forward to seeing you at the university."

As they turned back towards the road, Shira was full of questions to Reuven.

"You 'ave spoken with Yusuf about a project in this region. But Global Dawn, it will be in Jerusalem. Am I wrong?"

"Global Dawn has to be dynamic, always changing and

growing. I'm thinking of testing the big plan by building it in miniature in this area – maybe in Kadmon. We can make use of the regional survey I'm working on now to create the basic information layer for the project here. Eventually, I would like to develop it into a complete reference framework for all the local administrative, cultural and educational functions."

"And you think it can 'elp Yusuf's community, also?"

"Absolutely. The cooperation of someone like Yusuf could be a great asset both for the Bedouin around here and for us.

"And you do not worry about political problems?"

"I've never been one for politics or politicians. I defy any of them to drag me into their nasty mire. We can work within the political limits as far as possible, and where that fails, we'll find ways to work around them."

As they talked, they retraced their steps along the main highway and neared the entrance to Kadmon. On the opposite grassy verge, a Bedouin youth was herding his flock of sheep in poignant illustration of the gap between two worlds that Reuven hoped to bridge with his latest plan.

"Tell me more about the Bedouin students, Shira. Do you enjoy teaching them?"

"Oh yes. I like teaching them. They are polite and respectful. The girls, especially, are very serious. They wish only to succeed."

"Well, I'm really beginning to look forward to this opportunity. You've given me a tremendous amount of insight into the challenge and the obstacles I can expect to meet. When do I start?"

"Your contract will begin next week."

"On Tuesday?"

"Yes."

"Excellent. It'll give me a few days to remind my family of my existence, and to catch up on some things at home."

"When will you travel?"

"I think I ought to drive up there today. I'll contact you at the beginning of next week."

"If you need me, you know, you can ring me at the shop."

Shira moved to embrace Reuven, and he offered her a wide engulfing hug in response.

"Shira, these couple of days in your company have been momentous."

"I believe this is only a beginning, Reuven. You have much to offer us 'ere."

He smiled at her optimism.

Chapter 8

Reuven arrived home to find Tamar full of bottled up resentment and ready to explode.

"You ... you took off in the car! Not a thought for me! Oh, Tamar'll cope! It's always the same with you! Think of me at all, did you? Of course not!"

"But," he began, "you knew about my trip even before I did! If you needed the car, you should have said ..."

"Maybe I did know, but we've had no word from you in days!"

"So, it's not about the car, then?"

His protest fell on deaf ears. She was too absorbed in releasing her grievances to really listen.

"Left me here all on my own to cope, no money – or next to none!"

Oh, so the bottom line was the money, as usual. It was so demeaning to have his work reduced to such a petty level. And to think he had hoped to share his ideals and dreams with this woman! Tamar's outpouring was unstoppable, and the more agitated she grew the higher rose the pitch of her voice.

"... and I can never get hold of you! Your cell phone's never on!" she shrieked.

"Does that surprise you?" he asked acidly. "How do you think I can work with you behaving like this in the background?"

"Damned good at justifying yourself, aren't you? Don't you think I worry? People ask about you, and I don't know what to tell them."

"Oh, so that's your problem, is it? It's not me you're really worried about; it's what people will think. I bet the neighbours have a field day as soon as I'm away. What do they say? That I've got mistresses all over the place waiting upon my favours? And you, you'd believe their gossip before you'd trust me, wouldn't you?"

"Reuven, that's not fair! It's not true, and you know it! All your fancy language doesn't make it any more so, either! I can't carry on like this. I feel as if you're living in another world!"

"You know what, Tamar, I am. And from where I stand my world looks a whole lot more inviting than yours! Well, thanks for that warm homecoming. You're right. I acted inconsiderately. I'm home now, and I really don't have the energy for these stupid battles. I was actually looking forward to a few days with you and Shahar."

"Oh, right. In between project meetings, I bet. And that's the other thing. That damned project of yours! It's all you ever think about these days!"

Reuven's expression was stiff with fatigue.

"Believe it or not, I've been working really hard. Have you any idea at all what it's like trudging across the desert every day to earn your keep? I'm doing this bloody job for you! – It's you who's so obsessed with filling the fridge. I can tell you the money for that'll come in when the job's done and not before!"

"And when will that be, might one ask?"

"I've only just started this project, damn it! Can't you be the least bit reasonable? If you'd only listen instead of attacking me all the time you might get to hear what you want to know."

"Nu? What?" she asked, creasing her eyes sceptically.

"I've taken on some extra work to tide us over. If you'll just calm down, I'll tell you about it. First, I'd really appreciate it if you'd let me put my bag down, get out of these sweaty clothes and have a shower. By the way, where's Shahar? I was hoping she'd be around when I got back."

"Oh, she's busy with her friends as usual. Who knows where she is? Her father's daughter, that one – never troubles to call and say if she'll be home for a meal."

"There you go again. Please give it a rest. I can't cope with any more of this. I'm telling you, if you don't lay off me, I'll just leave!"

Tamar was on the verge of tears. She did not intend to greet him with such a vehement assault. She sat down on the rug and started pulling at her hair, but Reuven had no stomach for such pathetic hysteria. He felt no respect for her in such a state. He walked into the kitchen, filled a pitcher with cold water, returned to the hallway and emptied it over her head. Then, turning a deaf ear to the escalating hysterics behind him and the ugly tirade of curses that was issuing from his sweet-lipped spouse, he flung himself onto the couch in exhaustion. In less than two minutes, the sound of his snoring dominated the room.

A humiliated Tamar stood up, dripping wet and trembling. Sullenly, she dragged herself off to the bedroom to change her clothes. Several hours later, Reuven came to. He glanced through the open window. It was already pitch black outside. His stomach was rumbling. Of course, he realised, he had had nothing to eat since arriving home. He rolled off the couch and went to look for Tamar. He edged around a telltale pool of water on the tiles and headed towards the bedroom where he found her perched on the edge of the bed, head in hands, staring morosely at the floor.

"Surely you haven't been sitting like that all this time, have you?"

"What would you care if I had?" she asked frostily, shrugging her shoulders.

"You know I care, Tamar," he said.

To his relief, she did not seem in a hurry to rehash their earlier squabble.

"I did miss you both, you know. That's why I came home."

She wiped a few lingering tears from her eyes.

"Come here," he said, encircling her in reassuring arms. She seemed grateful for his change of attitude, and got up with a look of resolve. Then, with measured civility, she said,

"I haven't had a chance to tell you about Shahar's problem at school."

"What kind of problem?" he asked.

"Well, it's to do with the drama festival next month. The school's suddenly creating problems about her taking part and she's really upset."

"Look, my love, I really do need to shower now. Can we talk about it over dinner?"

While he was showering, he thought about the whole unpleasant incident that caught him off-guard when he walked through the door. His greatest worry was the way this kind of tension seemed to grow each time he went away. It had been happening gradually over the past few years, and it seemed that with each of his absences from home Tamar's need to cling to him became more extreme. He thought lovingly of Shahar. As long as he lived, he would be grateful to Tamar for bringing her into his world. When she was still an infant, he used to work long hours but still devoted all his free time to his daughter. Things changed, imperceptibly at first, as Shahar grew older. She began to keep a teenager's typically erratic social hours and wanted her freedom as kids of her age do. As for him, he was away from home so much, and Tamar was left lonely and insecure. Justifiably or not, she blamed all the recent turmoil in her life on Global Dawn.

As Reuven stepped out of the shower, the phone rang. It was Ora enquiring after him. It sounded as if she was offended that he had not contacted her since arriving home. He heard Tamar diplomatically assuring her he would call back as soon as he could. He tied a bath-towel around his waist and grabbed the phone to speak to her himself. His tone was cool and distant.

"I'm sorry, Ora. Do you think you can ring tomorrow? I'm really exhausted, right now."

"We need to meet soon ..."

"We can meet on Sunday," he said, cutting her short. "That's what I'd planned to do anyway, if it's alright with you. I'll have a few hours free then so we can catch up. By the way, have you fixed a date for another meeting of The Circle yet?"

"I wanted to make it some time in the next couple of weeks, but I didn't know if we could count on your being around!"

Ora's testiness irritated him. He had had quite enough arguments for one evening.

"This is getting us nowhere," he said. "You know full well how busy I am with my surveying work. It's my family's bread and butter. As for the meeting, just set a date. I'll be there. I haven't let you down up to now, have I?"

He understood the message in her silence. He had little patience for her hypersensitivity and struggled to keep his cool.

"Ora? Sunday?"

"Yes.   Okay," she replied reluctantly. "Give me a ring on Sunday morning, then."

He put down the phone and was starting towards the bedroom to put some clothes on before dinner when a mini-skirted, skinny-topped Shahar appeared in the hallway.

"Abba, I didn't know you were home!"

She raced up to him and threw both arms around his neck. He hugged her to his chest with one hand while securing the towel around his middle with the other.

"Finally, someone's actually glad to see me!   How've you been?"

She frowned.

"Didn't Ima tell you what happened with the drama festival?"

"No, she hasn't really had a chance to tell me anything much yet. She just mentioned you were upset.   Can we talk about it over dinner?"

"Sure," she said, cuddling up to him. "I'm famished!"

"Well, we're going to eat right away, so come and sit down," urged Tamar.

"Okay. Give me two minutes to get dressed, you two, and I'll be right there."

The smell of food and company brought Muki bounding in from the garden to claim his share of attention. He nestled contentedly at Reuven's feet, and Tamar tossed him a bone to chew on.

During the meal, they were all keen to catch up on each other's news, and the tension gradually began to relax between Reuven and Tamar.

"So who's going to tell me the story about this drama festival? What happened? Why's Shahar so upset?"

"You tell him, Shahar."

"It's just so unfair, Abba. After all my hard work on that show!"

"Of course, you wrote music specially for it."

"Yeah, and I spent hours helping behind the scenes, too!"

"So? Aren't they using all your work in the festival?"

"Oh, they're using it alright."

She got up from the table hands defiantly on her hips, then started waving her arms dramatically in the air as she strode about the room. Dumbfounded, Reuven asked,

"So? Aren't you pleased? Help me out here someone. Why the sour face, Pumpkin?"

He looked questioningly at Tamar.

"Hear her out, Reuven."

"Sure, I'm over the moon that they're using my work," she exclaimed. "Really cool about their not even asking me to come along, too!"

"What! You can't be serious! I've never heard of such a thing!"

"Well, that's the whole great story, Abba. D'you understand why I'm so delighted, now?"

"Don't you worry, angel. I'll sort them out! This is outrageous!"

Shahar pulled a chair up close to his.

"I feel better now you're here, Abba."

"Hmm," he said, reaching an arm out over the back of her chair. "Someone's got to look out for you, Pumpkin, haven't they?"

He lifted the mass of her long hair away from her neck and rubbed soothingly behind her ears with two fingers. Then, he looked across at Tamar. All sign of strain had vanished from her face.

"It's good to have you home, Reuven, my love," she said.

After dinner, he turned in early to the luxury of his own bed.

*   *   *

Saturday is not generally a working day in Israel. It is the seventh day of the week – the Sabbath or *Shabbat*, in Hebrew, when God rested from the work of the Creation, and Jews traditionally do likewise.

At ten o'clock on the second *Shabbat* morning in December, Reuven turned over in bed and retreated into the haven of its covers. He had risen earlier with a sore throat and a severe head chill, dosed himself with appropriate medicaments swilled down with hot tea and honey, and gone back to sleep. Pulling the blankets tightly around him, he shivered.

"Damn the flu," he groaned.

In the face of such pathos, Tamar's anger of the previous day dissolved into sympathy, and she set about nursing her husband back to better health and spirits. It is a widely known fact that a good broth and a home-baked strudel work wonders for a man's soul. While she set about these labours of love, he sought solace from the bedside radio.

However, as he lay in bed trying to escape from the world, the world was not so accommodating. Ora had done an excellent job of informing friends far and wide about Global Dawn. Among the first to respond was Charlotte Lavon all the way from Australia.

"Charlie, your voice hasn't changed in fifteen years!"

She and Reuven first crossed paths when she was still living in Israel. An attractive opening at the University of Adelaide prompted her return to Australia.

"How's life in the Land of Oz?"

"Good, thanks. I gather I'm lucky to catch you home."

"Either that wandering spirit of mine has lapsed or I had prior intuition you might call, today."

"Both seem pretty unlikely to me. I think I'll stick with the luck theory."

"How're your hubby and kids?"

"We're all fine. They're proud of my latest achievement."

"And what would that be? Opened a trendy bistro? Won the surfing seniors trophy?"

Charlotte laughed and Reuven's attempt to join her turned into a spluttering cough.

"What happened to you? You sound ill."

"Oh, it's nothing. Some stupid flu bug."

"You'd better get rid of that before the year's out. You don't want to begin a new millennium carrying an old bug!"

He managed a coughless laugh, and asked,

"So, Charlie. What have you done to make your family so proud?"

"You, Reuven Sofer, are speaking to a newly published author whose first novel is on the road to becoming a bestseller."

"Well, well. Congrats indeed. I always knew you'd be famous one day. Is your book on the shelves in Israel, yet? What name did you publish under?"

"Charlotte Lavon, and I will, of course, send you a complimentary copy."

"Signed by your own fair hand?"

"Signed by my own fair hand."

"You haven't told me the title."

"It's called 'Australian Timeline'.

"And the subject?"

"It's about the psychological effects of the new millennium on the average Australian."

"That's a pretty up-to-the-minute topic. What's your angle on it?"

"I show how the average Australian has been brainwashed by the media into utter confusion between fact and fiction. As a result, there's an escalation of unrealistic fears and even panic, as if the world's coming to an end. Isn't it like that in Israel, too?"

"Not really. Israelis are mostly quite cynical about the predictions of a great crash. They've taken precautions to protect their computers, but that's about all. People here have lived through wars and scud attacks. They've developed a philosophy of taking life as it comes."

"And on the spiritual side?"

"Religious Jews see certain universal events as heralds of the Messiah, but mostly the Gregorian calendar's irrelevant for them."

"And the non-religious people?"

"New Age philosophy has quite a following, here. For New Agers, the millennium's an important turning point. Still, the Israeli pop trade hasn't cashed in on the millennium as the English market has, for example."

"Oh, the British are famous for putting anything on a mug or a tea towel!"

Yes. They love kitsch! So, you rang me to tell me about your book? That's really impressive news, Charlie."

"Yes, but it's not the only reason I wanted to talk to you. I wanted to give you my reactions to the paper your friend, Ora, sent me about the Global Dawn project."

"Ah." Reuven sat up. Now, he was wide-awake and drawing deep breaths in anticipation.

"Your idea's dynamite, Reuven. I'm really sold on global

networking."

"So, you want to join our network?"

"Not if I have to be an information technology expert."

"Don't worry. You don't have to be a geek."

"As I understand it, the idea of Global Dawn is to provide easy access for everyone to a mountain of global data?"

"That's right."

"Researching my book made me see how tragically vulnerable most people are to the half-truths propagated by the media. Reuven, I reckon proper information's the only effective key to people's freedom."

"So you'd like to do something to help?"

"Mmm. I might be able to set up a Global Dawn branch out here."

"That would be incredible. Let's keep in touch on it."

"Okay, Reuven. Do, please. I'm serious. I want to start the ball rolling."

"Charlie, I always knew you and I would go places together."

"Right. Take care, then."

"Will do. You, too."

He felt elated. At last, a real sign that Global Dawn could reach out far and wide. He had faith in Charlotte, too. He rolled back into bed and fell asleep again in optimistic mood. The positive feeling carried itself into his dreams. He dreamed about a sapling with young roots pushing down into the soil. He watched it mature into a splendid tree. Then, he saw it scatter its blossom in a mist of white petals and golden pollen. A woman nearby had her feet rooted in the earth and her arms were stretched upwards. Her long curls bounced and swirled on the energy waves around her. He reached out to touch her, tears running down his cheeks, but the image evaporated.

When he woke up, the daylight was already fading into the early winter dusk. He sipped a little brandy from the glass at his bedside. He was overcome by an inexplicable sense of loss and lifted his hand to wipe his eyes. Powerful images floated into his consciousness: the silhouette of Tamar holding her ground tenaciously while projecting phenomenal energy; alongside her, the maturing tree taking root and spreading its branches. Clearly these images were connected, as were the destinies of Tamar and Global Dawn. In recognition of all Tamar had once been to him and must eventually be to Global Dawn, he resolved to be more attentive to her needs. Soon he would introduce her to the magic of the Negev where new hopes were germinating for the project.

*   *   *

Global Dawn was beginning to assert itself heavily in Ora's life. With the creation of the inner and outer circles, she had become their central communications link. Messages flooded her inbox every day ranging from superficial enquiries to real offers of cooperation. Fielding this lively rush of interest was thrilling work.

At the same time, her new passion for Jerusalem delighted Reuven. However, even he did not realise the extent to which that city had assailed her imagination. It came as quite a surprise to Ariella, too, when she confided in her.

On the Saturday afternoon after Reuven's return, Ariella was ensconced in her workshop, moulding, etching and soldering bracelets, rings and pendants with the aid of her jeweller's loupe. Away from the lively commerce of the *midrahov*, she enjoyed these quiet times when she could focus on her craft. Ora's call found her thus engaged. She sounded distracted.

"Whenever Reuven and I talk about Jerusalem, Ariella, he gets the strangest look in his eye," she said, "as if he's been transported into some other dimension. He talks cryptically about how people don't yet know who he is or the role he has to play. He says the days of prophets are gone, but I often think he really imagines himself to be one."

"I don't think I'd go that far."

"He believes he's been appointed to a sacred mission."

"I know, but actually he's not religious, is he?"

"Absolutely not. He thinks the world's religions have blinded us to the real truth."

"Which is?"

Ariella smiled to herself as she thought of her recent discussion with Reuven about the Maya and cosmic patterns.

"Hasn't he talked to you about the Master Plan?"

"Yes. I took it to mean a kind of fate or destiny."

"I think you'll find it's more than that. You need to listen more carefully to what he's really saying."

"What do you mean?"

"I don't think he's shared his whole vision with any of us. In my opinion, he sees Global Dawn as a minuscule part of something much, much bigger."

"I know his ideas are pretty mind-blowing. Still, he's won me over, you know. Global Dawn has become very important to me."

"Well, anyone can see you and he are close, these days."

"But I'm not always sure what he expects of me."

"Perhaps your faith in Global Dawn is all he needs. If it's constant, then eventually it'll start to influence other people, too."

Now, Ora was breathless with excitement,

"That's exactly the way I feel about it!"

"Easy, easy," laughed Ariella.

"Oh, I can't tell you how good it feels to be able to share things with someone who understands. Can I tell you something in absolute confidence? A gut feeling I have that no one else knows about."

"You can trust me. My lips are sealed."

She sounded almost conspiratorial as if savouring Ora's covert admissions. Nevertheless, her readiness to listen was reassuring. One really could tell her almost anything, Ora thought.

"I feel drawn towards Jerusalem," she said, with a hint of mystery in her voice.

"Meaning?"

"Obviously, Global Dawn is going to need a physical presence there pretty soon."

"Ye…es. But Reuven says Jerusalem's not ready for us yet."

This comment triggered an unexpectedly animated response.

"That's my point! What's he waiting for? – The Messiah to open the gate? You and I both know life's not like that. Has it occurred to you that maybe it's he who isn't ready?"

"Could be," chuckled Ariella. "Obviously, you think our Reuven's dragging his feet. So, what's your idea?"

"I'm thinking of moving to Jerusalem, myself," she declared.

At this, Ariella's eyebrows peaked dramatically.

"As a Global Dawn pioneer?"

An incredulous note had crept into her voice.

"Aha, and you mustn't breathe a word of this to anyone. I haven't even mentioned it to my family, yet!"

Now, Ariella's expression was stern.

"Have you thought about the implications for them of such a decision?"

"Of course. My kids are still at ages where changing schools is feasible. Neither of them is in upper school yet, and it's not as if we're leaving the country. They can keep in touch with their friends. They'll adapt soon enough."

"And Gadi? What about his work?"

"It's not a problem. He can commute from Jerusalem."

"And you're already an independent lady, so you have no local ties, at least from an economic point of view. Sounds as if you've got it all worked out. But what exactly do you hope to achieve by it?"

"A visible presence of Global Dawn in Jerusalem, Ariella. We'll be like catalysts to advance the city's readiness to receive the project."

"My, my, Ora, you're a brave woman."

Meanwhile, the Porath family, ignorant of the dramatic move Ora was nurturing, perceived Global Dawn as little more than an uncomfortable ripple in their ordered lives.

*   *   *

The following morning, Reuven pulled himself out of his sick bed to call on Ora. He found her surrounded by graphics downloaded from the NASA and Fuller Institute websites. He was surprised by a healthy influx of replies from the Outer Circle, as he termed his overseas contacts. The expected ripple effect had been slow to occur, and, even now, the people who were answering were mostly non-committal – with the dramatic exception of Charlie, of course. Nonetheless, the overall response was encouraging.

While Ora busied herself sorting through the mass of downloaded material, he took the opportunity to ring Shira. As he waited for her to answer, he kept an eye on Ora. She seemed more amiably disposed towards him, today. Perhaps she regretted the irritable reception she gave him?

"Reuven, 'ow wonderful to hear from you! Is everything okay?"

Reuven tried not to let Ora see how the seductive quality of Shira's voice affected him.

"Yes, everything's fine. It's been a demanding couple of days, though."

Shira responded with concern.

"Reuven? Something is wrong. I know it. You sound bizarre."

"Nothing slips by you, does it? I've got a touch of flu, but it's really not serious. Tamar's been spoiling me with home cooking, and she sent me to bed with a good dose of brandy yesterday."

"And nothing else is wrong? You sound so tense – not yourself."

"Now, how would you know what that self is when you've only known me for about two minutes?"

"Oh, maybe we 'ave met once before in another life, you know."

"Right, and maybe I was once your brother or your lover."

His comment revealed more of his familiarity with Shira than he intended. Ora gritted her teeth, pretending not to notice.

"So, I am mistaken?" she pressed.

Shira, on the other hand, unaware that their exchange had an audience, persisted in interrogating him about his bodily and spiritual health.

"No, but I really don't want to go into it just now," he said, trying to cut the conversation short.

"I understand, Reuven," Shira was saying. "Call me when you get back."

"I will. Bye for now, then."

"Who was that you were talking to, Reuven?" asked Ora with an innocent air. She wandered over to where he was sitting. "Everything okay?"

"Oh, it was just Shira. I rang her to let her know exactly when I'll be back in Kadmon."

As he said this, it dawned on him that, despite his resolution to take Tamar with him to Kadmon this time, he had said nothing about it to Shira. Perhaps, after all, this was not the best time for her to accompany him. After all, he would be just beginning his new teaching job and would need to devote himself to that, not to speak of the fact that he was already running behind schedule on the land survey. The next few days, his health permitting, were going to require a lot of dedication and long hours. He would explain that to Tamar. She would understand, and they could plan a visit together very soon. He looked up at Ora, and noted with some relief that she seemed to have regained her composure.

"Tell me more about the people you met in Kadmon, Reuven," she suggested, gently squeezing his shoulder.

"There are exciting new possibilities opening up there, Ora. Did I tell you about my meeting with Yusuf?"

"I don't think so. Is he an Arab?"

"He's one of the Bedouin students I'm going to be teaching."

"Oh?"

"I'm sorry, I thought I'd told you all about that."

"Sounds as if you've got a pretty full program in Kadmon, what with the survey and now this teaching. How're you going to find time for Global Dawn?"

"That's the beauty of it. It all ties in and, as it turns out, Yusuf wants to become involved, too!"

"You've lost me, I'm sorry."

"Kadmon is going to be the site of our first regional centre, and Yusuf is very excited about it because he thinks the project can help his community."

"Reuven, instead of your trying to tell me all about Kadmon, do you think you could take me there some time soon and show me?"

He smiled to himself before answering.

"I'm sure that could be arranged.   Your involvement is important to me. You know that."

She touched his hand with an unexpected fondness and went out to the kitchen to fix a hot toddy of a kind reserved for very special ailing friends.

Reuven stretched his feet across the sofa and rested, meditating on the latest turn of events. Also, with a mixture of concern and amusement, he thought about the intricate web he was weaving with all the women players in his life. Ora came to sit next to him, and asked,

"If I fix the meeting at Rikki's for sometime in the next two weeks, will you be able to come back from the Negev for it?"

"Yes. All being well."

"Then, can we work out a schedule for it?"

"I don't think we should plan in too much detail. Let's try to balance the action and the fun, shall we?"

"Okay. Is Rikki supposed to be preparing some kind of presentation?"

"I did suggest something like that to her, didn't I? But I haven't heard anything more about it from her. Actually, Nathan said he was going to see if she needed any help. I guess I should find out what's going on there."

He picked up his cell and began searching for her number."

"Rikki! How's tricks?"

"Reuven? Hi. Everything's swell around here, thanks."

"So, do we have a Global Dawn promotional team, yet?"

"I'm working on it. Slowly, slowly."

"Not too slowly, I hope?"

"Hey, we're talking about contacts that need to be carefully fostered."

"No chance of a presentation for our next meeting, then?"

"No way! I've already had this discussion with Nathan. Didn't he tell you? I can't pull something like that out of a hat. He thinks it's as easy as making a Web page. It's a whole different ball game. Needs time to prepare, not to speak of a budget, technical help …"

"Never mind. Don't worry about it. I think I have a solution. I'm relying on you for the big noise production, though. Okay?"

"Yes sir!"

He hung up.

"Rikki all talk and no action, as usual?"

"Now, now. Let's not start bad-mouthing her. She can be dynamite when she gets started."

"Oh, I bet she can," grinned Ora.

"Well, you've certainly perked up! Now, hush, I'm ringing Michael."

"How goes it, man?"

"That Reuven? Great to hear from you, man! The little wife and I are fine, thanks."

"So tell me, are you honourably employed, now, or are you still a liability to the State?"

"I'm saving myself for the right slot."

Reuven darted a knowing smile at Ora.

"You mean, like becoming Project Manager of Global Dawn?"

Michael laughed.

"I'm serious, Michael. That was a brainwave on Tamar's part. I want you to be our Project Manager."

"Is that what you rang to tell me?"

"No, this is a prelude. I want to give you a chance to show off your professional expertise to The Circle."

"What exactly do you want me to do?"

"Could you put together some kind of presentation? Something we can use, initially, to arouse interest among Global Dawn's potential investors?"

"Isn't that Rikki's territory?"

"In a way, but she doesn't have your technical knowledge. What do you say?"

"I should think I could prepare something. When the next meeting supposed to be?"

"Some time in the next couple of weeks. Ora's fixing it with Rikki."

"Wow! That's a tight schedule, but, okay, I'll do my best. Actually, I have a few ideas. It could be fun."

"You can ask Nathan to help, as well. He's already got some graphics together for the Website. He might have something you can use."

"Right."

"We're relying on you, then. By the way, Ora wants me to convey to you her everlasting affections."

"Ditto. Wait, before you hang up – don't you have any other news for me? I'm sure you haven't been dragging your feet with the project since we spoke."

"We most certainly haven't, but I think we'll keep you in suspense until the meeting. There'll be plenty to tell, then, so make sure your calendar's clear for us."

"I'll do my best. Bye for now."

*   *   *

Michael had a thousand questions, but somehow Reuven had
dominated the conversation and they remained unasked. Reuven was
an expert at evading issues that he felt unready to discuss. On the other
hand, his cryptic way of imparting knowledge did add a certain spice to
such interchanges.

He started thinking again about the idea of his becoming
Reuven's project manager. He could not shake the feeling that when it
came to the crunch Reuven would be reluctant to release the
management reins. Ora had done little to reassure him on that score.
She charmed him with compliments but did not actually provide any
straight answers.

With all this still weighing on him, he got down to the task of
preparing a winning presentation. As to the job, he was not about to
submit to pressure or manipulation. He would keep an open mind until
after the meeting.

*   *   *

*"The air over Jerusalem is saturated with prayers and dreams like the
air over industrial cities. It's hard to breathe and from time to time a new
shipment of history arrives and the houses and towers are its packing materials."*
                                                            Yehuda Amichai

On the Monday morning, when Reuven was preparing to return
to Kadmon, he received an unexpected visit from Menashe. Jerusalem
was the energetic hub of Reuven's vision, and Menashe's deep love of
that city created a unique bond between them.

"You know, I'm not a religious man," Reuven told him, "and
yet I feel there's a mystical aura about that city. It's as if some ancient
truth were locked away there."

"I agree. There's an otherworldly aura about the place that puts
it beyond our reach."

"There's something about Jerusalem we're not ready for yet."

"That's what I feel, too. Something has yet to be revealed."

"Religious people all over the world are waiting for the Messiah
to rise and walk through the Golden Gate. They wait and they pray; they
sigh and they hope. Jerusalem has carried its mystic burden for
thousands of years, and right now it hangs so heavy over the city that it's

almost choking it."

"Jerusalem is a golden bowl filled with scorpions", pronounced Menashe.

Reuven looked at him enquiringly.

"Those were the words of an Arab geographer. His name was Muqaddasi, and he lived in Jerusalem over a thousand years ago," he explained.

"An astute observer!"

"So, Reuven, you believe there's a great revelation simmering under Jerusalem's surface?"

"Yes. I believe the city's curtain of darkness will eventually be lifted, and then there will be no further obstacles to Global Dawn."

Chapter 9

The next meeting of The Circle was heralded by stormy weather. The early winter rain was welcome, but it caught Rikki's guests unprepared. They knocked on her door in urgent succession, each nursing donations of food and drink beneath inadequate layers of windproofing and rainproofing. Rikki had invested, the previous winter, in a fashionable wood-burning stove around which they huddled gratefully as she served them hot spiced red wine and cinnamon bread to take the edge off the sudden cold.

"Mmm. What a wonderful aroma. Like cedarwood."

"Actually, it's mostly oak, but I added a bit of orange wood for its sweet fragrance."

"Rikki, you're an angel. This is real pampering," said Ariella."

Reuven was conspicuously absent. Ora suspected him of purposely delaying his entrance for the sake of impact. Had he known, no doubt he would have been offended by her questioning of his integrity. She checked her watch anxiously then glanced out of the window, just in time to spot him getting out of his car. He slammed the door and swept around to the passenger side to gallantly usher his travelling companion under a large black umbrella. They crossed the road together into the shelter of Rikki's doorway. Once inside, all eyes were on them. There was a touch of complacency in his smile as he introduced Shira first to Rikki, then to Ora.

Ora sat by the fireside and watched the scene unfold. Rikki, she thought, seemed entirely unaware that the gathering had a serious purpose beyond partying. She was over-dramatizing her role as hostess and flaunting herself in front of the men, as usual. Reuven also seemed much caught up in the social scene – inappropriately so, she thought. She whispered in Michael's ear,

"Don't you think we should begin?"

But he just tantalised her in his usual way.

"You and me? Just name the hour and I'm yours, lovely lady!"

Determined to ignore his flippancy, she poured herself a cup of Rikki's brew, and meditated on the flames licking the front of the stove. Menashe came and sat next to her. He put a friendly arm around her.

"Why the sullen face? Looks like a wonderful gathering to me."

"Yes. It's great. It's just Reuven took forever to get here, and now he's here he's busy socializing. We're not going to get through half what we planned at this rate!"

"Take it easy, girl. Remember what I said about letting the project breathe?"

"Yeh, that's a fine philosophy. I just don't know if it's going to work for us."

"Ora, Ora. Loosen up. This is what networking's all about!"

"Networking?" echoed Rikki, who had sidled up to them. "Right. I guess that's one name for it!"

"Whatever are you talking about, Rikki?" asked Ora with tired irritation.

"Over there," she said, pointing at Reuven standing with a protective arm around Shira.

"Spit it out, Rikki. What's your point?"

"His latest conquest. Obvious."

"Shira? She's been helping him develop Global Dawn in the South."

"Oh, pl-ease! Your naïvety is touching."

With that, she sidled off leaving Ora to digest her poison. Ora turned back to where Menashe was sitting, but the chair was empty. She stared into the flames that suddenly seemed aggressive rather than comforting and fought back the unwelcome image of Shira and Reuven that Rikki had planted in her mind.

"This group is wonderful. I'm so very 'appy Reuven invited me."

Ora felt her face go extremely red in embarrassment as she stammered,

"We're all ... uhmm ... delighted to meet you, Shira."

At last, people began to settle. Michael had positioned a semi-circle of chairs facing the projection screen.

"What about Nathan? Isn't he coming?"

"Sure he is, but he works long hours. He'll be along a bit later."

As Reuven began to speak, his presence commanded the room. He began in grandiose style,

"First of all, those of you who have not yet met the lovely Shira, this is she."

Ora cringed.

"Until now, we've talked mainly about the Global Dawn centre in Jerusalem. Now, listen up, everyone. Shira and I have news for you. The Global Dawn regional project is under way in the little Negev town of Kadmon!" he announced.

"What exactly has been done there, so far?" asked Ora a little testily.

"Shira and I have begun negotiating with local partners."

Peeved by the sudden focus on Shira, Ora interrupted again, "With all due respect to you both, I think this is a bad idea."

"Oh?"

Ora took one look at Reuven's petulant expression and knew it was a mistake to say anything. Now, however, she had no choice but to explain herself.

"I think we need to have the central project nailed down in all its details before we start splitting our efforts elsewhere."

"I disagree with you. This has the makings of an excellent pilot. And while we're on the subject of regional pilots, there's more news. We have a Global Dawn branch starting in Australia!"

Reuven's eager announcement met with a disappointingly flat response, and in the pause Menashe asked, "Can I interrupt all this for a moment, Reuven?"

"Sure," he answered a little half-heartedly. "Open lines are our way, aren't they?"

"Well, I have a little pet idea of my own that I wanted to try out on you."

"Fire away, Menashe," said Reuven.

Nathan quietly slipped into the vacant seat in the semi-circle.

"Hey, Nathan. Good to see you, man."

"Sorry I'm so late, everyone. Heavy day at the office. Couldn't get away. What did I interrupt?"

"Menashe wants to share an idea with us."

"Actually, my focus is on Jerusalem, like Ora's. If we want to become a part of that city's life, then it will have to become central in our own lives."

"What are you getting at, Menash?

"A Global Dawn working community. A living fact within the city!"

Ora beamed with satisfaction but said nothing. Reuven's face, on the other hand, suddenly tensed, and the reply he gave seemed evasive.

"I have been advised to wait. Jerusalem is not ready for Global Dawn."

"Everything will happen at the appointed time," nodded Ariella. Ora thought she sounded like the voice of the Oracle.

"I like your idea, Menashe. It's just too soon," said Reuven.

"I think it's a great idea!" said Rikki. "We can all live and work there together like an extended family—"

"Whoa!! Steady on, Rikki!" laughed Michael. "I don't think Menashe meant the kind of community you have in mind!"

"Michael, if you've finished poking fun at poor Rikki, would you like to show us your presentation, now?" asked Reuven.

"Fine. Can everyone see the screen?"

There was some shuffling of chairs. Rikki and Ora moved onto the rug in front for a better view.

"Okay, so what I've tried to do here is to convey an overall concept for the project site in Jerusalem. Get the lights someone?"

The first slide was an aerial view of Epcot, zooming in on the geodesic dome of the Spaceship Earth exhibit.

"A theme park has to live and breathe its selected theme. In Disney's case it was the "Community of Tommorrow". In ours it could be something like "One Planet through Multiple Dimensions", but that's just an idea."

"Great stuff. I like it," said an excited Reuven.

"What we're looking at here is an aerial view of a typical theme park. This slide shows a classic shell architecture with a single path spiralling out from the centre. This next one, on the other hand, is like an eyeball with everything radiated out from the centre. There are lots of possibilities, of course. The central point is usually the highest, and you get a vista of the whole park from the top of it."

"Can I interrupt you here, Michael? Ora and I have taken a closer look at the dome idea and frankly, we've fallen in love with it. Isn't that right, Orale? Michael, I've slipped a couple of my own pictures in there. See them?"

What appeared next on the screen was a photograph of Lawrence's dome home.

Nathan started to gripe and rub his chin as he always did when he couldn't see the logic of things.

"What's the matter, Nathan?"

"You've lost me. What's on earth is the connection between that ugly contraption and the magnificent architecture Michael showed us before?"

This was Reuven's cue to tell the story of his lakeside dream and his discovery of Lawrence's dome home.

"At our last meeting, I showed you Lawrence's map and told

you a bit about his lifestyle. This "ugly contraption" as you called it, Nathan, is his home! I told you he's an expert in natural energy patterns. He actually used them to build his home and, as a result, it's an incredibly resilient structure."

"A geodesic dome, you say?"

"That's right. A more attractive and much better known example is the one that Disney designed for Epcot."

"Spaceship Earth!" called out Rikki in excitement.

"Exactly. Ora and I visualise a splendid geodesic dome at the centre of the Nebi Samwil project. Just like in my dream, it will transmit tremendous energy and bring unique life to our project. Michael, back to you. "

"It's really impossible to convey in a presentation like this the incredible energetic force Reuven's talking about. Of course, some of the most advanced virtual reality techniques can do a much better job. Like the ones NASA is using in their Digital Earth project, for example. In the next few slides you can how they're using the Digital Earth as a live education tool. Of course, NASA has state-of-the-art technology at its fingertips. That's why we'd like to get in there as a partner!"

Well, thank you, Michael. That was excellent," said Reuven.

"If you ask me, it was boring and flat! I think we can produce a much bigger splash," proclaimed Rikki.

"Yes, Rikki, dear," added Ariella. "Have you got something to show us or are you just slamming Michael for the sake of it?"

"Now, you two. Let's keep the tone impersonal here and save the rest for the stage!"

"This won't convince an investor to put any money into Global Dawn. Sorry, Michael."

"I know. It's just a beginning."

"I think this is very good, very good," volunteered Shira. "I like the flyover – it makes people want to go there, you know?"

"There!" said Rikki, triumphantly. "What did I tell you last time? It needs the dynamic imagery of film!"

"Talk's cheap, but we haven't seen any results from you so far, have we?" enquired Ariella.

For once, Ora felt sympathy for Rikki. Ariella was so judgmental! However, Rikki bounced back resilient as always.

"Hold on, I have something. I'll be right with you!"

Mutterings began as she hurried out of the room, reappearing a minute later with an email printout in hand.

"Listen to this, guys!"

She began to read aloud.

"Erica Darling, "

"Erica – that's me," she said, pointing her index finger towards her chest for emphasis. "When I was in Hollywood, years ago, they all used to call me Erica."

"Erica Darling,

How've you been? Sure, I remember you and

your hairclips. Whatever would I have done on

set without them? "

Ora could not resist a private snicker as Rikki hastened to explain how she was a tower of strength on the set in a thousand little ways.

"Your project sounds inspirational, my dear.

Global Dawn — such a spiritual name. Your

Kabbalistic rabbi sounds very wise.

Congratulations!

Of course, I love to support projects for a better

world. Bring your friends to my place in LA

whenever you can, and we'll talk some more!

Love and Light,

Shirley. "

"I take it that's Shirley MacLaine?" asked Ariella.

"The one and only."

"Well, Erica," said Michael with a smile. "You certainly seem to have won Shirley over. All we have to do now is gather enough funds to fly our whole team over to Hollywood for a while!"

"Don't pay any attention to Mr. Snide, over there, Rikki. He has his own plan to get in with the big boys," said Reuven.

"Actually, Michael and I did come up with an idea together," said Ora. "We want to canvass Al Gore's sponsorship."

"Yes, the Digital Earth project that NASA are developing – you know, the one Michael mentioned just now? We want to link Global Dawn to it. Actually, it's Al Gore's baby, so we're planning to make our pitch directly to him."

But Nathan was shaking his head vigorously.

"We're never going to win any of these people over unless we've got a real promotion package together," he said.

"What are you getting at, Nathan?" asked Ora.

"All we've got is a concept. It's fine as far as it goes, but investors are going to want to see some clear benefits."

"I hear you," replied Reuven, "but these aren't issues for a large forum like this one."

Aha, thought Ora, he's side-stepping the issue. Michael's right about his ploys; he hates not having all the answers. She caught a quizzical look in Michael's eye that affirmed her hunch.

"Actually," Reuven continued, "I think meetings of The Circle have served their purpose for the time being. Most of our work's going to be in small working groups from now on."

"Okay. Keep me posted, then."

Nathan picked up his coat and called out,

"Rikki, I'm on my way. Thanks for everything."

Michael embraced Ora and announced he was going to head home, too.

"Great meeting. Thanks, Rikki," he said. "Anyone need a lift?"

"Can you give Shira a lift to the station?"

"Sure, no problem, Reuven."

"Ora, coming with me?"

"Yes, thanks.

Ariella and Menashe slipped away arm in arm, noticed only by Rikki's watchful eye.

*   *   *

"Are you in a hurry to get home, Ora?" asked Reuven.

"Not particularly. What do you have in mind?"

The rain had stopped and the wind appeared to be whisking the remaining storm clouds seaward. It was the evening of the winter solstice which was due to coincide with the full moon at its closest to the earth for many years. Sky watchers had their telescopes poised while night ramblers looked forward to a brightly moonlit path.

Reuven headed north some way up the main coast road before turning off onto a dirt track and parking the car. He reached for Ora's uncertain hand, tucked a map under his arm, and directed a flashlight into the bushes in front of them. It was not yet completely dark. The raucous trill of crickets grew in intensity against the silence of the approaching night. Ora ducked her head to follow Reuven threading through the undergrowth that grew denser as the trail narrowed. She asked no questions, content to follow his lead.

He pushed aside a mass of reeds, and she gasped at the beautiful orange and rose sunset reflected across the dark expanse of water ahead. A lively population of mosquitoes circled in the beam of the flashlight, and a mist of water flies swarmed over the lake, hovering and skimming across its surface. Reuven nudged her towards the water's edge. A few metres away from it, a light pressure of his hands on her shoulders encouraged her to pause.

The top of the dome was not easy to spot being largely obscured by the trees on the opposite bank. He waited patiently for her to notice its dully-lit curve. As soon as she did so, she began to tread the path quickly and excitedly towards it, almost breaking into a run as they drew near.

The first to greet them was little Ilanit who raced into Reuven's arms in a great show of affection.

"Reuven, you came back!"

Rachel, fast in her wake, called out apprehensively.

"Ilanit, who're you talking to?"

"It's Reuven, Ima!"

"Reuven," she smiled. "How lovely to see you again, so soon."

"Rachel, this is Ora. She's my right-hand lady."

"Yes, I know. A pleasure, Ora. We've heard a lot about you."

"Reuven, Reuven, come and see! Abba's on the roof with his telescope. Look you can climb up, too!"

An iron ladder ran up the outer curve of the dome, and Ilanit skipped up and down it as nimbly as a little elf. Peering above her, they could make out the silhouette of Lawrence doubled over the telescope.

"Hey, there, Reuven! Er ... good to see you. Wait a minute! I'm coming down to join you."

He leapt off the third rung of the ladder.

"Don't tell me. Er ... I bet this is Ora!"

She grinned and accepted Lawrence's welcoming arm around her shoulder. He ushered them both inside where some herbal tea was brewing.

"You've chosen a very special night to be with us," said Rachel.

"Yes, indeed," said Lawrence. "I hope er ... you'll stay a bit. This night's got a story."

"Why is it so special?"

Reuven explained to Ora that Lawrence and Rachel were among the world's few remaining Druids. They believed everything in the universe was sacred.

"According to our tradition, everything has a soul and a

purpose. The human soul is the most advanced of all. Each of its incarnations brings it closer to its spiritual essence."

"So, are you saying that human beings are almost divine?"

"You can think of our spirituality in terms of God, if you like. To us, it's the sacred spirit of the universe."

"And why is the night of the solstice so special?"

"We're celebrating the end of a cycle. After this longest night comes the return of the light."

"Ah," Reuven mused, "the desire of Man to transcend mortal darkness into divine light; the eternal battle between good and evil, or between God and Satan. It's the foundation of all the world's religions, isn't it?"

However, his question so eloquently prefaced met with a quiet rebuff from Rachel.

"We don't like to think of life as a battleground," she said. "We see the light and the darkness as complementary in our lives."

Lawrence smiled and replied, sentimentally,

"I think er ... it was that philosophy that first er ... attracted me to our Rachel."

"You never told me that before," she replied.

Left thumb anchored under his chin, he stroked his jaw thoughtfully with his forefinger. Then he turned back towards his guests and continued Rachel's explanation.

"You see, er ... in the deep winter darkness are hidden the seeds er ... of new light."

"Today, we're at the end of a cycle," Rachel added. "It's a turning point. Our chance to review the old and prepare for the new with its unknown beginnings."

"So how do you celebrate this day, exactly?"

"That question's more complicated than you think," she laughed, handing round some corn chips.

"I don't know any two people who celebrate the solstice the same way. Each family has its own customs. For example, I only use herbs and essences that are sturdy enough to have survived the winter."

"Why?" asked Ora

"They're natural reservoirs of energy."

"And what do you use them for?"

"I use them in seasoning; I use them to clean our home, too."

Reuven began sniffing at the curved inner walls of the dome.

"Now that you mention it, there's an unusual aroma in here. What is it?"

"A mixture of pine and rosemary."

"Very refreshing," said Ora, nodding her head in approval.

"You feel that way because of the vital energy you're getting from it," said Rachel.

"So, what happens now?" Reuven asked, curious to know where all this universal philosophy was leading.

Now, we eat. So, find a comfortable position. Relax, breathe freely and partake of the fruits of Mother Earth."

Lawrence lit a few candles and Ilanit danced for her captive audience, bowing and curtseying for applause. Afterwards, Lawrence went out again and climbed back up to the top of the dome where he crouched behind the telescope, his gaze tilted skyward. The others followed him, positioning themselves at his side.

The moon rose to a magnificent fullness that night. As the moonlight bathed the whole surface of the dome, Lawrence and Rachel, Reuven and Ora received it as a blessing, both universal and divine.

Lawrence, closely observed by Reuven, mapped geometric patterns between visible stars and selected earth coordinates. Little Ilanit fell asleep in her mother's arms wrapped in her own private moonbeam.

*   *   *

That same night of the full December moon in a tiny Bedouin village due south of Kadmon, Fatima lay awake, eyes to the ceiling, in the heavily hand-carved bed she had shared since infancy with her younger sister.

She was the third oldest child of a family of eight children. Her two older brothers were employed in their father's carpentry business, and sought no further life challenge beyond it. Fatima's decision to participate in the university's English project was a first bold step towards her social and cultural emancipation. Her desire for a western-style education raised more than a few local eyebrows. She challenged the censorship of meddling tongues – a respectable young woman should not travel alone, they said, although it was really not far to Beersheva. Moreover, it was rumoured that women students conversed openly and shamelessly with young men at the university where liberalism knew no bounds.

Fatima persuaded her parents that the study of English would be her launching pad into the world of commerce. Her sole aim was to acquire skills that would benefit the local community. This was her trump card, and she played it well. In just a few weeks, aided by guile and spirit, she was to become the first female student to attend the university from her village.

*   *   *

On January 1st in the Year 2000, the Third Millennium sneaked in silently across the fearful backs of its end-time prophets, and the global machine moved onwards without perceptible alteration. Many partied as if there were no tomorrow; some held loved ones close as if in final embrace. Money gushed through casinos while the miserly secured their pocket books in a meaningless habit of restraint. And this next day followed its predecessor – the ultimate non-event.

Thus continued an unremarkable routine of working days through the month of January. February announced itself, and, in Kadmon, Reuven glanced around the cramped, basement room that had become his second home. The lack of windows in this confined space made it airless and oppressive. He lay on his back on the narrow sofa pouring mineral water down his throat from an extra-large Eden bottle. On the wall above him hung a copy of the Mabada Map. Next to it, a gift from Ora – a picture of his daughter balancing a globe on her head at the age of three, and beside her, the Global Dawn logo.

The phone rang and pulled him out of his daydream.

"Hi Orale. What's up?"

"There's something I've been hesitating to talk to you about for a while."

"So, tell me, nu?"

"Well, I might be wrong; maybe I'm being paranoid—."

"You're procrastinating."

"It's just an uneasy feeling I have."

"About Global Dawn?"

"About Menashe."

Reuven gathered his legs under him into a sitting position, spine flattened stiffly against the wall. He had some reservations of his own about Menashe, and he pursed his lips apprehensively.

"What's he been saying to you?"

"Reuven, he claims to share our dream, and he spouts philosophies and theories about its cosmic purpose, but something about him just doesn't ring true."

"Hmm. So, you don't think his interest is genuine? He says he wants to set up a residential Global Dawn community. What do you think of that idea?"

"Actually, I rather like it."

"But you have your doubts about him, nonetheless. Perhaps he has a private agenda?"

"What do you mean?"

"He never officially joined The Circle, you know. He just offered his place for the meeting and suddenly he was in."

"I guess. I hadn't thought of it quite like that. But a hidden agenda? That sounds so calculating."

"Well, what is it exactly that bothers you about him?"

"He makes loaded comments that seem designed to undermine us."

"Oh?"

She heard a coldness enter Reuven's tone.

"All his comments about how people are going to come and go in the project."

"Isn't that just his philosophy?"

"Maybe."

"You do have a point, though. He made it clear that he didn't see me leading the project through to the end."

"You're kidding!"

"Well, he made a good philosophical case for that, too."

"And he keeps hinting to me that I needn't go along with everything you say."

Reuven frowned. Although he was reluctant to jump to conclusions about Menashe on such a subjective basis, he had grown to trust Ora's instincts about people. He also had a very stubborn gut feeling that there was ambiguity lurking beneath Menashe's story.

"I think, before judging him too harshly, you should give him a chance to redeem himself. Maybe we're misinterpreting his intentions."

"Okay, Reuven", Ora replied in a half-persuaded tone and hung up.

*   *   *

Reuven was becoming an acknowledged force among the tutorial staff of the university. He entered the classroom punctually and greeted his students in English.   Even though their English comprehension was poor, they showed him deference and, for the most part, were ready to learn. He ran a finger down the class list and noted the names of a couple of additions.

Then he sought out the new faces with a cursory glance across the room, and he observed a young Bedouin woman edging towards an unobtrusively placed seat. She shyly lifted a black veil from around her olive-skinned cheeks and took a seat at the end of the fourth row. The flirtatious banter that naturally ensued between the other women in the class and their male student companions caused her to blush deeply in embarrassment, and her modesty quickly caught Reuven's eye. The other women all wore western-style clothing and sported a self-confidence and freedom of gait obviously quite alien to her. Most of them lived in urban communities where a more liberal attitude prevailed towards women's behaviour than in her village.

Reuven's first questions were directed beyond where she was sitting to the far corner of the room. He worked his way around the class systematically until his finger targeted the desk just next to hers. Then, came her turn,

"Now, you, please. Yes, the young lady next to Khaled."

She jumped from her seat and stammered uncertainly,

"Sorry, please, Mr. Teacher, sir ..."

"Reuven. I'm Reuven."

"Oh. I'm Fatima."

Fatima got up from her chair and, with a timid nod, acknowledged the rest of the class. There was a round of friendly applause that seemed to fluster her even more.

"Thank you, Fatima. Welcome to the university."

Above the blackboard, Reuven pinned a large photograph of a typical open market scene, and led the class in discussion of it. Names of foods and various household items began to fill the board. Then he entertained them with a comical rendering of traditional market folk. As always, Reuven's gift for spontaneity was heartily applauded by his students.

He kept a discrete eye on Fatima, noting the bewilderment in her eyes. He went up to Yusuf who had proudly claimed a place in the front row.

"Yusuf, can you help Fatima, please? Explain to her how we work in this class and so on?"

To the great amusement of the rest of the class, Yusuf got up and bowed with exaggerated courtesy first to Reuven, then to Fatima, saying,

"Certainly, Reuven. I am very happy to do this."

"Thank you, Yusuf. Please, sit down"

Reuven decided to consult Shira about paying a visit to Fatima's home.

*   *   *

By the end of the month, he had completed the bulk of his survey and had attained, he judged, a sound enough footing in his work at the university to be able to take another short break. He knew his

family was uneasy about his prolonged absence, and his occasional visits
were meagre compensation.

On his way out of Kadmon, he stopped in at Shira's shop and
came away laden with presents for Tamar and Shahar. These included a
set of stained olivewood pipes, some decorated leather house shoes and a
small etching by a desert artist. He was particularly taken with the sandy
textures and ruddy tones of the latter which conveyed the local ambience
with deceptive simplicity.

It was Friday morning and the roadside vendors were
conducting an excellent pre-Sabbath trade in fresh flowers, fruit and soft
sesame-covered pretzels. It was a clear road until just north of Kiryat
Gat where he ran into the unavoidable crawl towards the ugly
conglomeration of South Tel-Aviv. His journey home was otherwise
smooth, and he and his family spent a quiet evening together without
interruption or incident.

He slept in the following morning, and Tamar had been up for
hours when Shahar rushed excitedly into the bedroom finding him still
half asleep.

"Abba," she said, beginning her tale with a dramatic gasp, "My
friend, Meira, just called me from the hospital!"

"Hospital? Why?" he yawned.

"She woke up this morning with a strange numbness on her left
side. She says her left arm just lay in the bed like a dead weight beside
her!"

"So?" Reuven began," That's not so strange. It's just bad
circulation. It's happened to me lots of times."

"Abba, no, it's not what you think! It's much, much worse. Let
me tell you what happened to her!"

Muki bounded up to him through the open doorway while
Tamar lingered outside, coffee cup in hand.

"Yes, Reuven, do hear her out," she admonished, "but Shahar,
try not to make such a sensation out of it, will you?"

Shahar dropped her squeaky hyperventilating tone and assumed
one of hushed, conspiratorial mystery that left Reuven wondering how
much true concern for Meira lay behind her theatrics.

"Abba," she continued, "she tried to pick her left hand up with
her right and massage some feeling back into it, but it just hung all heavy
and limp. Can you imagine how frightening that was? Then, she
stumbled out of bed, clinging to the chair-back all the time. When saw
herself in the mirror, Abba, she was terrified!"

"Go on ..."

"Her face was all lopsided. One of her eyes was stuck wide open and when she tried to blink, she couldn't. She was so shocked. She fell back onto the bed and started to scream for her mother."

"Reuven," Tamar intervened, "Meira's been hospitalised. She called Shahar from the hospital just now. That's why Shahar's in such a state about it."

Shahar was the first of Meira's friends to rush to her bedside in Kaplan Hospital. The concern of the Sofer and Toledano families was accentuated by the strangeness of Meira's affliction. The doctors seemed to be hinting that her illness might be psychosomatic. Still, Tamar was alarmed.

"Even if she's not in danger of catching anything, this could all be very traumatic for her," she said.

"Tamar," said Reuven, "I think you're over-reacting. She's only doing what any caring friend would."

"But can't you see she's putting herself at risk?"

"What I see is that you're letting this get out of proportion."

"It's alright for you to say that. You'll be off back to Kadmon in a day or two!"

"Now, you know that nothing and no one is more important to me than Shahar. But I have obligations in Kadmon," came his stony reply.

"Ima, Abba, please stop it!" Shahar stood in the doorway fighting back her tears. "Abba, you're hardly ever home these days. Now that you're here, do you and Ima have to keep quarrelling?"

Reuven looked from one troubled face to the other. This whole scene was so melodramatic. Tamar was being quite illogical. After all, she was the one who so wanted him to earn some cash. Now he had a new job, and that was no good, either! Shahar was right. All this stress was doing no one any good. He reached out to her to pacify her."

"Abba, can't you please try to stay a bit longer this time?"

"Pumpkin, I'm not going anywhere until I know the two of you are okay. All the same, I think your mother's reaction is over the top about this thing with Meira."

"Of course it is. I'm sure you'd behave just like I am if a friend of yours was in hospital!"

"I think you're only doing what any good friend would and should do. The trouble is Ima's terrified for you, and I don't know how I can leave you both alone when she's so upset."

He began to panic. He had never seen Tamar in such a state. In all the years of his surveying work, she had never shown such stubborn opposition to his absence. She had always understood that it came with the territory, so to speak. Furthermore, he was concerned that gnawing at the fibre of their relationship were ugly factors such as jealousy and mistrust.

That night, neither he nor Tamar slept well. She tossed and turned. She kept getting up to drink, to throw open a window or to pace the room. Once she nudged him awake just as he was drifting back to sleep.

"Reuven, feel my pulse, will you? It's racing. I'm scared. Don't be angry, please."

She was suffering from palpitations, and he held her close to him to calm her. She started to sweat and rushed to the window again for air.

"Tamar, try to breathe steadily. I'll make you some sweet tea. It'll pass soon, I'm sure."

In the morning, he urged her to consult the family doctor.

"Oh, no. There's nothing wrong with me. I don't need a doctor."

"Tamar. We were both up half the night. You were feverish. It's not nothing!"

"Okay, I'll ring later for an appointment," she conceded.

"Sorry, my love, but later won't do! I'm taking you there now."

Finally, she relented and allowed him to drive her to the doctor's surgery. After examining her, the doctor asked Reuven to join them.

"Your wife is showing signs of stress. I'm prescribing a ten-day course of an anti-depressant drug."

"Okay"

"Now, here's my question. Can you possibly take a break from your work to look after her for a week or so?"

Reluctantly, he stifled his resentment and frustration at having to be away from Global Dawn at this critical time, and he agreed to stay with Tamar for as long as necessary. He called Shira to cancel his classes for the week and requested yet another extension to his surveying project deadline.

*   *   *

Meanwhile, Global Dawn was gathering its own momentum. In Reuven's absence, Shira and Jeanine came up with a scheme for setting up the Global Dawn centre in Kadmon. They even roped Yusuf into the search for a suitable, low rental location. To begin with, the main purpose of the centre would be to house Reuven's GIS. However, Jeanine was also looking to combine Global Dawn with a project for alternative healthcare and awareness – the baby of some close friends of hers. Shira envisaged the transfer of her shop to the new Global Dawn centre and the addition of a café-restaurant where students, researchers and other information seekers could socialise and exchange news and tips. The longer-term goal was for the centre to grow into a multi-faceted regional resource. Shira was undaunted by the lack of preliminary funding. She was sure the town council would back it. It should not be difficult to convince them of the potential benefits to Kadmon of such an innovation.

A few days later, the Kadmon town council was in session. The members were seated in their assigned places on either side of the long conference table. In the chair, laid-back and self-confident, was Chief Director of Planning, Arieh ben Moshe. He scooped up a handful of roasted sunflower seeds from a plastic bowl on the table and began deftly extracting the seeds from their husks with his teeth. His words of greeting to the assembly were punctuated by his coarse spitting of empty husks into his free hand. Two large fans at either end of the room provided inadequate ventilation, and the walls were covered in flies.

The council members included Tom Schechtman, member for population absorption and redistribution, Chich Hesed, Eran Mor and Adi Yaron. Hava Modan, sole female member and despotic guardian of the council's coffers, and Dr. Goldenberg, first Mayor of Kadmon and honorary council member, completed the regular quorum.

Eran held his right fist tightly clenched over the table as he thrust his jaw into an intense debate.

"What do you all think of Yusuf Nabari's latest rumblings? Vying for more cash, is he? All that drivel about community purpose – don't buy it, do you?"

The second speaker was Adi Yaron who had a permanent bee in his bonnet about the refusal of the Bedouin to budge from the villages.

"Community purpose, I'll give him! He harps on about the misery and distress of his village, but he turned a very generous re-housing offer down flat, didn't he?"

"Tell me, Chich, this Yusuf Nabari, is he an official resident of Kadmon?" enquired Hava officiously.

"No," said Chich. "He claims the land he occupies has been in his family for generations. Truth is they've squatted on it forever and a day. Some staying power, that's for sure."

"Well, yeah.   But how does any of this come to be our

problem?"

"It's not! It's the fault of the government! We don't have a budget to handle the likes of this Yusuf and his troublemaking clan!" replied Hava emphatically.

"Yeah, the government's to blame for not giving them their rights, not us! Ask me, that's what's at the bottom of this *Intifada*. All comes down to money in the end."

Tom Schechtman cut in abruptly to remind them that such inflammatory discussions of national politics were out of place at a town council meeting.

"Anyway," Adi pointed out, "seems Shira Argov's the one behind this latest project!"

"Shira, Shira. One of our little town's more cultured and respected young ladies," said the elderly Dr. Goldenberg. Dr. Goldenberg had a soft spot for Shira ever since he taught her as a new immigrant from France.

"Cultured and respected, oh sure. She and Jeanine Danan are Ben Gurion University's women's rights ringleaders!" replied Adi as if it was obvious that she was a troublemaker.

"You're making them sound like a couple of revolutionaries!" exclaimed Tom. "They do a lot of damn good work helping underprivileged women."

"Oh right," said Adi aggravating Tom with his cynicism.

"Have you any idea how hard Bedouin women have to fight to get an education in these parts? Without the help of the Women's Rights Organisation, I doubt any of them would ever leave home!"

"Just sounds like trouble to me," said Hava. "Filling simple girls' heads with fancy ideas ..."

"Right. And the papers said ..."

"The papers? The papers! I guess that's where you get all your shallow bigotry! You believe everything you read in those gossip rags!"

"I agree. Time you opened your eyes, Adi," put in Arieh with a touch of arrogance, "and you, Hava. Never thought I'd hear such narrow-mindedness from you!" He paused a moment for effect, ignoring her primitive objections, and said,

"I vote we give this project a chance."

Startled, questioning eyes were on him, now.

"Look, I've read Yusuf's request. It looks reasonable. We've got a Visitors' Centre we hardly use. What about giving it over to the project? According to him, it'll attract tourism here. Why not put him to the test? Perhaps it'll change the image of our town for the better? And if it helps his tribe, too, well where's the harm?"

Eran turned to Arieh,

"What exactly does he want?"

"As far as I understand, he's looking for a low-rental location. Somewhere central to attract visitors passing through."

Hava Modan addressed her imposing bosom to the debate.

"And what's his real interest in it? How do we know we're not setting up an incubator for anarchy?"

"Look, I really don't think those three are anarchists! Anyway, once we've tied them to a deal, they'll have too much at stake to risk playing politics."

Dr. Goldenberg asked for clarification of what was being proposed. Arieh explained briefly the idea of a regional resource centre, upon which the honorary member responded enthusiastically,

"Sounds like a marvellous venture; definitely deserves our support!"

"Is Yusuf the project's only spokesman?"

"No, Eran. Global Dawn is the brainchild of one Reuven Sofer."

"Well, I think there are still too many open questions for us to decide anything tonight."

"I agree," said Arieh. "I propose we invite the key people involved to formally present their scheme to us."

The same evening, Yusuf received an excited call from Shira.

"The town council likes the idea of Global Dawn! They want us to go there and talk about it."

"*Hamdu lilah*! God be praised! I pray this will be successful."

"It will, it will! Of course, it will! It is wonderful! Reuven will be very 'appy!"

*   *   *

A few days later, Shira, Jeanine and Yusuf were sitting together over coffee in the campus social club when they were interrupted by a call from Reuven. Jeanine and Shira exchanged conspiratorial smiles as Shira's cell phone displayed his number. They had made a pact to keep all their plans secret until his return. With family matters uppermost in his mind, nothing was further, indeed, from his expectations than the joint initiative of these three.

"Hello, Shira," droned a depressed tone.

"Voilà, Reuven, we were just talking about you. Did you feel it?"

"We?"

"Jeanine, Yusuf and me."

"Well, I'm afraid I'm not the best topic for lively conversation, right now."

"Why do you say such a thing?"

"Accept it, Shira. It's the truth."

"Poor Reuven, you 'ad a bad day?"

Jeanine nudged her to pass over the phone.

"Listen," said Shira. "Jeanine, she wants to say 'ello."

"Reuven, darling, we miss you."

"Hey, Jeanine. How's it going?"

"I'm helping with your classes, but the students all want to know when you'll be back."

"Ah," he said, consoled by the thought that he had been missed. "And what about that new girl? You know, the shy one from the village – What's her name now?"

"Fatima?"

"Yes, Fatima. How's she coping?"

"She's doing okay. Yusuf's been helping her, and, by the way, she's really not so very shy. Given her background, I reckon she's pretty brave."

"I'll try to give her some extra attention when I get back."

Shira grabbed the phone from Jeanine.

"Now, tell me about your daughter's friend. Is she feeling better?"

"She's not really improving at all. Some kind of psychological trauma, I think. At least I'm not so worried now about Shahar, but this has all taken quite a toll on Tamar. I'm afraid I have to stay a bit longer to be sure she's okay."

"So now it is Tamar you must care for?"

"Yup. For a week or so. After that I should be back in Kadmon."

"We'll be waiting for you, Reuven!" shouted Jeanine.

"Hey, you guys have really cheered me up, you know. When I get back, we'll get Global Dawn moving. That's a promise!"

Yusuf whispered to Jeanine the positive news about the council. She winked at Shira, then hurriedly whispered back,

"Shhh. That's terrific. Let's surprise him and not say anything just yet, okay?

*   *   *

The following afternoon, Shira wrapped things up early in the shop. Yoram was surprised to see her home.

"You're back early! Everything alright?"

"I closed up. I was worn out."

She lit some incense tapers, and they began to give out a soothing aroma of sandalwood.

"Nava's teacher rang. She wants to talk to us."

"What about?"

"No idea."

"You, didn't ask?"

"No."

She tried to quell her irritation at his passivity. Were all men like that? Reuven certainly was not. He would never have left a message hanging in the air like that. Especially where his daughter was concerned …

"So, why were you so tired?" he asked edgily. "A lot of business in the shop today?"

"Oh, no. Not really. I don't know."

"Must be that project then, taking it out of you. I don't like the way that Reuven fellow pushed his way into your life with all his demands and warped ideas."

"Stop it, Yoram! It is not your business! Anyway, Reuven is not 'ere, he's in Tel-Aviv!"

"Still affects you."

"I told 'im I would help 'im. Why should I not do it? Are you so jealous of 'im?"

"That's ridiculous."

"Is it? You were not very polite when 'e was at our table. You made a lot of critique of 'ow he was behaving. It was very embarrassing!"

"Deserved it. Had no right to go stirring things up like that."

Shira began to rub her forehead. She felt a migraine coming on and held her open palm towards Yoram to halt the escalating argument. His primitive possessiveness was becoming insufferable. It seemed as if another man had only so much as to look at her, and he would get hysterical. Of course, Reuven's adamant support for women's independence made things worse with Yoram. It was so ironic that she was known in Kadmon as a spokeswoman on women's issues, yet her own husband's treatment of her was quite bigoted. At least she did manage to get away on business trips from time to time. And then there was her teaching … but she came home each time to Yoram's crude attitudes. His typical behaviour was so raw …

"I tell you," he was ranting, "that man's a lousy influence on you and this family!"

"Yoram, please, enough. I am not feeling well."

"You don't feel well! What about me?"

She knew where all this garbage was leading. Somehow, each discussion would be turned around so that he was the wounded victim. He would start getting depressed, and before she knew it, she would be taking care of him. That was how it was with him. He used psychological blackmail to force her to pay attention to him, and it worked. Her attitude would mellow, and she would take the time to smother him with affection for the sake of *shlom bayit* – a peaceful house.

But this time, she needed her own space. It was too much. It was no good confiding in neighbours or relatives. To them, Yoram's primitive ways were acceptable. Even though his family hailed from Eastern Europe, they had absorbed a levantine ethos and mentality. Her job, it was intimated, was to wait on him, soothe him and cosset him. He was the king, resplendent on his throne; his authority was never questioned. No, this time she had to get away.

*   *   *

Within a week, she began to prepare for another African spree – not to Morocco, this time, but to Kenya. Her husband's possessive dependence on her was becoming a tightening noose around her free spirit, and this business trip would be a timely break from all her marital pressures. Her mind drifted to memories of a previous Kenyan trip – her first sight of Mombassa, the warmth of its people and the excitement of her first safari. She thought of the luxury of the Indian Ocean with its sandy beaches and coral reefs. But the doorbell interrupted her daydream. It was Jeanine.

"Jeanine, *quelle surprise!*"

"Great news!"

"Come in, come in. What is 'appening?"

"Reuven's going to be back in Kadmon next week, and I want to plan a welcome party for him. What do you say?"

"Terrific idea! He will need a strong cognac when we tell him everything."

"He still knows nothing about it?"

"Oh no. I don't think so. I 'ave said nothing to 'im. 'Ave you?"

"No."

"Listen, Jeanine, I'm taking a little trip, so maybe we will 'ave to delay this party a few days."

"Sounds impulsive. How long will you be gone? What about our presentation to the council?"

"I 'ave to get away. It is personal ... well, and business too, of course. The council, they will not call us yet. They are busy with some twin city visit from 'olland. And Reuven? When will 'e be back?"

"In time for his Tuesday class. Will I be able to contact you while you're away?"

"I can call you, maybe. Anyway, I will be back by Monday. Oh yes, I think so."

"Sounds as if I'll be organizing this party all alone."

"Jeanine, I think this is not a problem for you. You are a terrific 'ostess!"

"I do throw a pretty good party, don't I? Should I invite some other members of Global Dawn?"

"Why not? Reuven will like this. Why don't you speak with Ora?"

"Have I met her?"

"Ora, she lives in Tel-Aviv. She has been working with Reuven on Global Dawn from the very beginning. You know, she is in touch with all the members of The Circle. I told you about them."

"The meeting you went to?"

"Aha. She and Reuven, they organised it all together."

"Well, it'll certainly be interesting to talk to her. Yes, do give me her number."

Shira finished her packing. She habitually travelled light, though she expected to return well laden. Her sister had generously volunteered to keep an eye on Nava and the two younger boys in her absence. As for her eldest son, between his studies and his girlfriends, he was rarely at home these days except to ravage the well-stocked Argov kitchen; grab a shower and collapse into bed. Yoram would assume command of the shop, and her English students would be handed over to a substitute. She would leave for Mombassa at noon the following day.

Chapter 10

Reuven had given Ora a free hand in the part of the project she was dealing with. Still she wished he were more personally involved. While she valued the trust he placed in her, she missed the intimacy and excitement of their earlier work together. Reuven's spark was irreplaceable.

Michael had gathered a technical mini-forum including himself, Nathan, Rikki, and a couple of university students, one of whom offered his small north Tel-Aviv apartment for the first meeting. Ora was also invited along. Nathan sent last-minute apologies. His busy schedule left no space, right now, for Global Dawn. Michael concluded somewhat scathingly from this that Nathan's scepticism had finally won him over.

"I think it's a good thing that we've discovered his lack of commitment now rather than later," he commented to Ora.

"Maybe," she said, "but that leaves us without an effective working group."

"What about Rikki? Didn't she want to join us?"

"Well, yes." Ora concurred. "Do you think we can rely on her, though?"

"Hi, guys!"

Rikki walked through the open door leaving Ora with a look of stunned embarrassment on her face. Quickly pulling together her expression and her wits, Ora turned to greet her.

The purpose of the meeting was to plan a set of promotional tools. Michael had connected a PC to a projection set-up and was outlining the concept to the newcomers.

"This is my very sketchy idea of the project architecture. What we need is for you guys to build on this rough beginning to create a stunning image that will blow the minds of our audience. See these images? These are pictures of geodesic domes. We want to use a construction like this for our central graphic, right?"

"Hey, Michael," began Rikki, "what about your flyover of

Jerusalem for the beginning? We could zoom in on a magnificent view of the dome above Nebi Samwil."

"Steady on! Don't forget the whole Nebi Samwil thing is fantasy until all the politics surrounding it are resolved. Right now, a controversial image like that could smash to smithereens any chance we might have with investors."

Ora quietly added,

"I agree with Michael. What we want to convey here is the global character of the project. The theme should be networking."

The two students were beginning to look bewildered by the grandiose concepts being tossed around. The job was obviously more complex than they anticipated. Michael tried to put it to them more simply. Meanwhile, Ora's phone rang.

"Hello, that Ora?"

"Yes, who is this?"

"My name's Jeanine. You don't know me."

Something in her commanding tone gripped Ora's lower stomach. This was not the dispirited bereaved mother she had imagined.

"I've heard about you from Reuven."

"Of course. Reuven is an old friend and ex-lover of mine with whom I recently renewed contact."

Ora's jaw dropped open at this unsolicited admission and asked warily,

"Look, can I ring you back later? I'm right in the middle of a meeting with the project team."

"Excellent. What I have to say to you will interest them, too. Please put me on speaker phone."

In spite of her annoyance at the intrusion, Ora found herself submitting to Jeanine's imperious manner.

"Reuven's project, Global Dawn, will very soon be opening its doors in Kadmon."

Ora was beside herself. How could she be about to open Global Dawn in Kadmon when Reuven was not even there? Her question was promptly answered.

"Shira Argov and I have personally persuaded our town council to provide facilities for this venture. Their final approval will be granted upon Reuven's presentation of a project plan."

Ora summoned all her powers of self-restraint into a cool reply,

"Why didn't Shira ring me herself, then?"

"She's gone to Africa on Global Dawn business."

Ora wondered what on earth she meant. Whatever did Africa

have to do with this project?

"She'll be back early next week," Jeanine continued, "in time to welcome Reuven back to Kadmon. I'm sure you know that family reasons have detained him for the last few weeks."

Ora, seething at Jeanine's arrogance, struggled to maintain her calm. It was Michael, however, who asked Jeanine indignantly if she was aware that she was speaking to Global Dawn's active core.

"Sure. You must be either Nathan or Mikey. Reuven and Shira have told me all about The Circle. You have my deepest respect."

Ora could not help wondering if the last comment was meant ironically, but Michael simply corrected her.

"It's Michael. Rikki's here too, by the way."

"My pleasure. Shira and I are throwing a party for Reuven next Tuesday, and we want you all to come. Ora, I'll email you the details. I've got to rush, now. Not a word of this to Reuven! We want to surprise him. See you all at the party, then!"

Before any of the team could catch their breath, the line went dead. Jeanine had said her piece and hung up.

"Any liquor in that drinks cabinet? Could use a drink," said Rikki breaking the silence. It seemed that the moment called for something stronger than coffee.

*   *   *

Ora was disgruntled. She wanted to be glad about Global Dawn's success in the Negev, but found herself captive to far less altruistic sentiments. She decided to stop by Reuven's house and tell him about the meeting with the technical team. Luckily, she found him strolling in the local park with Muki. Muki was racing around, yelping with delight in the freshness of the warm winter's day. Reuven's mood was predictably dark. He began to talk about his latest clash with Tamar and the bitter disharmony Global Dawn seemed to be causing between them.

Ora reached out to comfort him, and he embraced her affectionately in return. They stretched out on the grass in the shade of a large oak and gazed up through its open branches at the clear midday sky. She began to tell him about some of the encouraging reactions she had received from the Outer Circle. In particular, she was keen to share with him the news of a new Global Dawn discussion and action group being set up in Paris.

"I logged onto some international mapping forum, and suddenly the name of Global Dawn popped up. The message was from a student called Jean Marcel."

"That'll be the work of Yvette. Don't you remember we sent her an email? She's an old friend of mine."

"But we didn't hear anything from her, did we?"

"She was never one for writing."

"I thought perhaps we should write to Jean Marcel."

"Absolutely. I'm fascinated to hear about this Paris group. Let's take Muki back, and then we can drive over to your place and draft an email together, okay?"

"Great idea.'

She was heartened by his more positive frame of mind.

As soon as they reached her house, Reuven made himself at home in the kitchen and brewed some strong coffee for them both. Ora, meanwhile, loaded a web page she wanted him to see.

"Here, come and look at this. It's another Parisian surprise for you!"

"La Géode – Science City, Parc de la Villette, Paris? What's all this about, Ora?"

"Take a deep breath, and look at the photographs. Then, tell me if this isn't a mirror image of your dream for Jerusalem!"

Reuven began to look, but his concentration seemed to flag.

"Looks interesting ..."

They were interrupted by a call on his cell. It was Jeanine. Ora cursed inwardly. She heard Reuven tell Jeanine he planned to return to Kadmon on Monday.

"Truth is," he said, "my land-surveying project is now desperately overdue, and I'm afraid I've jeopardised my prospects for future field work."

He listened to Jeanine's brief response, then added,

"I've really missed Kadmon and all of you. Until Monday, then!"

He turned back to Ora. She was still sitting at the computer with her back to him, so he could not see the corners of her lips quivering. She was breathing deeply to control her feelings about what she had overheard. His impatience to return to Kadmon was clear and required little explanation, she thought.

"Oh, Reuven, I've printed out those few pages about the Géode as I can see you're not into reading them, right now. Try to look at them soon. You'll find them electrifying."

"That's great, Ora. You're terrific."

"Oh, and by the way, about your workload. I had an idea."

"You did?"

"Yes. Perhaps you should consider taking on a field worker to help you."

"Good idea. Shouldn't be too difficult to find someone – maybe a student keen to earn a bit of cash and gain some lively experience."

"Well, working with you would most certainly be that."

"Speaking of which, we have an email to draft, don't we?"

*　　*　　*

By Friday morning, Ora was becoming concerned that the technical team was dragging its feet. Reuven, of course, still knew nothing of the urgent need to prepare a presentation for the Kadmon Town Council. Jeanine, meanwhile, had emailed her, pressing her for assurances of the team's preparedness. Despite her dislike of Jeanine's controlling disposition, she wanted Global Dawn's image to be professionally presented in Kadmon. To achieve this, however, some serious changes would have to occur quickly. Her train of thought was interrupted by the unexpected arrival of a visitor.

Gadi answered the door to an ample, rotund figure of a middle-aged man with long, greasy hair pulled tightly back into a rubber band. His eyebrows seemed to be set in an inquisitive arch and his mouth in a supercilious half-grin.

"Menashe, isn't it? Don't think we've met, but you fit Ora's description exactly!"

"Who's that at the door, Gadi?" she called out.

"It's one of your friends from the project."

"I'll be right there."

"She's just getting dressed. I'm afraid we're a bit disorganised on Friday mornings. The kids go off to school early, and it's our chance to take things easy."

"Hi there, Menashe. What brings you to our neck of the woods?" asked Ora, buttoning her shirt as she came towards him. "Join us for breakfast?"

However, Gadi excused himself. He had some errands to run.

I'll be off, Ora," he said, semi-apologetically. "I'll leave you two to your business. Be back around eleven, okay?"

"Fine, Gadi. Sorry, Menashe. Just you and me for breakfast, then. You were saying?"

"I'm starting a new seminar at the Alternative Medicine Centre not far from here, and I thought I'd take the opportunity to call on you."

She summoned her most gracious smile and enquired,

"What's the seminar on?"

"A new kind of therapy that uses meditation to reach the deeper motivating forces of self. Why don't you come along?"

She tactfully avoided rejecting him outright.

"I'm afraid my timetable's tight, just now. Global Dawn's turning into a full-time occupation."

"Oh, really? So much has happened since our last discussion? I thought it was stagnating from what I heard at the last meeting."

Again, his cynicism struck a discordant note.

"There've been developments since then from quarters you'd never imagine."

"Hmm. It doesn't surprise me. Things happen at their destined hour by the appointed agent, do they not?"

"I'm sure you're right in theory."

"So things are going well?"

"Yes and no. On the one hand, we've gathered support in a lot of new places."

"And on the other hand?"

"I'm afraid some of the people I thought we could depend upon have let us down."

She lowered her eyes as she spoke in order to avoid his questioning glance.

"In what way?" he asked.

"They claim they support Global Dawn, but they're really passive about volunteering any of their time."

"By they, you mean?"

"Members of The Circle."

Nothing in his manner, she observed, indicated that he felt himself in any way implicated. Instead, he took it upon himself to pass judgement.

"I think this is really about your expectations of others, Ora. You don't find it easy to accept them without judging them, do you?"

He was a fine one to talk, she thought. Struggling to maintain her polite cool, she got up to refill the coffee pot.

"What's your point?" she asked.

"I think you need to awaken their curiosity. Show them more clearly what Global Dawn can offer them."

"And how do you suggest I do that?"

"Look at your own motivation. Why are you doing it?"

"Because I believe in it, and I want to have a hand in improving the world my children are going to inherit."

"Hmm. What about your emotional motivation? Idealism isn't enough to generate your kind of devotion to Global Dawn."

Ora thought back to her conversation about Menashe with Reuven, and their mutual agreement to give him a fair chance. She fought to subdue her resentment of his demeaning presumptions.

"Reuven shared his dream with me long before The Circle ever existed. I feel a very personal connection with it," she replied haughtily.

"Okay. So, you've got your answer now, haven't you? Look how deep your personal involvement is with Reuven and his dream. Do you think it's realistic to compare yourself with the others?"

"So what am I supposed to do? Lower my expectations of them?"

"On the contrary. Let your example be their inspiration."

"I don't think I have the patience to wait for them to be inspired."

"I understand. It seems we now know what you need to work on. You need to learn to be more patient, and let things take their natural course."

Momentarily flushed, she hoped that her twinge of guilt was not over-apparent. Menashe's next suggestion, however, only strengthened her doubts about him.

"If you ask me, it would do you good to take some time out from all of this. Why don't you come to one of my courses?"

So that was it, she thought. He really was trying to coax her away from Global Dawn. She projected her best hostess smile and answered him,

"You've given me a lot of food for thought. I need to mull it over for a while."

"Well, you do so and be in touch when you're ready."

"Thanks, I will. I'm really glad you stopped by. Your timing was impeccable."

*   *   *

The next couple of days passed by, and Monday dawned without particular distinction. Ora caught the morning train to Beersheva. Her drifting gaze embraced the hills of the northern Negev that were unusually verdant after the rain. Eagles were circling high in the greyish sky, and local workers were going about their business, warmly clad against the desert cool. Further south, she saw enclaves of anemones flashing by as scarlet patches beneath the feet of almond trees in blossom.

From Beersheva, she travelled on by local bus to Kadmon where Michael had agreed to meet her.

Unaware of their parallel journeys, Reuven was also on his way to Kadmon. As was his habit on such long drives, he had turned up the music, rolled the windows down and was testing the health of his vocal chords. He was puzzled by the lack of word from Shira in the last few days. And another thing, Ora had mentioned that Jeanine had called her. He wondered why. After all, Ora had never met Jeanine. What could Jeanine possibly have to talk to her about, and why Jeanine and not Shira?

That evening, Jeanine's guests arrived armed with assorted bottles and party fare. Among them were university students, neighbours and friends. She greeted them in exotic dark purple silk, cut high at the throat above provocatively bare shoulders and a deeply scooped back. Drama being her middle name, she carried her attention-craving mania to all the excess that good taste would allow.

Ora had resolved not to be intimidated either by Jeanine with her aura of command or by Shira when she eventually swept in from her African travels. The long Perspex table had been moved to one side of the room, and upon it flared an assortment of decorative candles. On a second table, more centrally placed, were amassed delights to both tongue and palate for which she suddenly discovered a rampant appetite. As she motioned to Michael to accompany her to the table, they were stalled by the arrival of an astonished Reuven. Jeanine had invited him on the pretext that they needed to go over his teaching schedule. Now, he stood in the doorway, innocently laden with files and a giant notepad and began to absorb the ambush they had laid for him. He read the large "Welcome Home Reuven" banner strung above the entrance and tossed aside his load to offer his hostess a great hug of gratitude. Allowing himself to be ushered inside on the arm of that same elegant escort, he stopped in further surprise to greet Menashe.

"Menashe?   Whatever is going on? Jeanine, an explanation, please, now!"

However, Jeanine just shoved a glass into his hand saying, "Shhh. No questions. Enjoy."

Ora was also surprised by Menashe's arrival from Ein Karem. He was standing a little awkwardly to one side rolling a cloth cap between his fingers. Jeanine's gushing artificiality and the contrived atmosphere she engendered were plainly making him feel ill at ease. As soon as he spotted Ora, he exclaimed,

"Ora, dear, I'm so glad you're here. I feel like a duck out of water among all these pretentious young intellectuals."

"Don't worry," she replied, a trifle stiffly. "This will be an interesting evening, I promise."

As she spoke, Shira appeared in the doorway, and his attention was diverted. She circulated among the guests until she found Reuven.

"Shira, what a wonderful surprise!"

"It is Jeanine you 'ave to thank for all of this. It was 'er idea. She organised everything – she even called our Global Dawn friends."

"And I'll have to find a special way to thank her."

"I shall look forward to that," smiled Jeanine, catching him off his guard with a seductive glint in her eye.

"Now, everyone," she continued, "Shira and I have an announcement to make."

The clamour faded to whispers and then into a pregnant silence.

"Most of you already know Reuven. He has become an important part of the life of this town. The real purpose of this evening is not only to welcome him, but also to announce the opening, very soon, of his Global Dawn project at the Kadmon Visitors' Centre. Reuven's project will bring new life to this town by providing information resources for all and attracting tourists here from all over the country."

The applause was deafening. It seemed to Reuven that only he was left bewildered as to exactly what was being announced here. He sat down to catch his breath and was quickly joined by Jeanine and Shira, Menashe, Ora and Michael.

"Help me out, here, someone, please. Whatever have you all been up to behind my back?"

"Actually, Reuven, you should ask Yusuf," replied Shira.

"Oh?"

"He has talked with the town council about Global Dawn."

"You mean to tell me that Yusuf has single-handedly taken on that whole embassy of senility?"

"Oh, they are not so bad," Shira countered.

"So, they've voted in favour of our project?" pressed Reuven, with one hand calming his palpitating heart and the other reaching for a second whisky.

"We haven't passed the final vote yet," replied Jeanine turning to Michael with an enquiring look.

"How's the presentation coming along, Mikey?"

Coolly, he corrected her for a second time.

"It's Michael. We still have some work to do on it. We were

delayed by some differences of opinion between members of the team."

"Okay, guys. Listen," said Jeanine." We're expecting the town council to call us any day now, and they want you, Reuven, to come and personally present the project to them. We almost have them in our hands. This is our final step to clinch the deal. Our presentation must be very persuasive, and leave them no doubt whatsoever of the professionalism of our team and the benefit of Global Dawn to this town."

Reuven appeared quite traumatised and said nothing.

"Reuven, come over here. There are some people I want you to meet."

He followed Jeanine as obediently as a lapdog.

Shira, meanwhile, had gathered a group of students around her and was recounting various episodes of her African trip. There was a gentle radiance about her. She held out artefact samples to a captive audience while excitedly advertising the forthcoming move of her shop to the Visitors' Centre. Ora edged her way into the circle.

Reuven approached Shira's circle of admirers from the other side and waited patiently for a hiatus in her attention to them. There was none, however, until one of Jeanine's entourage called everyone over to participate in a game. The idea was to break the ice between them by challenging their inhibitions. The lights were dimmed, and some candles lit.

The game involved the telling of dreams, and Jeanine was appointed to interpret them. A first volunteer came forward. Ora looked anxiously around for Reuven. She sat between Menashe and Jeanine's friend, Arik. Her attention was focused more on the players than on the game itself. She noted the reverence with which so many of them seemed to hang on Jeanine's every word.

Arik stood up and volunteered the next dream that he claimed had haunted him since childhood. The atmosphere became quite tense as he described a dramatic scene of vertigo reminiscent of a Hitchcock drama. Jeanine said his dream was obviously the replay of a terrifying childhood experience with which he had never come to terms. He would have to return to the place where it occurred to exorcise its memory.

Ora was unimpressed by this response. It seemed devoid of any unusual insight.

Jeanine stood up and looked around for another volunteer. She pointed a finger at Ora and declared,

"Ora, I sense you have a story for us."

Ora froze. All eyes were on her. In the next instant, however, her self-controlling scepticism slipped away, and, as if in subordination to Jeanine's will, she rose to her feet and began to speak.

"My dream has recurred over many years, but until now I've never told anyone about it. Actually, I dreamed it again last night for the first time in about two years. It begins in my own home on a regular afternoon. I'm re-arranging the chairs in the living room. I look up at the wall. In place of the ceiling-to-floor tapestry that usually fills it, I see a door. It swings open to reveal an entire room larger than any other in the house, L-shaped and fully furnished in solid, traditional style. Heavy sofas upholstered in faded pink, shelves full of classic literature and law books, quality carpets and a chest displaying an incomplete porcelain tea service.

I enter the room; walk to the end, and around the corner into the hidden wing where there are several beds, each with a fringed cover, pillows and a bedside cabinet. I tug one of the drawers open, lifting it right out of its compartment. Inside is a yellowed set of local maps. I leaf quickly through them – could be valuable. I shove the drawer and its contents hastily back in place and rub the dust off my fingers. My children come home from school to find me still gazing in amazement at this newly discovered space. They're enchanted by it. Then, my husband joins us and sets about calculating the increased market value of our house with the addition of this room.

I'm troubled by conjecture as to why the room might have been closed for so many years and why it was not even listed in the deeds of the house. My overriding feeling here, however, is one of well-being."

Trembling slightly, she sat down and Jeanine began to analyse the symbolism of her dream. She found a very strong message of changing realities. The fact that the opened room was fully furnished indicated riches in store for her. A long-hidden treasure trove was just waiting to be unlocked.

"How do you explain the dream's recurrence?"

"Opportunities for change arise frequently in life, but they can only be of real value to us when we're emotionally prepared for them. In the past, you blocked your door to change. That's why the meaning of the dream wasn't clear to you. Now, you've not only recognised the door, but you've publicly declared it open. I've no doubt your courage will have its reward."

Reuven retired to a quiet corner in order to gather his thoughts and slowly take the measure of the evening. He now appeared next to Ora, and she wondered how much of her story he had heard. A subtle nod of his head was sufficient for her to understand that he, at least, had faith in Jeanine's insightful wisdom. She also detected a look of exhaustion on his face. The evening had taken a high toll on their emotions.

He turned around to speak with Shira, but finding her preparing to leave, he just whispered a few words in her ear to which she responded with a soft smile.

Ora took her leave of Jeanine and Shira and gratefully accepted an offer of a ride home with Michael. By way of farewell to Reuven, she pressed both his hands firmly between hers. All being well, their next meeting would be at the Kadmon Town Hall to make their bid for the opening of Global Dawn's southern branch.

*   *   *

Reuven's present disposition could be categorised as one of volatile incredulity. The chain of events that was so rapidly pounding a forward trail for Global Dawn left him suspended between euphoria and disbelief. Intruding unpleasantly upon his elation, however, were his and Ora's misgivings about Menashe's involvement in Global Dawn. During the early meetings of The Circle, he held himself aloof as if he were blessed with some higher than average insight. This guru-type attitude irritated Reuven as it was the antithesis of the Global Dawn ideal, but it was only later that his suspicions deepened about the true motive for Menashe's involvement.

Latterly, since Ora had added fuel to the fire, he was even more determined to find redeeming qualities in Menashe's behaviour. It saddened him, therefore, to observe Menashe's undisguised envy of his partnership with Ora and to hear from Ora of how repeatedly, under guise of friendship, he tried to lure her into his domain and away from Global Dawn. Regretfully, he concluded that Menashe did indeed represent an undermining force with an independent agenda thatch must be distanced from The Circle and from Global Dawn. In a brief and businesslike telephone call to Ora, he asked her to remove Menashe henceforth from all mailings and project communications. The absence of any surprise in Ora's tone as she received his decision in itself constituted its acceptance, and thus the matter was laid to rest.

Thursday evening brought Reuven an official summons to present Global Dawn to a town council meeting the following Sunday morning. He slept fitfully during the intervening period. Sunday would be judgement day – a "one shot, win or lose" chance for his lifelong dream to touch a portion of reality. He had entrusted the technical preparation to Michael and Rikki. Would their creativity hit the mark?

His thoughts moved to Charlotte. Distanced though she was, geographically, she was the first to react and to absorb the essence of his intent. He had heard she was already making headway with her plans to start a Global Dawn group among the students in Adelaide. Then, there was Yvette, too. She was obviously operating behind the scenes to get things moving in Paris. Ah, Yvette ... So many years ... Finally, he cast his mind back to his first meeting with Shira and how they had talked about the routes we choose and the signs that guide us. He was stunned by the innate energies now surfacing in Global Dawn and already profoundly affecting the lives of a whole network of his friends and associates. This joining of spirits had a tangible value far beyond a project built or a computer framework activated. This was the intended path.

Slowly, tension receded from his forehead, neck and jaws, and his eyes stirred with a tender new spark. Creator and servant of Global Dawn, he rested awhile reflecting on a prophecy uttered long ago in a near wordless encounter among these same ancient hills and deeply flowing sands.

*   *   *

The events of Sunday proceeded rapidly and without undue commotion. Michael dazzled the council with an impressive presentation, blinded them with science and, most importantly, succeeded in presenting Global Dawn as a highly beneficial potential investment for the town. The project's original opponents found themselves artfully undermined by the project team's professionally persuasive manner, and the vote was carried in Global Dawn's favour. Moreover, in addition to the provision of low-rental space at the Visitors' Centre, it was agreed to grant Reuven a start-up loan to cover the initial running expenses.

Dr. Goldenberg offered congratulations to Shira, while Tom Schechtman and Arieh ben Moshe wished Reuven success. The opening of Global Dawn in Kadmon was provisionally scheduled for the beginning of May.

Chapter 11

A fierce and hot April wind was driving its dust against Shira's shop front as she wrestled with the windows to block the blustery intrusion from her display shelves. She blew the grit off her fingers and began to whip a polishing cloth around a few ornaments, when the door flew open. It was Reuven. Letting the door swing rhythmically against its hinges, he stamped some clogged sand from the worn tread of his work shoes and raised the low brim of his hat to Shira.

"Phew! Quite a sand storm brewing out there!" he exclaimed.

"I know. I love the wind and 'ow it 'owls round the square on days like this one."

"Mmm. Appeals to the wilder side of your nature, does it?"

She beamed back at him as they pressed the door to and locked the elements firmly out. He headed immediately for his favourite corner at the back of the room, and she joined him with a welcome mug of steaming coffee. He patted the cushion next to him motioning to her to sit next to him.

"Now, I want to hear about your trip and what prompted you to take off so suddenly for Mombassa."

"Oh, I 'ad to restock the shop."

"That the only reason?"

"I needed a break. Also, I 'ad to meet with a new supplier. You know it is very important to me to do these things myself."

"So do you feel better after your trip, Shiri?"

"Well, yes, I suppose so. It was good for me."

"Was it what you needed?"

"Yes. I needed that time alone, you know. I needed to think about some problems."

"Go on ..."

"It was because of Yoram, Reuven. Really, 'e's a very nice father and 'e loves me ..."

"But?"

"All my activities, 'e thinks everything is a menace to 'im. 'e's so possessive about me, like an obsession."

"Especially now that you're so involved in Global Dawn?"

"Yes. 'e says ugly things about you."

"So, how can you cope with it? Do you think it's just a passing phase?"

She glanced up at him, took a deep breath as though about to explain, but instead of replying she gave a little shrug and turned away.

Reuven flexed his forefinger and thumb into a reassuring massage above her left shoulder blade.

"Shira? Talk to me," he coaxed.

Still averting his eyes, she turned towards him again. Then, abruptly conquering her reticence, she drew herself up to full height and flatly declared,

"I 'ave decided something in Mombassa, Reuven. I 'ave to leave Yoram."

*   *   *

Alongside Shira's rift with Yoram was her deepening connection with Reuven that quietly intensified despite thinly disguised envy on the part of Ora and the obvious ambivalence of Jeanine. Reuven was aware of these undercurrents between the three women but did not choose to be sucked into them. His own marital bed was too thorny for him to seek further complications in his personal life. The southern land survey was at last nearing completion. This freed him to concentrate on the May opening of the Global Dawn centre. By thus occupying his mind with practical matters, he was able to let the emotional tide flow over him.

Shira also appeared to be immersing herself totally in the building of their mutual dream and revealed no outward hint of her private trauma. She began to widen her Global Dawn agenda. She called Ora to get the latest news from the Outer Circle and was thrilled to hear about the new action group forming in France.

"Ora," she said, "I 'ave a fantastic idea. We should send a group of our members from 'ere to Paris."

Ora surprised Shira on this occasion by not only agreeing with her but by sounding extremely excited about the suggestion into the bargain.

"I'm going to send an email to Jean Marcel, right away!" she said.

Within the hour, an invitation to the group arrived from Yvette.

*   *   *

The next day, Reuven and Shira were busy as usual with renovation work at the Visitors' Centre. Shira had reached an agreement with Jeanine's friends to locate her new shop and café in the Centre's forecourt, and Reuven was helping her to redecorate her allocated space. His trusted blue bag lay gaping open on the edge of a stepladder, and from one of its side pockets rang out the cellular tones of Ravel's 'Bolero'.

"It's your phone, Reuven," called Shira.

He hurriedly wiped the plaster off his hands and strode over to investigate the interruption.

"Damn, I missed it," he exclaimed. "Looks like Ora's number. I wonder what she wanted."

"I am sure she will ring you again. Anyway, the two of you speak almost every day, don't you?"

Shira's dismissive attitude struck a discordant tone with him, and he threw her a questioning look as he redialled.

"Hi, there, Ora. Were you just trying to reach me?"

He was still watching Shira, who was now, most uncharacteristically, pouting. Ora heard him heave a loud sigh and asked what was wrong.

"Nothing for you to worry your pretty head about, Ora."

"Hey, I phoned with terrific news. We're going to Paris!"

Reuven paused a long moment before replying, leaving Ora suspended in anticipation of his reaction. Only an occasional audible breath affirmed his presence at the other end of the line.

"Reuven?"

"Well, well. So, you've heard from Yvette."

"Yes. She wants us all to come to Paris."

"So. Global Dawn is to have its first international meeting!"

Shira nudged Reuven.

"Let me talk to Ora. This sounds like a job for me."

"Just a moment, Ora," said Reuven, and quickly covered the mouthpiece before addressing Shira.

"Can you girls be trusted to work on this together?"

She gave a rather awkward nod. However, instead of passing her the phone, he kept his eyes fixed sternly on her as he told Ora to thank Yvette for the invitation and to say they'd be in Paris just as soon as Shira could arrange the tickets.

"Tell her we'll be in touch with all the details very soon!"

Reuven dug his fingers deep into the bucket of plaster and

slapped some aggressively onto the partition wall. The warm spring breeze was rapidly drying the first layer out, and it would soon be ready for sanding. The jealousy between the women in his life was becoming oppressive and completely contrary to the spirit of Global Dawn. Even Shira was now demonstrating herself prone to this venom.

The sound of forceful slugging of plaster clods stopped Jeanine in her tracks.

"Reuven! Good therapy for an angry heart, I see!"

He swung around on the spot, and she leapt back.

"Slow down. If I want you to help me get plastered, I'll let you know!"

He fell back laughing onto an old grey-striped mattress and picked up a plastic canteen from which he took several gulps of water. Shira raced over to tell Jeanine all about the Paris plan, and with yelps of delight, the two of them landed on either side of him as seductive in their shorts and skimpy T-shirts as a couple of frivolous teenagers.

"So, when is the group due to fly off to *La Belle France*?"

"I am going to enquire about flights and so on tomorrow. We want to do this as soon as we can – I think it will be wonderful for the Global Dawn team. Do you agree with me?"

"Yes, but Shira," began Jeanine cautiously, "what about all the work you guys still have to do to get this place ready for the opening?"

"I think we can manage everything even if we stay in Paris for a week. What do you think about this, Reuven?"

Reuven was surprised by Jeanine's hesitation, but all he said was,

"I think, as long as we concentrate all our energies on working together, we'll be fine."

Sure enough, it turned out that there was more behind Jeanine's reluctance than she was telling them. Suddenly, her animation dwindled and an apologetic look crept over her face.

"Look, guys, I think this is great news about Paris, but I'm afraid I can't come with you."

Reuven and Shira exchanged puzzled looks, but she volunteered no clarification.

*   *   *

And so it was that, less than a month before Global Dawn's opening in Kadmon, a group of Global Dawn's key members gathered at the Roissy Airport terminal to wait for transport into the centre of Paris. In Jeanine's absence, Antoine had volunteered to be the group's

exclusive Paris guide. Paris through the eyes of Antoine was likely to be
a unique and colourful experience, indeed.

It was a forty-minute ride by airport bus into central Paris where
Jean Marcel was to meet them. Rikki was already flaunting herself in
front of Antoine, who appeared to be swallowing her whole with his
eyes, enraptured by her every move.

Ariella nudged Ora.

"Take a look at that wild pair. A match made in Heaven, you
mark my words."

"Speaking of which, you must be sorry that Menashe backed out
of the trip at the last minute."

Ariella shrugged her shoulders, then answered quite bluntly,

"Oh, some things are just not meant to be, Ora."

"But I thought ..."

"You're right. We did get rather close. I'd even begun to pin a
few hopes on our relationship."

"So, what went wrong?"

"We just didn't see life the same way, you know."

"Did you two have an argument?"

"Actually, yes. Things became quite unpleasant between us."

"Oh, I'm sorry, I had no idea ..."

"No one did, Ora. He began to make demands on me I just
wasn't prepared for. But, please, I beg of you, keep this between us. I
wouldn't want him to hear rumours that I'd been gossiping, you know."

Ora fell silent as they reached a flyover on the outskirts of Paris.
Below it, she could already see the characteristic boulevards teaming
with mid-day traffic.

Reuven leaned against the high-backed bus seat, and sank into
nostalgic reveries of the time he spent in Paris when he was a student.
Very soon, he glimpsed the white silhouette of the Sacré Coeur on the
horizon. He yearned to amble through the streets of this glamorous and
elegant city, to linger under the perfectly pruned oaks and chestnuts of
the Tuileries, to gaze up to the columned heights of the Place Vendôme,
then, crossing over the river onto the Left Bank, to wander into studios
and galleries of lesser artists in the narrowly winding side streets near the
Sorbonne. He recalled a small corner café in Saint Germain des Prés
overlooking the old walls of the Cluny Museum where he had sipped a
Perrier Citron from a tall glass at a tiny wooden table.

His memories of Paris were filled with the dust of second-hand
books purchased at the open canopied stalls of Gibert Jeune. Paris, in his
mind's eye, was squeezing through the great iron doors of the métro
platform to be crushed like a sardine between the Franklin Roosevelt

station and the Trocadéro. It was fountains and spires, backstreet jazz and a carafe of red house wine on a hot summer night.

Disembarking from the bus in the Opera Square, they were met by the suave, casually jacketed Jean Marcel who smiled as he approached them. Reuven was jolted out of his daydream and extended a warm handshake to Jean Marcel.

"Terrific to meet you! Where's Yvette?"

"Oh, she's waiting for you in Neuilly."

"Is that where you're taking us, now?"

"Yes. Let's take all your baggage over there," he said, pointing across the road, "and we'll divide you up between my car and the jeep."

The jeep was parked on the other side of the rue Auber. Its driver, Robert, beckoned them across.

"Hi there. Three with me; the rest in the car. Okay?"

Jean Marcel quickly explained, as a few of the party climbed into his back seat.

"We're going to our temporary meeting house at the Kaplan Centre. It's about twenty minutes ride from here, in Neuilly. That's where we'll meet your various hosts and sort out some accommodation."

"That sounds wonderful," said Ora, introducing herself.

"So you're Ora – At last, a face to fit the messages!"

"That's me. This is all so exciting."

"You speak very good English, Ora. You don't have an Israeli accent at all."

Ora laughed,

"That's because I grew up in England. Reuven did, too, by the way. What about you?

Your English is also excellent."

"I'm a bit like you. My mother is from South Africa. She came to Paris as a child, but we've always spoken English at home. Do you have any *francophones* in your group?"

"Well, my French isn't very good, but we do have a couple of real French speakers with us – Antoine and Shira. Their both Moroccan by birth, although I think Shira actually grew up in France. Then there's Reuven. Of course, his French is very good, too."

"Wonderful! So, you'll all manage fine to converse with our little action group."

"Yes. We can't wait to meet them."

"You won't have to wait very long at all for that. We'll have our first meeting tonight over dinner, which, by the way, they're preparing specially. I think it's going to be quite a feast!"

As they reached the Kaplan Centre, Reuven was overcome by the eagerness of the welcome party that aligned itself along the kerb. Yvette rushed out of a side door in the austere brick building to find Reuven whom she had not seen for many years. He anticipated her, engulfing her in his wide-open arms. Her tiny figure was entirely lost inside his embrace, leaving only a few trailing locks of her straight, ash-blond hair as evidence of her presence. Her dynamism more than compensated for her miniature physique, and it became quickly evident that she was the driving force behind the Paris action group.

All the luggage was piled into a corner of the lobby, and Yvette led her guests into a large meeting room where the host group were already assembled. Jean Marcel took charge of the formal introductions and, as he spoke, there was a continual background murmur of translations from English into French and Hebrew for those who required it.

The Paris action group was mainly made up of students who answered Yvette and Jean Marcel's initiative at the university. Ariella enquired about some of their reasons for joining the group, and found them to be very varied – several were peace activists, a few were GIS specialists and one was on the fringe of local cinema.

"What about you, Yvette? Do you have a special connection with Global Dawn?" she asked.

"I agree totally with Reuven. His idea of a global network, it's very good, very good."

"So, you read about Reuven's project and decided to test the idea on some university students?"

"Well, yes, more or less it happened this way."

"And where do you see yourself in Global Dawn?"

"Actually, I'm a professional artiste. I would like to do something creative in this project."

"Yvette uses all sorts of experimental media in her art, don't you, Yvette?" added Jean Marcel. "Her talent's going to be a great asset."

"And what about you, Jean Marcel? What's your Global Dawn story?" asked Michael.

"I read the project summary together with Yvette. It connects beautifully with my own ideology for technological interchange."

Jean Marcel turned to Yvette.

"I think it's time to let our action group ask the Israeli delegation some questions."

Throughout the evening, the Paris group tossed questions at their guests who tried in their answers to convey the whole process of the project's transformation from a dream into a global reality. Apparently, Yvette had found Charlotte via the Internet, and it was their hope that the two groups would meet in Jerusalem before the end of the year.

The cohesion of the two groups at this first meeting was quite amazing. It was almost as if they had discovered long lost family, and nothing stood in the way of their bonding, not language, not culture, not expectations. The group from Israel heard their hosts' plans to show them around Paris, and Ora's face lit up at Jean Marcel's mention of a visit to the Géode. She shot a glance across at Reuven, which he reciprocated with a nod of elated recognition.

After dinner, the group split up to spend the night in the homes of various volunteer hosts. Shira was invited to stay with her cousin in Saint Cloud, and Antoine and Rikki slipped away, apparently to find their own solution for the night.

Ora awoke the following morning to the tantalizing aroma of freshly percolated coffee wafting up the staircase to the atelier she was sharing with Ariella in the central Paris apartment of Jean Marcel's older brother, Eduard. She could hear the noises of the street below – cars hooting impatiently, shutters being shoved open, and slash windows hauled up to greet the day. She drew the lace curtain aside and peeped down to watch the café owners offering breakfast to early customers – businessmen in well-adjusted suits at flimsy cross-legged metal tables on the flagstones of the narrow pavement.

She pulled on jeans and a close-fitting turtleneck sweater, gathered her hair into a tortoiseshell clip, and ventured downstairs. At the bottom of the stairs, a decorative wrought iron gate swung out onto the tiled hallway. Eduard wished her *bonjour* and turned to open the heavy front door to none other than the familiar lively faces of Antoine and Rikki.

"Surprise!"

"Did you sleep well? It seems we have breakfast guests."

Antoine enquired after Ariella who was still fast asleep upstairs. Eduard served them all hot croissants, and they began to discuss their plans for the day. First, there was to be a round table meeting in which both groups would participate.

"When will we be going to see the Géode?" asked Ora.

Eduard, obviously puzzled by her stubborn interest in an amusement park, replied in an indifferent tone,

"*Demain, je pense ...*"

Ora looked questioningly at Antoine, who smiled and translated, "My brother say we should perhaps go there tomorrow."

"Oh, but we must!"

"*Mais pourquoi elle s'y préoccupe tellement?*"

"He wants to know why are you so interested in this place?"

"I'm sorry. I should have explained. I'd rather wait though and tell the whole group, later."

"*Non, non!*" replied Eduard, his unaccepting finger swaying back and forth in front of her face like a pendulum

To which, hand on heart in feigned sufferance, Antoine added his own plea,

"Yes, Ora. We are in *grande suspense*. This is not very kind of you. Will you tell us your big secret now, please?"

Ora laughed, "Okay, you two, I'll tell you now. It's not so mysterious, really. You see, Reuven's been talking about building a geodesic dome for Global Dawn in Jerusalem. That's why I'm so interested in seeing the one here in the Science City."

"*Eh bien*, we *parisiens* are very proud of this Géode. It is unique."

Ora continued to explain how the Géode's synthesis between education, culture and entertainment was just what Reuven was aiming for in his project.

"And so, you want to make for the Géode a twin sister in Jerusalem?"

"Well, we need to see it to be able to answer that question properly."

As things turned out, Ora was obliged to contain her excitement about the Géode until the following morning when crisp air and a clear sky promised perfect visiting conditions. She checked her watch. It was 7.30. Downstairs the phone was ringing and Eduard picked it up.

"*Yvette! Bonjour ... Eh, oui. Tout va bien ... Vers neuf heures, alors? Formidable.*"

In very stilted English, he informed Ora that Yvette and the others would be meeting them at nine o'clock.

*   *   *

A little later that same morning, Jeanine stood in her acupuncture therapist's treatment room in Kadmon. She twirled a buttonhole rosette between two fingers before carefully removing it, slipped off her sleek black shirt and trousers, and lay face down on the therapy table.

"Go easy on me, today, Dudu, please."

"You are very tense. We will relax all these muscles. It will be fine."

He ran his firm, practised fingers down her spine and outwards over the hip-line. The first fine needle was inserted and she tried to shift her thoughts to sunny beaches and ocean spray. The whole acupuncture procedure involved symmetrical insertion of extremely fine and flexible needles the length of her spine up to the base of her neck. It gave her a strange tingling sensation that she found quite stimulating.

"If the lamp's too hot you must tell me."

"No, no," she smiled, "it's fine. You must be really looking forward to having your own space at the Visitor's Centre. How're your preparations for the new clinic coming along?"

"I'm nearly ready. I just need some publicity."

"Oh. Maybe I can help you with that."

"Shhh. No more talk. We must help the needles work. I leave you now with nice music for fifteen minutes, OK?"

"Mmm."

As she lay there, she turned over in her mind the shallow excuses she gave for not travelling to Paris. It was okay. No one suspected her real reason for staying behind. On the day the Paris invitation arrived, she received another much more personal message – Yoni's father had arrived in Israel and wanted to spend a few days with her. It was to be their first contact since the funeral, and she began to feel a disconcerting stirring of buried emotions. In the months after Yoni died, she steadfastly avoided her pain. Even at the memorial meeting, a whole year later, she scarcely allowed herself the luxury of mourning. She convinced herself that there was a purpose to Yoni's death within the cosmic pattern of things. Such rationalisation was a comfort, it was true, but it denied her the simple relief of crying. Of course, she agreed to see Yoni's father, but said nothing of the visit to anyone else. Not even to Shira. This was not a matter for the gossip columns of Kadmon.

Now she thought back over the few intimate days they spent together. How different he seemed from her once passionate lover. A chasm had opened between them. Since his bereavement, he had immersed himself in fast moving commerce, risk-taking in stock markets and casinos, property building and fashionable living. His accumulated wealth was of no more interest to her than were the women who lately fed his sexual appetite. He dropped into her life from another world.

No matter. They shared an immense outpouring through which, at last, they confronted their grief. Through a tearful recounting of Yoni's life, they bridged and tended the abyss of their loss. It was a healing process long overdue. Just three days later, he was gone. Alone again, she discovered in herself a new acceptance that would allow her to move on to the next phase of her life. Her decision to remain in

Kadmon had been wise, she told herself. She needed this private time.

The peace of mind she gained by opting out of the Paris trip was not, however, entirely without disturbance. For one thing, she was more troubled than she was willing to admit by Reuven's re-entry into her life. There was no denying his impact on her at this emotionally vulnerable time. Then, there was the unsolicited intervention of his sister, Michaela. The two women first crossed paths as students, and they never really found a common wavelength. Jeanine was far too flamboyant and manipulative for Michaela's taste, and Jeanine thought Michaela ridiculously over-protective of her brother and embarrassingly unfeminine in her comportment. Michaela's approach to Jeanine soon after Reuven left for Paris was ostensibly for professional reasons. As chief researcher for the second television channel's national news, she wanted to put together a documentary on Global Dawn. Had the initiative come from any other source, Jeanine would have welcomed such publicity, but she feared Michaela's motives – Perhaps this was nothing more than a ploy to meddle in Reuven's affairs?

Her thoughts were interrupted by Dudu's return.

"I'm afraid I'm a poor subject for you today."

"It's okay," he grinned. "You're a challenge."

"So, are you going to electrocute me, now?"

He laughed. "No, Jeanine, it will be a very small electric pulse. It will make good energy for your muscles."

That process complete, he began to remove the needles systematically from her back. The last part of the treatment would be pure pampering with a generous massage by his large and beautiful masculine hands. She let out a sigh of satisfaction and allowed herself to melt into the soothing ambience.

*   *   *

The dome is easily the most prominent and impressive structure in La Villette Science City. Access to it is along a walkway, past several other exhibition buildings. Its geometric composition is partially camouflaged by a smooth silver reflective surface that mirrors the various park views in each direction. It houses the main attraction for the many children who visit the site each day – the IMAX theatre, offering simulation cinema on a giant, hemispherical screen for an audience of up to four hundred.

"Care for an escort into Fantasyland, pretty lady?"

Ora turned around to find Michael sporting his most provocative expression.

"Oh, it's you!"

"I see you're disappointed. Expecting a suave French courtesan, were you?"

She returned a reproachful look towards him as they inched forward in the entrance queue.

Antoine and Rikki sauntered up to claim their places in the line, ignoring vociferous objections from behind them. Reuven, meanwhile, had fallen silent, once again. Inside the dome, he felt an almost childish thrill of anticipation. He was not disappointed. The show transported its audience from their physical surroundings into the ultimate virtual reality. They traversed forests, jungles, rivers, seas and mountains, becoming totally immersed in the Planet Earth's environmental changes, past present and future. These fantastic visions were entirely built upon real geographic imagery – the work of researchers, scientists and historians.

Yes, thought Reuven, stunned by what he had seen. We're going to need this kind of creative genius and more to build our project in Jerusalem.

Not far from the Géode, they entered the Explora, a science and technology discovery area, where computer facilities were provided to visitors for investigation into specific topics such as space, the ocean, rocks and volcanoes, light or medicine.

"Yvette, d'you think we could get to talk with the managers of this place?" Reuven asked. "I'd like to hear about the planning behind it."

She agreed to help him look for the administrative offices. They walked back through the park to the other side of the complex where they found the site engineer's office. The chief engineer was not around, but his deputy was clearly delighted to receive such an enthusiastic delegation. He launched into a complete history of Science City, and Antoine improvised a translation for the non-*francophone* members of the group. Towards the end of his explanation, the chief engineer arrived. Yvette introduced the group, and quickly filled him in on Reuven's special interest in the Géode.

"I admire your courage," said the chief engineer addressing Reuven. "Of course, this is a multi-million dollar venture – You'll need to find some very serious investors to establish such a thing in Israel."

"We realise that, sir."

"Well, I don't really know how I can help you."

"I'd like to keep this contact with the Géode alive, and perhaps later on you might consider twinning our project with yours?"

"It is a possibility."

"That would certainly add to our credibility in the cutting world of finance."

"*Eh bien,* for how long will you be in Paris? Would you like to meet the project director?"

"That would be wonderful, but we're only here until tomorrow night. Will there be enough time?"

"I think not. He's out of the country until next week. Can we contact you by email?"

Ora rushed forward.

"Here's our card."

As they wandered out of the office complex, a light spring rain had fresh-washed the walkway. It glistened under foot in the mid-morning sun. Antoine and Rikki strolled up the path, leaving behind them a pungent trail of Gitane smoke. Ora ran from point to point, camera poised to capture the Géode and all the reflections in it from every angle.

Reuven wore an air of reverence as if he were retreating from a shrine. He glanced at Ora and then at Shira, who clutched his arm and shot him a warm smile.

*   *   *

A tour of Paris by the inimitable Antoine was scheduled for the next day. The two groups met outside Boulangerie Manon near the Porte Maillot métro station. From there, it would be a straight ride into the centre of the city. Antoine arrived laden with crisp baguettes and cartons of milk to start the day. He waved his white beret in the air as a sign to the little group to gather round, then demonstrated the ritual devouring of the baguette.

"You see, this bread is not for the 'igh society," he asserted. "You must to taste it fresh, *comme ça!*" So declaring, he tore it into rough hunks, the outer crusts fragmenting themselves generously over body and entourage as he did so.

"Pass it around, please, pass it around!"

As they ate, he enquired,

"So, you want to see Paris in the boring touristique way, or you want to see it in Antoine's special style?"

Without waiting for a reply to this rhetorical question, he dived into the métro station leaving the group to follow. By the time they were all reassembled below, Antoine was waving several carnets of tickets for their transportation into and around the city. He resumed his introductory speech, declaring that he intended to give everyone –

including the Parisians amongst them – a unique insight into the real soul of Paris. Paris was, of course, an artists' milieu, par excellence. The most genuine and dynamic view of the worlds of these artists could be found not in the great museums, but by peeking behind the façades of their residences and workshops, and into the galleries and courtyards of their private displays.

The itinerary was to include non-orthodox routes around the streets, the parks, bookshops, galleries, markets and cafés of the Latin Quarter and Montparnasse. They would venture in the tracks of Quasimodo to the highest dark steps of Notre Dame. They would observe the elegant chic of Parisian women whose cool and distant beauty drove many a French poet to intoxication and despair. They would witness the dramas of impassioned argument between Parisian drivers, bartenders and bystanders – a traditional street entertainment provided free of charge by the city's veterans. Antoine also hoped to find time to educate his wards in the extraordinary ambience of a Paris street market where serious shoppers fastidiously inspect before purchasing the perfect cut of meat, a selection of choice cheeses and array of vegetables to feast both eye and palate.

Reuven, meanwhile, excused himself from the Paris tour. He felt an urgent need to gather his thoughts and feelings in solitude. Jean Marcel offered him the use of his car and he headed out of Paris through its south-eastern suburbs via the Porte d'Orléans. It was about an hour's drive to the Forest of Fontainebleau.

Until now, he had managed to conceal his natural aversion to travelling in groups. He was deeply grateful to his friends, who arranged the Paris trip, and to Antoine for being their inspiration and guide. For his own part, however, he knew that the most treasured moments and experiences of his life were the product of his personal exploration and discovery – not something fed to him on the general platter served up to the tourist trade.

He half-wished he had invited Shira to join him, but then again, the peace and seclusion he sought today carried its own conditions. He entered the forest by the main avenue, drew into a side road and stopped the car. He paid little heed to the warning signs of the danger of falling rocks as he skipped across scattered boulders and continued through the woods. Here and there, he crossed paths with mushroom pickers – Fontainebleau was well known for its excellent growth of mushrooms, edible and otherwise. The threat of a poisonous variety deterred not these professionals who were well prepared and intent on their targets. It being a weekday, there were few other people to be found in this part of the forest, unlike the section bordering on the palace grounds that tended to be inundated with visitors. He idled among the towering pines and oaks, inspired by their awesome grandeur and beauty. Impulsively, he pulled off his shoes and socks, and stretched his toes at the feet of these natural giants. The mushroom seekers moved on, and a light haze began to spread across the glade. Only, the occasional swish of a squirrel tail among the dry leaves broke the silence of strangely absent birdsong. He leaned back onto a mass of tangled ferns and lay staring into the face of the mist. Someday, he mused, tall and strong as Fontainebleau, Global Dawn would stand rooted deep in the rock of Jerusalem, and its name would echo far across the planet.

A breeze coaxed the treetops into circular motion producing a faint hum. With the strengthening of the wind in the lofty branches, the sound intensified. He cupped his hands against his ears to muffle the insistent drone. Out of the mist at the far end of the glade emerged the grey silhouette of a roughly clad man. Index finger curled towards his chest, he gestured to Reuven, while raising a finger of his other hand to his lips in tribute to the surrounding silence. Reuven tried to follow him, but found himself unable to stand. He had read about the hermit of Fontainebleau. If this was he, he was likely to be a harmless soul. Nevertheless, his appearance was unnerving.

The humming grew faster and stronger, rising above the glade in shrill crescendo. It forced Reuven's attention dizzily upwards as into the vacant hollow of his gaze reared another shadowy form – this time, the ghostly figure of a horseback rider. Holding tightly onto a rein with its left hand, it leaned outwards from the saddle and beckoned with the forefinger of its right before speeding on. Again, the excruciating rushing sound and the merciless, pounding hum. Reuven held his fists tightly against his temples, and struggled to stand, only to fall back again, flushed, his head spinning.

In the next instant, the mist evaporated and he regained his balance. A couple of mushroom pickers were examining the mossy verge just a few metres away.

"... *alors, tu pense que c'était lui?*" ("So, you think it was him?")

"... *sans doute, Le Grand Veneur, oui ...*" ("Yes, without a doubt, the Great Hunter ...")

They wandered on and, stunned by what he had heard, Reuven grabbed at the nearest tree trunk for support. He had heard tell of the 'Wild Hunter of Fontainebleau'. Some said he was Death in disguise. He trembled with foreboding.

The humming subsided and the space ahead of him cleared. He lay back against the tree and burrowed his bare toes into the knotted undergrowth. The hermit and the hunter – signs the meanings of which he must fathom. Death and its messenger had passed him by and left him unscathed. Surely, it was a reminder that his work was not yet done. Today he had sought to escape like the hermit behind the misty veil of the forest. The vision of the recluse played on his conscience reminding him his purpose was not to be lightly revoked.

The sky remained overhung with grey. His eyes were fixed on the spot where the hermit had appeared, obliterated now by the merging forms of trees and foliage. He picked up his shoes and, swinging them by the laces, wandered down a meandering path covered with freshly fallen pine needles.

The grey spectres had laid bare a lesion in his subconscious. Just like the unhealing wound of the proverbial seeker of the Holy Grail, a scar on Reuven's soul was keeping him from the target of his mission. Whether in Achziv, Kadmon, Jerusalem or Paris, the same dark shadows stood as stubborn barriers to its realisation. Born of the hollow wretchedness of the unloved child inside him, an inner voice now emerged full of self-questioning.

"Don't you recognise those images?" it nagged.

He shivered as he recalled the figure of Death riding so close yet failing to claim him.

"You need to get your act together and fast," chided the voice. "You make fancy speeches, but where are you when there's real work to be done? Chickening out and doing nought! Just like a bloody hermit! Don't you see?"

He kicked at the pine needles underfoot.

"Look," he told himself. "I know I'm a worthless piece of shit. I can change, though. Just need time ..."

"You think you can bargain with the Reaper? He'll come for you soon enough. And, just as Menashe said, Global Dawn's not going to wait for you!"

He wandered aimlessly across a thicket of browning ferns. He inhaled the pungent fragrance of the pines as he trod a silent carpet of closely packed needles. Suddenly, he felt the needle bed slipping away beneath him, and he clutched frantically at the nearest tree trunk. The needles were eddying downwards into a rapidly widening hole. The power of the swirling mass grew. It was sucking at his feet!"

"Get a grip on yourself!" admonished his inner voice. "Is that what you want? For the earth to swallow you up?"

"Why not? I'm a fucking impotent leader of my mission!" he shouted, stamping out his rage on what was surprisingly firm ground, after all. Again, his emotional outpouring was readily answered, "Let go of those demons before it's too late!"

He watched the falling needles. Each time, a few more shook themselves free of the mother twig and joined the accumulated softness of the bed below. He contemplated this natural process of release and enrichment. Letting go. It seemed so simple. Let go of the blackness in his heart. The spectres of Fontainebleau were mirrors of the darkness of his soul. He had to finally let go of his fears and show firm leadership of Global Dawn. The clock was ticking.

Cool sunlight began to radiate through the treetops, and he stretched his arms upwards to receive it. He drank the last of the water from his flask. It was time to head back towards Paris before the after-work traffic jammed the bridges. There was a new sense of calm about him – his spirit recharged and his personal challenge clarified.

*   *   *

It was the group's final evening in Paris, and a farewell dinner was arranged at a restaurant of Jean Marcel's choosing. On the way there, Ora sat in the back of the jeep. Quietly, she watched Reuven. His behaviour during the trip had been a disappointment to her. For the most part, he seemed so self-absorbed as to be unapproachable. The trip only widened the gap arisen inexplicably between them, she thought.

The restaurant had the unassuming name of *Chez Lucien*, but Jean Marcel assured his friends that dining there was excellent. Reuven and Jean Marcel sat elbow to elbow at the top of a long wooden table. They chose a bottle of select Chablis and another of Beaujolais to accompany the meal of pepper steak and lamb cutlets in finely chopped rosemary, parsley and dill. The meat was served with green salad and a choice of spring vegetables doused in olive oil and garlic.

"Let's toast this historic meeting," said Jean Marcel.

Reuven raised the smooth red wine to his lips. His reply was characteristically esoteric.

"Global Dawn's history was written thousands of years ago. Our meeting was inevitable."

"So, Reuven, dear," began Yvette, "you still believe we're pawns in a universal plot?"

"As the years go by, I'm more and more certain of it. Please don't tell me you've outgrown those cosmic truths you used to be so sure of?"

"Hmm … I was so much older then, I'm younger than that

now..."

"At least you haven't forgotten the old songs!"

"Absolutely not," she smiled.

Ariella turned to Yvette.

"So, you don't think our meeting here in Paris is symbolic in any way?"

"A meeting of interests and common directions. Nothing more."

"No universal truth bringing us together?"

"Doesn't exist. We each have our own truths," said Jean Marcel.

"Then," commented Rikki, "there's not much point in exchanging views around a dinner table, is there?"

"It's a good intellectual exercise," smiled Jean Marcel.

"And you don't believe in global networking?" asked Reuven.

"*Mais si*, Reuven! I think this is the *raison d'être* of Global Dawn!"

"But not because of a common purpose."

"Not a predetermined one. Only the one we create, ourselves."

"So, you think we're creators, Jean Marcel? Like Gods?" queried Rikki with sudden excitement.

"In the image of God," Ariella corrected her.

"Could be. What do you say, Reuven?" asked Jean Marcel.

"I think there are universal forces we know nothing of. In the past, cosmic messengers have dropped in now and then to guide us, but we mostly ignored them. Now, all that's about to change. There's going to be a massive shift in our perceptions – a new beginning for whoever's prepared."

"My, my. You make it sound like some messianic event," said Michael.

Reuven smiled and said nothing.

"You're not denying that, are you?"

"You can find it predicted in almost every biblical and traditional source. Have a good look at the hieroglyphic texts of the Maya."

"Hard to explain away their predictions," agreed Ariella, always a willing advocate.

"So, you really see some universal significance in our little meeting here in Paris?" asked Ora.

"I do. It's like a massive puzzle. From our limited viewpoint, we can't see how all the tiny pieces fit together. When we've built our live Global Dawn network, new dimensions will enhance our vision."

With Reuven's prophetic words seeping into their minds, they fell silent over black coffee with cream, fourrées and Cognac. It was a peaceful conclusion to this phase of their journey.

Chapter 12

On his return from Paris, Reuven began to sleep badly. In his nightmares, he saw the menacing finger of a phantom rider pointing to familiar landscapes laid waste. Sometimes the ghost of Fontainebleau was replaced by a dramatic image of a riderless horse saddled with a melted watch – Dali's famous symbol of fleeting Time. The more threatened he felt by the power of these visions, the greater, he believed, was the urgency to act. His fragile emotional condition paralysed him, however; instead of taking action, he turned in upon himself rejecting even those who should be closest to him.

Tamar observed his growing turmoil with foreboding. She tried to reassure him, but her efforts fell on unfertile ground. Sometimes he would absent himself from home for days and nights without any word of explanation. On the rare occasions when she dared to question him about his work, he would give a mysterious and knowing half-smile and say his direction was now confirmed. All would be revealed when the time was right. Once, she begged to let her come with him to Kadmon, but he refused. He claimed her presence would diminish his focus on the project at this crucial time. The more she pressured him, the more withdrawn he became.

In Kadmon, as the day of the Global Dawn opening approached, the media began to seek him out, and Jeanine and Shira struggled to conceal his state of mind from the public eye. They shielded him from prying enquirers saying his heavy workload and the weight of community activity left no time for interviews.

Finishing touches were being made to the façade of the Visitors' Centre. A 'bio-garden' was planted along one side of the entry path; on the other side ran the shaded patio of Shira's new café. Here, a charming array of handcrafted wooden tables and stools encouraged visitors to linger. Inside, a small study area was set up for free surfing of the embryo Global Dawn portal. Jeanine had worked on a schedule of events for the opening day.

She knew he would be suspicious of her motives. However, there was no denying she had done a first class job on publicity – Attractive flyers in the centre of town promised a splendid event. Still, Jeanine prayed that the television interview to which she had agreed would not explode in their faces like a backfiring cannon.

On the morning of the event, avoiding the tide of peak hour traffic, Ariella picked Ora up from her home at crack of dawn, and they drove a clear road down to Kadmon. By mid-morning, the entire town was assembled for the opening. At the Centre, rowdy lower and middle school children arrived in procession, and were ushered into the front rows of the reception hall. The aisles were cluttered with the overwired paraphernalia of the press. Ceiling fans did little to ease the airlessness while a local technician tried to coax the rarely used air conditioner into operation. It exuded thick dust, eventually clearing to give a measure of cool relief. The seasoned press reps stood making tactless wise cracks about the gauche provinciality of the setting. Luckily, Jeanine managed to prevail on them to temper their attitude.

The inaugural ceremony began with a speech by the venerable Dr. Goldenberg, first Mayor of Kadmon. He praised Shira for her work in launching the project. Ora glanced at Jeanine. Wasn't she annoyed that Shira had stolen centre stage? However, Jeanine was otherwise distracted. Reuven was due to speak next, and he had just spotted his sister briefing the TV crew in the foyer. It looked as if Jeanine was going to have to physically restrain him from throwing an ugly fit. She had dragged him aside and was feverishly whispering in his ear, all the while maintaining a firm grip on his wrist. Finally, he wrenched himself free, ran his fingers through his dishevelled hair and adjusted his shirt. Just in time. Ora let out an overloud sigh of relief and looked around anxiously to make sure no one else had noticed Reuven's compromising behaviour.

He was called to the dais to introduce the project and he explained in simple terms how Global Dawn was going to create a new information world for residents of the town. The momentum of his speech was interrupted by another surprise in the audience. Tamar and Shahar had come into view beyond the glare of the footlights. In astonished delight, he smiled at them across the chaos of the crowd and then publicly invited them to join him on the podium. Michaela presumed to follow suit, leaving Ora appalled at her insensitivity. She flinched awkwardly at the memory of their fracas then, feeling Michaela's eyes on her, blushed in deep embarrassment.

Meanwhile, some interview chairs and microphones had

been set up for the next part of the proceedings that would be going out on national TV. Reuven ceded the floor to Jeanine, who surprised everyone by graciously deferring in turn to a young student member of the technical team. This was Michaela's agreed cue to conduct a formal interview.

"Tell us about your part in the project," she began.

"I'm creating a virtual town."

"Mmm. Sounds ambitious. What exactly is a virtual town?"

"Well, we've built a portal with a whole lot of local information, and there's a special study area here at the Visitors' Centre, where people can come in and surf."

"Really. Is it open today? Can we try it?"

"Yes. It's not finished, but you can use what we've put together so far."

"Mmm. Can you tell us more about what you're working on?"

It's going to be an open framework connecting all the most important information sources at the town hall like the electricity company, the statistical office, the university, and so on."

"Pretty cool!" responded Michaela. Above the loud applause from the audience, she added. "Reuven, you must be proud of your assistant, here."

"How right you are. He's a godsend. Under that modest exterior lurks an intellectual powerhouse."

"Well, thank you, young man and good luck!"

Next, she called on Jeanine.

"Jeanine Danan. Your name is associated with mysticism and fringe activities, is it not? Is this the direction you hope to take Global Dawn here in Kadmon?"

"Our project will derive its energy from the spirit of the land. I shall be developing a centre for spiritual therapies here, based on the wisdom of kabbalistic tradition. An enlightened team will guide our students to embrace natural balance and harmony in all their work."

"Will your guidance include such tools as the Tarot?" asked Michaela with a sensationalist twist to her tone.

"Certainly," replied Jeanine refusing to be provoked. "The Tarot is an ancient art of great value," she added.

"So the leadership of Global Dawn in Kadmon is of divine emanation?"

"That would depend on one's standpoint, wouldn't you say, Michaela?"

Ignoring Jeanine's backlash, Michaela addressed Reuven again.

"Is there anyone else you'd like me to call to the platform?"

"Ah, yes. Yusuf Nabari."

There was some commotion as Yusuf was called, and the microphone was aggressively shoved towards him.

"Yusuf Nabari of the Nabari Bedouin tribe?"

"Nabari family live here many generations, ma'am."

"Mmm. Yusuf, what can you tell us about Reuven's project?"

"Reuven, he is very blessed man. I believe he will help my people in the village very much. He's wonderful teacher, also. I want to thank you, my friend. That's all. Thank you."

He gave a little bow and retired from the podium. The hall was silent, and the audience waited for Reuven to respond. He made no comment, however. Instead, he asked his daughter to step forward and offered her his hand. Next, he reached out to Tamar and finally to Michaela. His closing words were directed to this intimate circle.

"Tamar, Shahar, Michaela, you can't even begin to imagine what it means to me to have you all here at my side on this momentous day."

Ora thought back to Achziv where he had declaimed the names and roles of three women, and she was struck by the potency of the present moment.

Yusuf began to play a set of goatskin drums in practised rhythm. Then Shahar's voice rose with extraordinary clarity above the drumming in a prayer set to her own music. There was a tremor in Reuven's voice as he harmonised with her. Finally, Jeanine joined in their song of welcome to the spirit of Global Dawn in its new home. The cameras faded on this intimate circle as they stood together even after the crowd dispersed.

*   *   *

A week or so later, Reuven stood on the terrace at the back of the house and threw a well-rubbed brown leather ball to Muki who raced to the garden fence to bring it back and begin the game of "fetch" all over again. The dog was in playful mood and pulled at Reuven's trouser-leg to coax him into joining in. He was preoccupied, however, and wandered across the lawn to the hammock into which he pitched himself, one leg folded back at the knee, the other slung lazily out onto the grass. He tossed the ball towards the fence and sank back into the hammock to gather his thoughts about the latest events and their implications.

Despite Michaela's public display of support for Global Dawn, he was slow to trust her change of heart. He wanted desperately to believe in her loyalty, but could not so easily disregard her earlier lack of faith. In the same way, he was finding it hard to rationalise Tamar's sudden appearance in Kadmon, so contrary to the resentment she had previously demonstrated towards the project. Then again, there was the added complication of two other women, each of whom, while ostensibly investing altruistic energies into the project, was becoming emotionally attached to him in ways that he had not knowingly fermented. He was growing increasingly frustrated by such feminine machinations and manipulations. He was weary of the unceasing inner struggle, and the only effective way he found to deal with it was by adopting the impermeable mindset of the hermit against which Fontainebleau offered him clear warning.

Impulsively, he called a quick goodbye to Tamar. Without checking if she heard him or not, he grabbed his keys from the kitchen drawer and went out to the car. He set out along the main southbound highway. He had scarcely slept the previous night, and his whole body was racked with fatigue. In the suffocating mid-July heat, he resorted to loud rock music to keep his senses sharp. The cell phone rang a few times, but he ignored it, glancing casually at its display panel to gauge the source of the disturbance. The battery was low. Soon it would cease to function, cease to bother him, and give him some peace which was actually all he asked of the world right now. The music faded from his consciousness, as did the road, and he felt his eyes closing, his head lolling forwards ...

His cutout from reality was the briefest of moments. During that half instant, he lost control of the car. It skidded and rolled over into the oncoming traffic lane – empty by some timely act of God. Now he was fully alert. He reacted with swift skill to pull the car over and steer it hard onto the grass verge.

A short while later, the phone rang in Tamar's hallway.

"May I speak to Tamar Sofer?"

The official tone of the caller's voice provoked a spasm of fear in her belly.

"I'm calling from Soroka Hospital. Please, don't be alarmed. Your husband has had an accident."

She felt an involuntary shaking take hold of her body as she tried to restrain her instinctive panic.

Shahar had entered the room and was staring questioningly at her mother's face, drained of colour and tense with anxiety. She pulled her daughter protectively close.

By the grace of God, Reuven had escaped with minor surface wounds and a little concussion. The car, they told her, was a complete wreck. As she slowly absorbed the news, anger began to take the place of her fear. She was furious at him for having contrived yet again to complicate their lives.

Then, she felt Shahar shiver and clutched her more tightly to her chest. Her eyes were wide with fright, and the strangled quasi-falsetto voice that pleaded to go and see her father straight away made any other option unthinkable.

"Of course, dear. We'll leave at once. We'll take the first train to Beersheva."

A neighbour offered to drive them to the station, and they were soon on their way.

*   *   *

Flat on his back in the anonymity of the hospital ward, Reuven slowly began to take stock of his situation. He was deeply shaken by the knowledge of his narrow escape. He reached for his cell, then finding it battery dead recalled in a flash the final moments before his collapse behind the wheel. He tried to get up, but a domineering representative of nursing officialdom restrained him.

"I have to ring my family. Let me get to the phone!" he shouted in frustration.

"No need. All taken care of," came her imperious voice. "Your wife's been informed about the accident. Suggest you stay put for now."

Having issued her orders, she adjusted her cap, tidied her uniform and bustled off.

Reuven tried to calm himself a little, but questions and troubling images were invading his mind like battering rams against a time-weathered gate and threatening his sanity. How could such a thing have happened to him? He was an extremely skilled driver. He had swift reactions and keen instincts about the vagaries of the road. He had survived driving in hellish weather conditions and in worse states of fatigue. How could he have fallen asleep at the wheel? Tamar would be sure to blame him for this latest blow to the family cashbox, he thought. Could their marriage take any more strain?

Within the hour, Tamar arrived and at least some of his questions were answered. He knew she was livid. He could see her swallowing hard and sucking her cheeks into hollow cavities in her effort to hide her vexation from Shahar. She was assisted in this by the sight of his pathetic, pale figure, and could not help but let out a sigh of relief at his miraculous survival. Shahar fell on him in a sudden flood of tears. He patted the back of her head and said with a tender smile,

"Pumpkin, look at me. I'm fine."

After the round of doctors' examinations, his release was approved. The hospital was too crowded with the seriously ill or wounded to hold him there another night, and he, for his part, was more than ready to go home. The bureaucratic procedures of hospital release were lengthy, but by late afternoon they were able to leave.

They travelled to Tel-Aviv by *sherut*, a shared intercity taxi, and arrived home just before sundown. Reuven uttered scarcely a word the entire hour-long journey. His expression was morose.

Over the next few days, Tamar's attitude began to change. Thankfulness at having him by her side diminished her bitterness over their financial predicament. She began to lavish attention on him. It was a kind of perverse compensation for the preceding months of her pent up resentment and frustration.

However, Reuven's emotional confusion did not abate. The memory of the accident continued to haunt him. He was convinced his brutal swerving from the road was a warning sign. The hiatus it caused in his Global Dawn journey was undoubtedly an omen; it was time for him to take stock of his responsibilities. Tamar's appearance in Kadmon was an act of good faith that must be recognised. Her implicit role in the future of Global Dawn could no longer be ignored. He could no more abandon her than he could his daughter. And if not for Shahar, for whom was he building the project?

At that time, Shahar was nearing the end of her final school year and was looking to discover life's options on her own terms. The prevailing atmosphere in Israel was bleak. The economy was in a slump, the job market at an all-time low. Technocrats were rolling in fools' gold while economists predicted the impending doomsday of the hi-tech euphoria. In short, Shahar and her peers found little inspiration on the home front, and they began to look further afield for challenge and opportunity. Cautiously, she broached the subject with her parents.

"Abba," she began.

"Yes, my treasure."

"Abba, y'know I've got a few months before the army, now."

"A few months of well-earned freedom now all your exams are over, Pumpkin."

"Exactly."

"You could come and work with me on the project for a while.

It would be wonderful ..."

"Abba, listen! Ima's right, you're obsessed with your Global Dawn!"

"Now, Shahar," came her mother's voice. "That's not what I said. It wouldn't hurt you to give your father a little support, and whether you do or you don't, that's no way to talk to him."

"But Ima! I'm eighteen years old! I need a life of my own!"

With the palms of his hands, Reuven motioned them both to quieten down. Then with a crooked index finger, he beckoned to Shahar. He pointed to the chair next to him, and she sat down hands folded primly in her lap in a semblance of obedience while her expression remained defiant.

"Okay, okay. Tell us what's on your mind."

"I want to go on a trek."

"On your own? Out of the question."

"No, wait!"

She sprang out of the chair and began pacing the room, gesticulating frantically in her desperation to make them understand.

"There's a whole group of us. We've got it all planned. We'll have to work for a month or so to pay for the flight, and then we'll travel together. It's going to be so cool. Ima, Abba, please say I can go!"

There was no decision made on that day or on the next. As the week neared its end, Shahar began to despair of ever getting her parents to agree her plan. They were so over-protective. If her mother had her way, she would keep her tied and cosseted forever. Her father was no better. He talked about his little angel spreading her wings, but the greatest barrier to her flight was his own possessive adoration. In fact, it came as a surprise to all when he suddenly relented and made the following pronouncement,

"Our daughter must begin her journey, now. So it is written in the Master Plan and so it shall be."

The finality with which he presented his decision made it impossible for Tamar to argue with him. Thus it was that, at the beginning of the following month, Shahar left home with a little saved cash in her pocket and a backpack on her back.

Soon after her departure, the situation in the country worsened rapidly. Extreme factions, Arab and Jewish, bared their ugly teeth, and the year's opening hopes for peace were crushed by escalating violence that caught innocent civilians, adults and children alike, in its crossfire. On both sides of the conflict, the disparity grew between politicians and the popular will.

Reuven looked to Jerusalem for inspiration. The scene that met his eyes there was no brighter than anywhere else. Sanctimonious wardens of the city were paying suffocating homage to its history. The city's golden light was subdued under an all-embracing cloak of religious fervour, and innumerable zealots were revered and worshipped by a thronging, swaying multitude, clothed in black.

*   *   *

Gadi had surprised Ora by his willingness to go along with her idea of moving to Jerusalem. It was agreed that they would make a trial run of it with the option to return to Tel-Aviv at the end of the year, if difficulties arose, either emotional or practical. She was delighted by his positive attitude, and the new spirit of togetherness this new challenge seemed to have injected into the family as a whole.

The beginning of the new academic year found Ora, Gadi and the boys fairly well settled in a rented apartment in Jerusalem's German Colony. It was on the third floor of a traditional Jerusalem stone building with private access to a large flat roof. There was a communal garden shared by all the residents – not overly well kept, but a pleasant play area for the kids.

A strange circumstance had precipitated their decision to take that particular place. They followed a newspaper lead. The initial description and location suited them. The moment they walked into the apartment, however, Ora's face paled. She clung to Gadi's hand like a frightened child, saying,

"I feel dizzy. I think I'd better sit down."

He presumed it was the heat,

"Come and sit by the window. I'll ask the landlady for a glass of water."

She overheard them whispering about her in the next room. The gist of it being the landlady's chiding.

"Dangerous thing, dehydration."

"Right."

"Most people don't realise …" she went on.

"Yes, well, thanks again. Kind of you …"

Gadi managed to cut her amateur medical advice short and rushed back to Ora with the water.

"Gadi," she said in a shaky voice. "It's not dehydration …"

"I know, couldn't stop the woman from sermonising."

"Gadi, it's not that. It's this place …"

"You don't like it? We'll go. No problem," he said turning

towards the door.

"No, you don't understand. I adore it. It felt like home straight away!"

"Okay, so ..."

"Gadi ..."

He caught the distracted look in her eyes.

"Ora, what's the matter with you? You're acting really weird."

He began to lose patience. She had already embarrassed him in front of the landlady with her bizarre behaviour. She emptied the glass and quickly put it down. Then she began to look around.

"I've been here before," she replied flatly.

He became exasperated. He checked his watch and wandered out into the garden. He could not cope with her fantasies.

Meanwhile, she ventured around the furthest corner of the L-shaped living room, and that was when she understood. It was the room of her dream – just as she had described it at Jeanine's party. She raced out into the garden to explain to Gadi.

"I know you think I'm crazy but this is the place I told you about. The one I keep dreaming about!"

"Ora, honestly, I think you need your head examined if ..."

"Listen to me! I told you about that game we played in Kadmon. Remember?"

"Hmm. So?"

"Jeanine interpreted my dream. She said it represented riches in store for me – a treasure trove just waiting to be unlocked."

"Ora, I'm damned if I understand what you're babbling about," he replied, infuriated.

"Gadi. It all suddenly makes such sense to me."

"Never mind. I gather you like the place?"

"I love it," she said with an enraptured smile.

"Well, in that case, I think we'd better find the landlady and close the deal. Just try not to hug her. I don't think it's her style."

Ora pouted a little at his sarcasm, but the sight of a contract in his hands soon washed away all negative thoughts. The deal was smoothly concluded and within a month, they received the keys.

Soon after the move, Ora began planning and arranging the available space to include a small administrative office from which her Global Dawn business could be conducted. Michael was again making motions of interest in taking over management of the project, but the question of payment for his services could scarcely be raised with Reuven whose own account was barely covered by his unpredictable income.

Ora rang Michael.

"Hi."

"Hello, beautiful."

"Please be serious. We need to talk. Reuven's in no frame of mind right now to help me manage things here in Jerusalem."

"I noticed," replied Michael.

"We're going to have to take the initiative ourselves to find sponsors for our work just like Shira and Jeanine did in Kadmon. What do you think?"

"Fine. The question is how we're going to tackle the people with the real money?"

"Mmm. We can start by talking to NASA and the Digital Earth people. Once we have a few names like those under our belts, our job's going to be much easier."

"That's for sure. Those people we met in Paris are worth contacting, too. I reckon they liked Reuven's twinning idea, don't you?"

"Yup. You're right. That's something we can get onto right away."

"Fine. Why don't you follow that one up while I explore some other tricks?"

"Okay. Don't forget I'm relying on you, though."

"Honey, just call and I'll spring into action. You can count on Mikey."

"Words, Michael, words. Now, get off the line will you, and prove your worth!"

Ora had been feeling quite abandoned by Reuven. Gadi, on the other hand, had risen in her esteem by his acquiescence to the move. The change actually added a new spark to their marital relations. If only Michael and his wife would join them, she thought, she would feel so much less isolated. However, she knew there was no real chance of that happening until there was a budget for their relocation. Nonetheless, she was encouraged by his supportive attitude. She prayed his ingenuity would serve them as well in Jerusalem as it had in Kadmon.

*   *   *

A new *Intifada* brought increased violence and economic hardship to the country, and Reuven and Tamar were badly hit by the downturn. With a major slump in the construction industry, there was little GIS work to be had. Reuven was still teaching twice a week at the university, but the *Intifada* was throwing a question mark over the stability of that job, too. Tamar realised that her small early retirement pension would no longer suffice, and she began to look for ways to bring in some extra cash herself. Eventually, she took on some evening work as a dental assistant, and Reuven's undisguised relief at her decision confirmed its wisdom.

When Reuven was asked to perform at a beachfront venue for the up-to-thirties, he accepted gladly. The place was called 'Ginger' and combined a British-style pub atmosphere with a lively country, rock and blues stage. On the evening of the performance, Tamar asked if she could come along, and the look of genuine interest on her face delighted him even more than the question itself. They arrived early, and took a table towards the centre. Reuven's spot would not be before eleven-thirty. In the meantime, they ordered a couple of beers, and sat back to enjoy the bright mood of the place. A woman in her mid-twenties was sitting at the table next to theirs. She was wearing a long kaftan, her hair was covered with a scarf and she had the kind of large gypsy-style earrings that were fashionable back in the 60s. Strapped across her chest was a baby carrier with a tiny infant cosily asleep inside. Amazing how a child could sleep so soundly in the midst of the loud music and the throng of people. The stage manager of 'Ginger' came up to Reuven and Tamar.

"Looks like a good audience for you tonight, Rube," he said.

"Right. Got a few surprises in store for them, too!"

"Yeah, we can always count on you for a great show."

"Hey, Rube, Tam, good to see you guys," said his partner, slapping Reuven's hand amiably.

"Reckon Arnie'll turn up with his harmonica, do you?"

"Sure. Not before midnight, though. Races from one gig t'another like a bloody spitfire, he does," he shouted.

There was a hard rock band playing, and the sound was phenomenal. There was no choice but to shout. Tamar preferred not to compete with the noise, so she nursed her drink quietly giving Reuven's hand the occasional affectionate squeeze.

The young crowd continued to pile in, pushing excitedly towards the front and waving their hands in the air to get the attention of the over-worked waiters. The vibrancy of the place put Reuven in youthful spirit, too. He rocked jauntily in his seat and sang out the lyrics of the songs with gusto. Impulsively, he pulled Tamar to her feet, and they began to dance a comical jig together right there in the aisle.

"Oh, Reuven," she laughed, "you're such an exhibitionist!"

He had scarcely caught his breath when the manager of the joint called on him.

"Okay, you're up now. Hey, everyone, let's give a big welcome to Rube!"

Cheering and foot tapping accompanied him to the stage, and he launched into a bold and witty first number. Immediately, he had the audience in the palm of his hand. He indulged their taste for heavy rock, thrilling them with his extravagant stage presence like some wild pop idol of the sixties. His performance lasted for about twenty minutes and ended in raucous applause. Tamar beamed proudly as he returned to his seat next to her.

The next one up was a visiting singer from Denmark. A couple of the regular performers had slipped out for a breath of fresh air and were hovering around the entrance joking with the security guard.

Suddenly, there was the most ear-splitting crash as if a gas main had burst just outside. Reuven was thrown from his chair. In the uncanny silence that followed, he looked up to see Tamar catapulting through the air above him.

"Oh, my God!" he screamed as she slammed into his stomach. "Tamar? Tamar!"

"I'm okay," she answered faintly, and laid her head on the reassuring expanse of his chest.

A sickening stench of burning flesh and vomit mixed with spilled beer now pervaded the air making it hard to breathe. The atmosphere was filled with dust and debris.

"Reuven!" shrieked Tamar in sudden horror, "next to you!"

She was pointing at a bloodstained garment lodged between his thigh and the upturned table-leg.

"That woman. The one with the baby, it's hers. It's her scarf. Oh, dear God in Heaven, where is she?"

They could hear the baby crying but could not make out where the sound was coming from.

"Got to find that poor woman," whispered Tamar, trembling yet assertive. She tried to get up, but Reuven persistently tugged her back.

Searchlights were on them, now, and the communal terror seemed to escalate as the extent of the horror was illuminated. Reuven covered Tamar's eyes with his hands to shield her from the spectacle of people and body parts strewn all over the floor in a confusion of uncertain survival or death. She tore his hand away again and tried to pull away from him.

"It's too late. You can't help her, my love," came Reuven's desperate answer.

The hollow sound of a megaphone invaded the room urging all those who were in good shape to leave quickly.

"It's the paramedics. Thank God they got here quickly. We have to get out, now."

"But that baby ..."

"The rescue workers'll know what to do."

Amid the screams and hysteria, they clutched onto one another and tried to get through the chaos into the street. The walls were all smeared with blood. The doorway was completely blown away, leaving only broken glass and twisted metal hanging from the ceiling. Suddenly, Tamar grabbed Reuven and began to scream uncontrollably. Hanging from a beam in the wreckage of the entrance was a coat. A hand was protruding from the pocket and a severed leg lay in a pool of blood on the step below it. Reuven felt her turn cold. Trembling, he hugged her closer to him and manoeuvred her away from the foul carnage. They passed by a couple of stretchers on which two bodies were laid out, unconscious.

"It's those two performers who were talking to the security guard before," said Reuven, shakily.

"Do you know them?"

"No, not really. Popular guys, though, both of them."

Their faces were criss-crossed with lesions from the flying glass, and it was impossible to tell if they were alive or dead.

"Wait here a second, my love. Maybe I can do something ..."

But the police kept pushing the crowd back and he was unable to get near enough to help. He returned to where Tamar stood nervously waiting for him and led her out into the road. They looked back and saw the two stretchers covered over with black sheets. She shivered at the sight.

Outside, the flashing emergency lights and whining sirens seemed to heighten the drama. They had to walk some way along the promenade before they were able to find a cab to take them home.

"Nasty business," said the driver. "Lucky to get out the way you did, you two."

A news report came over the car radio.

"... Four people are known to have died including the bomber ..."

"Pure evil, that is. Attacking innocent people like that. And the Government's got no backbone. Out of control. Where will it all end?"

He turned the radio up.

"... reported to have wrestled with the security guard before detonating his explosives. Evidence of his identity was discovered in a coat hanging at the entrance ..." As they heard this, they shivered in unison.

The following day, Reuven and Tamar went to the funerals of the two performers. Reuven terrified Tamar by turning to her with a stony face and remarking,

"This is only the beginning. There's much more suffering to come. It will be a long road."

She hated it when he got that prophetic look in his eye, as if he knew what his and her fates were going to be.

Phone calls streamed into their home from Ora, Michael, Rikki and Antoine, from Jeanine, from Shira, even from Yvette in Paris and Charlotte all the way from Australia.

"Thank God you're both okay," each of them cried.

To each, he answered with the same chilling words that there would be more pain before it was over.

Often now, Reuven lingered at Tamar's side. She welcomed his return to the hearth, and she accepted without question his conciliatory motions towards her. He was, apparently, setting his house in order. In anticipation of what, she knew not.

One evening during this period of his waiting upon destiny, they were sitting on their garden terrace. Tamar shivered slightly as he took her hand. He gazed into the infinite blackness of the night and began to tell of a strange new vision.

"It happened on one of these chill nights when I was unable to sleep, and I came out here to meditate for a while," he said. "The high-risen moon had thrown its elongated shadow onto the grass in front of me. The street was silent; you were in your bed. Muki was slumbering right here next to me. Suddenly, I felt a companion at my side, though he moved not a muscle to affirm his presence. After some immeasurable time, he turned to look at me. Then, softly as the faintest whisper on the breeze, he said, 'It's **Time** ...' There was no further exchange between us, and he faded back into the night."

"Still holding onto her husband's hand, Tamar pulled a blanket tightly around her.

"Don't you worry, my love," she said to him in pacifying tone. "It was just a strange dream. Our hearts are troubled in these unholy times."

"It's a sign, Tamar," he insisted, "a sign of the inevitable."

*   *   *

Little by little, things began to move ahead at the new Global Dawn location in Jerusalem. Ora slipped into the role of project coordinator as if she were born to it. Time had afforded her an assured and skilful demeanour that elevated her above the pettiness of jealousies or insecurity that might once have hampered her. She began to command respect and even to attract her own society of followers. She initiated an electronic forum that became the mouthpiece of Global Dawn's new groups around Europe and elsewhere. From her little office in the German Colony, she now effectively controlled all the interaction between project members in Israel and abroad.

One of her regular correspondents was Yvette with whom she had developed a friendly email rapport.

"Yvette," she wrote, "I need your honest opinion."

"*D'accord*, Ora," came her immediate reply.

"This is a bit embarrassing ...."

"No, no," she insisted. "Tell me, please."

"Well, I've been asked to represent Global Dawn in a peace workers' forum in Copenhagen, next October."

"Terrific!"

"Of course, it's very flattering to be approached ..."

"I think this is not flattery. *Pas du tout. Enfin*, who could possibly speak for Global Dawn better than you?"

Ora paused a moment as she read Yvette's message. She got up from the computer chair and began pacing the room.

Gadi popped his head round the door and, seeing her thus distracted, asked what was on her mind.

She swung around on her heels to face him.

"Gadi, have I changed since we moved here?"

"You mean, are you more or less impossible to live with?" he grinned.

"Mmm. Guess I deserved that, didn't I?" she answered good-humouredly.

"What prompted this impulse for self-analysis?"

"They want me to go to Denmark on behalf of Global Dawn."

"Fantastic! Think you'll go?"

"Maybe. I'm just so taken aback by the invitation."

"Seems natural enough to me."

"So, you agree with Yvette. But why me and not Reuven?"

"That's easy. He's the figurehead. Action's your territory."

"Is that really how you see it?"

"Well, of course! Look how Michael pumps energy from you, too. He thinks your every word is gold dust. Don't you know that?"

Somewhere in Ora's subconscious she supposed she did know that. Hearing Gadi state it as an obvious fact made her wonder, though.

"You're not just the tiniest bit envious of Michael, are you Gadi?"

"Not at all! It's time someone made you sit up and take a good, long look at yourself! You're a powerful energy ball, and I'm proud to call you my wife."

Her eyes sparkled at this rare piece of undiluted praise from him.

A knock at the door interrupted them. Gadi answered. It was the landlady.

"I'll be right there, Gadi," called Ora.

"No need," he replied. He came back into the living room holding a postcard invitation to a lecture. "Hey, turns out our landlady's some kind of antiquities expert. Did you know that?"

Ora had a sudden flashback to the strangest part of the dream that had led her to the place they now called home. The drawer of old prints. They had not come across it. She looked up at the artwork on the walls.

"She didn't say, but it makes me wonder if any of the pictures hanging around the flat are valuable?"

The walls were hung with a number of prints of old masters.

"Doubt it," said Gadi. "They all look like repros. Come on, she's not going to leave some family heirloom in the dubious hands of tenants like us, is she?"

"Mmm. S'pose not." Ora was still looking a bit spaced out.

"Mind you, this one looks interesting, Orush."

"What is it?"

He was rummaging around in the farthest corner of the "L' and had dusted off a framed print that looked quite old.

"This. It was lying on the shelf over there. Never noticed it before."

He hung his find on an empty wall-hook above the shelf. It was a map. Rather like some of the old Jerusalem maps Ora had pulled off the Internet.

"I know what this is, Gadi," she exclaimed. "It's a copy of one of those early engravings. You know, like the famous Templar one that shows the old city of Jerusalem as if it's the centre of everything and has its layout all tweaked to fit into an ideal geometry?"

"Wow, I reckon you're right. It's got symbols on it, too, like the Templars used to use."

"What symbols? I thought all their stuff was secret, so no one knew about it unless they were inducted into the rites."

"There were symbols that they wore publicly."

"Like the five-pointed star? Is that what you can see?"

"The pentacle? No, but there are double Templar crosses. Look."

"There's even a crude drawing of a knight at the side, there. Just outside the wall."

Gadi was busy examining the Latin lettering at the centre of the map. The map showed the old, walled city of Jerusalem over to the right-hand side. At the centre was a hill with a fortress on it.

"Unbelievable! Ora, this is going to take your breath away!"

"What have you found? A crusader fortress? They built plenty of those. What does the writing say?"

"Mons Gaudii!"

"Mons Gaudii? Hill of Joy?"

"Ora, sit down and listen to me. Don't you know what Mons Gaudii was? It was the Latin name for a place you've heard plenty about from Reuven. Don't forget that twelfth century maps completely distorted the distances and proportions of things. If the centre of Jerusalem is over there, what's the highest hill that overlooks it on this side?"

"Nebi Samwil! Oh my God! First the dream, now this; it's hard not to believe in destiny guiding us here, isn't it, Gadi?"

He said nothing. It was an interesting coincidence.

"So," said Ora, picking up the landlady's invitation. "Curious about her lecture? Enough to go along?"

"What's it about, anyway?"

"Doesn't say, really. It's called 'The Tilted Square'."

While the modest Porath home continued to serve as the main nerve centre of Global Dawn, the need for permanent premises for the project was growing daily. Eventually, it was decided to pool the limited resources of the key activists and rent the whole ground floor of the building. Welcome though the additional office space was, it remained clear that it was no more than a stopgap solution.

In the following month, the Visitors' Centre in Kadmon declared a profit, and Shira and Jeanine were able to cream some of their surplus to help the Jerusalem venture. It proved enough to cover the cost of some modest publicity for which Ora reluctantly found herself seeking Michaela's professional touch. As it turned out, she was spared the humiliation as Michaela had pre-empted her. She and a small TV crew were already in Europe with Global Dawn uppermost on their agenda. The most dramatic breakthrough, however, came from Charlotte whose canvassing of Global Dawn in Melbourne, Sidney and Adelaide actually brought sufficient donations both for the commissioning of a feasibility study and for the salaried appointment of Michael, at long last, as project director.

Michael quickly proved himself an impressive power source. Within a few months, he put together a formidable working team, had the web image of Global Dawn completely revamped in hi-tech style, and added the necessary spark to the promotion package to enthuse targeted partners.

One morning, he arrived in the office and, after helping himself to a large coffee, sat down at his desk, hardly acknowledging Ora's presence by more than a grunt. She was already accustomed to his antisocial, early morning behaviour and thought little of it. She was, however, itching to ask whether he and his wife had decided to take over the newly available living space on the ground floor. She hovered over him asking a million petty questions but avoiding the big one. Eventually, he gave in, and with a large grin declared,

"It's okay, Ora. You've got a couple of new neighbours!"

She threw her arms around him with a yelp of delight. At last, her family had real partners in their venture.

*   *   *

On the afternoon of the landlady's lecture, Ora and Gadi had cleared their schedules and were ready to explore the meaning behind its intriguing title. The event was to be held at a private gallery in the centre of town, so they left early to avoid the hassle of traffic jams and parking problems. On temporary display there was a valuable fine art collection.

"Do you think this can all belong to her?" whispered Gadi.

"Certainly looks as if she's got quite a stash here, doesn't it?"

Most of the audience were elderly, so Ora and Gadi stood out as the attractive delegates of Youth.

"Shh. Here she is."

"Our subject today," she began with a formal clearing of her throat, "is 'The Tilted Square'. The logical progression of what I'm about to expose to you will be aided by some drawings that my assistant here will kindly project."

The talk lasted about an hour. Gadi's concentration soon lapsed, and he dosed off. Ora, on the other hand, was transfixed from start to finish. Copies of the drawings were distributed in handy folders; useful, she thought as a subsequent memory-jogger.

"So, what did you make of all that?" asked Gadi sleepily as they drove home. "Dry, theoretical stuff, I thought. Couldn't honestly see the point of it – or the proof, for that matter."

"Maybe that's because you had your eyes closed!"

"Hmm."

When they got home, the boys were busy, as usual, making the typical noise and mess of a healthy pair of teenagers.

"Hey, kids!" Ora called.

"Hey, Mum," answered Shai, immediately pouncing on her bag to see what goodies it might contain. Ora smacked his hand out of the way.

"All in good time. There's something interesting for you in there, though."

"Candy?" came Omer's cheeky reply.

"Oh, so you're here, too, then. Great, I've got something to show you both."

But Shai had already dashed off to attack his father.

"Hey, Dad," he said, jumping up and down in front of him. "You're home early!"

"Shai, will you let him get into the house! Listen, you two. Dad and I have just been to a lecture."

"Boring!" they shouted out in unison.

"It's about a REAL treasure hunt! Does that sound boring?"

They looked at each other and shrugged their shoulders.

"Okay, let's see it then," said Omer.

She opened the folder and began to lay out the first drawing. It was quite simply a square with another square up-angled inside it.

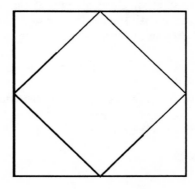

"Oh, no, it's more Druid rubbish and sacred bullshit," moaned Omer and started to walk away.

"Actually, he's right," laughed Gadi. "That's exactly what it is!"

The two of them walked out of the room, arm in arm, making fun of Ora's obsessions with crazy theories. Shai, meanwhile, was leafing through the folder and wanting to know more.

"I'll show you, but you'll need to get a compass, ruler and set square to make all the measurements exactly. Go on, hurry up and get them."

Meanwhile, she took out some blank sheets of folio and began experimenting with some of the shapes. As she pencilled in a circle inside the inner square, carefully so as to be at a tangent to all sides, her precisely calculated drawing stirred memories of Reuven and his scratchings in the sand. It was the strangest feeling as if she were following a prelaid mystery trail; one that he had followed a long time before her.

"I've got them. Here, Mum." Shai held out his school geometry set for her to see.

"Great, now the first thing you have to do is to copy those shapes. Make sure it's a true square with all the sides exactly equal, then everything else will fit."

He sprawled on the floor and set to work.

"Hey, Mum, this is fun, isn't it? Reckon I'll get good marks in geometry at school after this?"

"Maybe," she smiled. "Okay, now we're going to draw the most important shape of all. It's called the Tilted Triangle, and it's the one that's going to guide all the other lines and points into position."

"So, we can use them to make a treasure map?"

"Yeah. Exactly. Do you know what an equilateral triangle is?"

"Aha," he answered, chest all puffed out with pride. "It's one with all the sides equal and all the angles the same."

"Right, and do you know what those angles are?"

"No."

"Well, get out your compass and set square, and you can measure one of them."

Ora, meanwhile was sketching in the triangle so that it was pointing evenly into the top left corner of the outer square. She measured exactly a fifteen-degree angle on either side.

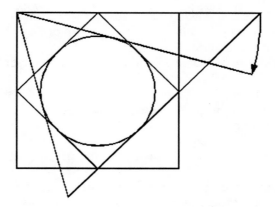

"Sixty!" said Shai, triumphantly.

"What?" said Ora, who had forgotten her question.

"The angles of the triangle are all sixty degrees!"

"Right, now you remember that, because it's going to be very important."

"And that tilted point of the triangle is the famous North-West Point," added Gadi, back in the room and looking over Shai's shoulder.

"I thought you weren't interested?" said Ora.

"Well, the lecture had its moments ..."

"Yeah, in between snores!"

The doorbell rang.

"Gadi, be a love and get that, will you?"

It was Michael.

"Hey, neighbour! Come in, come in."

"Yes, but Michael, we're in the middle of a complex geometric exercise, here, so look and learn in silence," warned Ora, knowing that her request was close to impossible where he was concerned.

"Mum! Come on! What's next?" nagged Shai impatiently.

"Next," she said baiting him with an enigmatic answer "is the key. Watch ve...ry carefully."

Michael had begun to leaf through the folder.

"'The Tilted Square: Secrets of the Great Masters'– I've heard about this," he said. "It's like the stuff that Da Vinci and co used to get their lines straight. Supposed to have mysterious links with Kabbalism. Goes way back. Heavy stuff for kids, Ora!"

"Why, Mum? What does he mean?"

"That's real magic your dabbling in there, mate."

"Real magic? Can I do some, too?" piped up Omer, skating into the room on his roller-blades.

"Take those skates off and grab a piece of paper."

"Now, watch, all of you!"

Following the line of the top of the triangle, she carefully drew the shape of the magical Tilted Square. Then she added a second equilateral triangle.

"Hey, it's a *Magen David*!"

"So it is," she smiled. "Some people call it the Seal of Solomon."

"But the artists who used this geometry weren't Jewish. Why would they want to put a *Magen David* in the middle of their paintings?" asked Shai.

"Maybe they did it by accident," said Omer.

"No, no," said Michael. "No accident. It's all part of the magic! It's not just a Jewish symbol."

"What do you mean?" asked the two boys in chorus.

"Like I said. It's a central clue to old pagan magic. We didn't invent it, but it's been part of Jewish tradition for a long time."

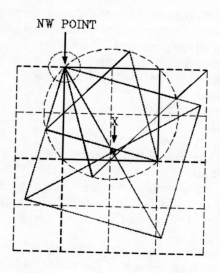

NW POINT

"So, was Leonardo da Vinci a pagan?"

"No, he was a Christian."

"Look, the thing about his sacred geometry is that it belongs to the whole world. The pagans knew about it. So did the Jews. The Kabbalists used a lot of the same symbols, too. Then, there were lots of Christians who got excited by the Kabbalah. Mysticism is a powerful thing."

"What do you mean, powerful, Michael," asked Omer, looking a bit scared. "Is it dangerous, like black magic?"

Then he asked Ora in a shaky voice,

"It is dangerous, isn't it, Mum?"

"No, darling." But, he was already running out of the room.

Shai's eyes were gleaming. He looked up at Gadi who was frowning in disapproval of Michael's talent for sensationalism.

"What do you think, Dad?"

"I don't believe in all this magical eyewash."

Suddenly Shai exclaimed,

"Hey, Mum, I've done it! Look, I've got the whole thing worked out! See that centre-point of the square, down there? It says that's the secret spot where the treasure's supposed to be hidden! Cool! Now I can have a real, geometric treasure hunt with my friends."

"You'll have to map out your hiding-place pretty carefully."

"Yeah, but I'm the only one with the magic key! Wow! This is so cool!"

Ora meanwhile had reached a large book down from the top of the chest. It contained true-scale reproductions of old masters, and she was engrossed in tracking the 'Tilted Square' theory in Vermeer's famous 'Lady Writing a Letter with her Maid'.

"Don't you think it's a bit contrived as a theory?" asked Gadi, watching her. "After all, I'm sure you could locate any number of triangles to connect different points in that picture."

"You're right, but she said in the lecture that this has been proven in at least fifteen of his paintings. That's pretty convincing, don't you think?"

"So, this is meant to be an ideally balanced picture? Is that what she was trying to say?"

"Well, she sees more in it than that, I think. She sees it as a mark of genius and perfection. I mean, she didn't actually use the word divine, but ..."

"I guess it's uplifting like a perfect composition of music."

Ora continued mapping and measuring and seemed quite ecstatic at seeing how the theory really worked.

Chapter 13

"This is the land which I swore unto Abraham, Isaac and Jacob, saying: I will give it to your seed; I have caused you to see it with your eyes, but you shall not go thither."

Deuteronomy 34:4

As Global Dawn began to expand its reach inside Israel and beyond, Reuven found himself an abstracted onlooker upon the germination of his own brainchild. His withdrawal from project activity became acute, and he was rarely to be seen at any of the Global Dawn sites.

In Kadmon, every spare moment in which Jeanine was not busy at the university she dedicated to project promotion activities among the visitors to the Centre. As for Shira, since the *Intifada* had finally led to the suspension of the Bedouin project, the shop and adjacent café had become her prime sources of income and she put in long hours developing her business in its new Global Dawn location.

On one of Reuven's now rare visits to Kadmon, he strayed in the direction of Shira's house. He stood hesitantly contemplating the doorbell before ringing it. Their friendship had been strained of late by her false expectations of a love affair that did not figure on his agenda. He had voluntarily distanced himself from her, as she put it. Under the circumstances, he was relieved when it was Nava who came to the door.

Nava was approaching her mid-teens, and there were coy hints of sexual awakening about her. She seemed a little daunted by the indefinable change in Reuven and asked if he was feeling alright.

"I'm fine," he answered, although his grave tone was unconvincing. "Is Ima home?"

"No. She's over at the Centre. Pop in, she'd love to see you."

"Maybe I'll do that later," he said. "I'd like to rest here for a bit first, though, if you don't mind?"

"Of course not," she smiled. "I'll get you a drink."

He could see she was confused by the unfamiliar gravity of his manner, but he did not feel up to putting on a special show of good cheer for her.

She brought him a glass of fresh orange juice, then, with an awkwardly apologetic look, she slipped out of the room again. In an instant, however, she was back with one of her brothers in tow. The two sat opposite him with expectant looks on their faces, but he said nothing. It was only after Nava's brother kicked her in the shin that she found her tongue and started to chat about her latest contretemps with a school teacher. The crux of the story was her indignation at the teacher having called her lazy.

"What right did she have to say that about me?" she asked. "I hate it when teachers judge us without bothering to find out what's really going on! Don't you think it's a *chutzpah*?"

"Mmm. Hard to say," answered Reuven.

"I think it's disgusting!" chipped in her brother. "We're supposed to show respect for our teachers, but what about them respecting us? They make up their minds about us at the beginning of the year and never even notice when we change."

"Right! So what if I was a bit wild last year?"

"More than a bit, Nava!" giggled her brother.

"Well, alright, then, very wild. But this year I'm completely different."

"Yeah, right. You're a real angel, now!"

Shira walked in and they dropped the subject.

"Hi Shiri."

"Reuven, how wonderful to see you! We missed you, you know. What are you all talking about?"

"School."

"Oh, Nava is angry with 'er teacher."

"So I understand."

"Why do we never see you in Kadmon any more, Reuven? Many beautiful things are 'appening in our Global Dawn Centre. You should come and see it."

"Yes, I know. I ought to look in on the students working on the database, too."

"Would you like to go there, now?"

"But you just came home ..."

"It's okay. We can go together. We should talk also."

"What about?"

"I will tell you on the way."

"Are you going out again, Ima?"

"Yes. I will be back soon," she called.

"Shall we go in my car, then?"

Alone in the car with Shira, he was reminded of all the reasons he had been avoiding her. It was so tempting to accept her uncomplicated affections, her maternal cosseting – like the mother he had never had. Without judging him, she simply loved him with a trusting innocence that quieted his soul. Her understated scent of sweet rose oil floated seductively towards him and he reached for her hand.

"You're such a giving person, Shira. I don't think I've ever known anyone quite like you. I could so easily fall in love with you, you know, but the timing's all wrong."

She kissed her forefinger and laid it on his lips to silence him.

"It is not necessary to explain these things."

"I don't want to hurt you ..."

"Shh. I know that. These have been terrible times for you – the accident and then the bomb attack."

"They were signs, Shiri. There's more trouble still to come. I need to stay the course.

If I flee from these challenges, then my role in Global Dawn will be over."

"What are you saying?"

"I haven't been a good husband to Tamar. I should have had more faith in her."

"But she did not share your dream. How could you?"

"It took great courage for her to come to Kadmon. One day she'll also come to Jerusalem. It's written in the Master Plan."

"You are a good man. Your belief is a great inspiration to all of us."

"I'm leaving the southern project in your hands, Shira. You and Jeanine will carry its burden, now. But tell me about Yoram. Is it really over between you?"

"There is some bureaucracy, you know. And 'e's very sad and angry. He keeps pleading with me to change my mind, but I will never do that."

"And Jeanine? How is she?"

"There is a rumour in Kadmon. You remember 'er story about why she did not come to Paris?"

"Of course I do. It didn't seem at all logical, but she wouldn't open up about it, so I let it be."

"They are saying she stayed because of a man."

"Well, good for her," smiled Reuven, but Shira quickly corrected him.

"No, no. It was not like that. They say the man was Yoni's father."

"And what does she say?"

"Nothing."

"Have you met him?"

"No."

"His name?"

"No," she shook her head.

There was no time for any more questions. The car drew up at the Centre, and they went inside. Fatima stopped Reuven in the corridor. She wanted him to commend her for a scholarship program in the United States. He was amazed by her transfiguration. Gone was the shy village girl. She addressed him with the confident air of one whose choices in life were clear. He gave her the papers she needed and congratulated her on her success.

"I am very sorry you were in the hospital, Mr. Reuven, sir," she said.

"It was the will of God. Thank Heaven it's history, now. Anyway, I wish you good luck in America."

"*In sh'Allah*. Thank you."

Reuven finished the few administrative tasks he came to take care of. Shira showed him around the new garden and offered him some aromatherapy in the treatment centre. He declined, however, and went straight back into the building by the main passageway leading out towards the lobby. On the wall by the entrance, he noticed a new plaque.

> "*To the memory of our beloved son, Yoni, who was taken from us too soon, we dedicate this entrance hall. May the Global Dawn project become an inspiration to many future generations of cherished youth as they embark upon their individual voyages through new dimensions of life.*"
>
> Jeanine & Avraham Danan.
> 30th May 2000

He paused a few moments in silent contemplation of the plaque. Then, he bade Shira farewell and headed home.

*   *   *

A new morning was born in North Tel-Aviv. Thinly streaked
clouds traversed the eastern sky. Solitary flies hovered on the warm
airwaves. A couple of uncouth ravens squawked noisily by. A housecat
padded niftily onto the balcony, ears and nose twitching. She snatched at
a close-flying insect, played it to death tossing it between her paws, and
then discarding it like an old toy.

Muki did not flinch as Reuven let out a leonine waking roar. He
had spent the night on the terrace catching the odd hour of sleep in
between studious pouring over maps and books. Nava's comments about
her teacher were plaguing his mind. The responsibilities of a teacher and
those of a project leader were similar, he thought. A leader who is out of
touch with the changing spirit of his followers can no longer guide them.
This was exactly Nava's complaint about her teacher. "What right does
she have to judge me?" she had asked.

Lawrence's map was spread out on the table. On it was
highlighted the site of Nebi Samwil, the designated home of Global
Dawn. Next to the map an annotated Bible lay open at a page of
rabbinical commentary on the story of Moses and his exclusion from the
Promised Land. Reuven read it again carefully. The first time Moses hit
a rock for water, his act was applauded. When he did the same some
years later, however, he was severely punished. Why was that? The
second time he lashed out angrily at the rock. Was that it? Did he
deserve such a penalty just for giving vent to his frustration? Reuven
groped around for the notebook in which he had scribbled his thoughts
on the subject.

"It's not the act itself but his insensitivity to his audience that's
the key," he had written. "The ethic's quite clear. During all those years
in Sinai, he was so forcefully driven by his passion that it blinded him to
the spiritual growth of his people."

He put the notebook down on the table.

"That's it," he said to himself. "I'm just like Moses. I've been
too preoccupied with myself to be able to lead anyone else."

He got up, went over to his study area and pulled his diary from
the drawer. He tugged at the satin marker, and it fell open at the current
date; February 10th, 2001 – exactly a year and half since he had
wandered with Ora on the beach at Achziv and told her of his dream. He
hunched himself over the diary and began to write passionately. His pen
did not leave the paper for over an hour. When he finally closed the little
book, he secured it under lock and key in his private cabinet. Then, he
replaced the map and the reference books – the annotated Bible, works

of kabbalistic interpreters, 'The Mayan Prophecy', a study of symbols in Salvador Dali, 'The Madaba Mosaic and Maps in Antiquity', 'The Little Prince' by Antoine de St. Exupéry, 'The Theories of Pythagoras' – all these and so many more sources of wisdom and inspiration returned to their designated spaces in his bookshelf. He reached Muki's worn leather lead down from its hook and whistled for him.

That same night Ora could not sleep. She got up at about two in the morning and looked out at the wisp of a new moon. The sky was clear. She wandered down into the little courtyard, shivering as she walked in the chill of the night air. A couple of bats were swooping about the shaggy palm. Instinctively, she ducked as their ominous black forms dived against the creaking branches.

"Hateful creatures," she shrieked in revulsion and ran back inside. She lay down on the couch and dozed off around three, but her sleep was still troubled. She dreamed of Reuven's desert tale but with a disturbing twist. In her variation, it was not he but she who stood silent watch over the cool night scene. The high-risen moon threw its shadow across the ridge ahead. Scarcely visible against the dark sky was the minarets of Nebi Samwil. Someone joined her, and, although aware of him, she did not move. At last, he turned towards her. She recognised the low voice and the bulk of his figure beside her.

"Reuven?" she whispered but barely caught his reply, so softly it travelled on the wind. There was no further exchange between them. He slipped back into the darkness, and she fell into a deep sleep that carried her through to morning.

*   *   *

It quickly became apparent that the hitherto leadership of Global Dawn had profoundly underestimated the power source that was Michael. Within a few months of accepting the position as project manager, he had put together a formidable working team and revamped the project's web image in hi-tech style. Breezing in from another European fundraising spree, Michaela set about bringing Global Dawn into the public eye within Israel. She contracted first-rate designers of flash ads for cable television. The same images were posted in street ads at key points around the country. The impact was astounding as the name of Global Dawn began to infiltrate into the local vernacular and culture. Reuven, still looked upon as the project's figurehead, was besieged by requests for interviews, public lectures and appearances. He rejected them all, unable to deal with such acclaim.

Michael, by contrast, was busy gearing up his latest innovation to blow the minds of major players – a sensational geovision roadshow that immersed its viewers in a stunning VR simulation of the vast Global Dawn Park envisaged for Nebi Samwil. The architectural concept was modelled entirely to a natural geometry formula with an almost complete geodesic sphere as its centrepiece. A hand-held control shift provided real-time interactive dimensions to the experience. Investment in this new bag of tricks had been a gamble that was already paying off. One by one, Michael's targets fell prey to its persuasive magic. The first hint of its success was a letter from NASA's Digital Earth team in which they officially recognised Global Dawn as their middle-eastern partner. Domestic and foreign cinema and entertainment agents were hot on NASA's tail with offers of sponsorship for the proposed Global Dawn Geovisualization Centre and Theme Park. Before long, the following press release appeared, causing no small sensation among the followers of the Global Dawn story.

Investment Pours into a Visionary Project for Jerusalem

"Global Dawn, a Visionary Project headed by one Reuven Sofer, is attracting the attention of the press community these days as megabucks pour into it from international donors and investors.

The project appears as a speck of moonshine in the midst of the turmoil that presently dominates the middle-eastern scene. Could this, the people ask themselves, be a point of hope in their wilderness of despair?

Sofer claims, we are told, that Global Dawn was conceived in another dimension. He has been labelled a dreamer, a missionary (both divine and satanic), an alchemist and a trickster, but the sceptics cannot deny the reality of the sudden flood of capital his project has generated.

Sofer is camera-shy and even aggressively opposed to meeting with the media. We were, however, able to obtain an exclusive interview with his sister, Michaela, herself a journalist and the leading light in the project's publicity campaign. She stated that the project is to be built on the controversial territory that politically divides Jerusalem's East from its West. No word has so far reached the press of the exact location referred to.

Ms. Sofer describes Global Dawn as a mega-project, which will unite on a single campus a planetary discovery centre, several global representational offices, a supertech theme park and residential facilities for the project's permanent *and floating associates."*

With the *Intifada* raging on, Global Dawn was developing into a blessed oasis in the midst of conflict. Reuven sank into watchful meditation of his vision emerging resilient alongside burgeoning strife and warmongering close to anarchy.

Towards the end of winter, Nature opened her floodgates and torrential rains swept across the whole country causing flooding and damage to property and utilities. Among the worst hit were the farming communities by the coast. News came in of a drowning incident. A huge wave of water overturned a jeep on the coast road and the driver fell into the surging current. Several more drownings were reported, as the sea became a fierce opponent to any bold venturer onto its surf. Navy divers were called in to extricate bodies from the raging waters. Most of the villages in the Galilee were evacuated. Along the coastal plain, the rains were incessant, and soon whole districts of Tel-Aviv were entirely submerged under the flood. The municipal drainage systems proved useless against the aggressively rising tide.

As the drama escalated, a state of national emergency was declared. Hundreds were dead or missing, and the toll kept rising. Gale-force winds uprooted trees, and destroyed roads and bridges. A ship was wrecked in the storm outside the southern port of Ashdod; the wind lifted entire shacks from the ground in the port area and swept them away. Rural settlements were cut off without electricity or any means of communication, and the army, the police and civilian volunteers worked around the clock to fly food in to the worst hit areas.

The horror continued for over a week before the winds and the rain finally subsided. In their wake, they left a vast floating population. Penury educated many in the art of scavenging. They preyed upon homes of modest defences, seeking bread and ready cash. Infiltrations of this kind became commonplace in Reuven's neighbourhood. The residents began to improvise deterrent plans and devices to prevent incursions into their homes, but without any aid from official sources, their desperation grew and violence kept it frequent company. Thousands marched upon the seat of government demanding action, but the country's rulers remained silent. In Kadmon, the emergency affected Shira's supply sources. Her shipments from North Africa were mostly lost, and the little merchandise that arrived was severely damaged in transit. Only Jerusalem escaped the devastation turning that city into a real haven for the destitute.

These dire circumstances necessitated the engagement of Global

Dawn's leaders in provision of shelter and basic resources for the needy.
At the hub of this activity was Ora. The Global Dawn effort was aided
by magnanimous donations from concerned supporters overseas. An
improvised network of soup kitchens and makeshift lodgings gave
temporary relief to the growing multitude of streetfarers. The plan for a
Global Dawn residential community began to acquire new significance,
and Ora recalled uneasily how Reuven and she, hearts loaded with
suspicion, had ousted its initiator from the forum.

*   *   *

Reuven had known for some time that his role as mission leader
was over. Now, it was time to set Tamar free to fulfil her destined role
according to the Master Plan. He knew what he had to do and explained
his decision to her in these brief words,

"I have to leave you," he told her. "It's Time. Global Dawn will
continue its course now without me. Shahar has already begun her own
journey of discovery far across the globe. She will be my messenger and
travelling spirit. It is enough for me to know that one such as she was
born. And you, my love, must also discover your own way now. It's
time to release my burden from your back."

"Where will you go, Reuven?"

"I'll follow my conscience, far from here, to a quiet place in the
country."

At their parting, he held her in a timeless embrace. He took
Muki and walked northward to a point in the Lower Galilee hills where
several tributaries of the river merged into a fast course before resurging
out towards the sea.

More days of turmoil and terror followed his departure. The
floodwaters had scarcely subsided when the skies once again grew dark
and menacing, and a rumbling was heard underfoot, from the depths of
the earth. Giant crevices appeared like gaping jaws across the northern
valleys. The whole topology of the region was changing. Planet Earth
heaved a great sigh as its shuddering intensified. Hills exploded into
rubble, and the landslide shifted great rocks to menacing angles. In Tel-
Aviv's homes and offices, objects began to rock and slide. Windows
shattered and the residents trembled. Soon the whole metropolis was
creaking and moaning. People ran into the streets. In whichsoever
direction they chose to flee, great land waves rose up in front of them
blocking their paths. Then, at last, the quake subsided leaving its victims

to take stock of their battered lives.

In Kadmon, Shira and Jeanine sadly unscrewed the dedication plaque to Yoni and closed the doors on the southern project. They made ready to flee their broken township. Shira gathered her children to her, and together they walked for two days across rock-strewn and cruelly ripped terrain. In Hebron, they joined a mixed procession of travellers and took a further day and a half to cross the hills into Jerusalem. There they gained the merciful sanctuary of Global Dawn.

Tamar stood shaking in the ruins of her home. A whole section of the ceiling had caved in, and the bathroom had made sudden acquaintance with the kitchen floor beneath it. It was as if a giant wrench had crunched the house between its arms. There was little left to salvage. She stooped to gather a few portable treasures from an upturned drawer. Beside her, still pinned to the terrace wall, was a tiny key. The cabinet to which it belonged had been flung from the desktop and lay on its side near the drawer. The fall had jammed the lock so that the key failed to catch. Stubbornly, she set about forcing it open with a blunt knife. It surely contained documents or items of value, she thought. She prised an opening in the frame, and eventually the whole cabinet door gave way. She was astounded to discover inside just one solitary item – Reuven's diary. Apprehensively, she began to read the pages into which he had poured his anguish the night of his departure.

"The blindness of my passion has prevented me from being a good leader of Global Dawn. Like the seekers of the Holy Grail, I carry unhealing scars on my soul. In these catastrophic times, I am neither angry nor remorseful. A judgment is upon us all. Like Moses, I am barred from Jerusalem. I am called to account for failure in my mission. I look to my beloved Tamar and Shahar to continue the work I have begun. When the time is right – and it will be so very soon, each will accept her mission in the knowledge that ultimately our roads all lead to the Jerusalem of our destinies. Global Dawn will carry the chosen into a new and better world. It will be their guardian and their inspiration."

Upon reading these predictions issued from the depths of his shattered soul, Tamar wept for her faithlessness and for the weight of his burden. She looked with self-disdain upon the history of her weakness and wiped a last tear of remorse from her face before moving on. Of the material loves she once held dear, only fragments remained. With a strong, new whisper in her heart, she slipped away from her ruined homestead. Her direction and her mission at last were clear.

*   *   *

Armed with an impressive project plan and financial credentials, Michael was ready to tackle the governing legal and political eminences regarding site clearance and construction approval at Nebi Samwil. The latest Global Dawn project plan included an artistic rendering of the completed site and implementation milestones for all its commercial, administrative and residential facets. It aimed to serve, equally and without prejudice, all the region's splintered and conflicted factions whom the brutalities of war and acts of God had claimed as victims. The completed project would span a vast area north-west of the city's centre. Free harmony and balance were essential to the Global Dawn ideal; it would belong to no man and to all. Bolstered by the support of powerful movers of finance and opinion, he was confident that the formal licence would easily get its rubber stamp.

As things turned out, it was not so easy to get such clearance from the resident bureaucracies and theocracies holding dominion over Nebi Samwil. For all the power of the project's formidable sponsors, it took protracted negotiations by expert consultants to achieve the release of those strangleholds. Neither was this legal battle to be Global Dawn's last. When the construction permit was finally in hand, still more obstacles presented themselves. Israeli law stipulated that no new stone could be laid before its intended ground was excavated!

Nebi Samwil was an officially declared nature reserve and historic interest area. Its archaeological significance was well known; richly layered evidence of its habitation back to the Iron Age had already been unearthed there. Situated on the crest of the Benjamin Plateau, one theory connected it with the biblical town of Mitzna. The main historic vestiges in evidence to Global Dawn planners were a crusader fortress and a church, the former in ruins; the latter converted into a mosque. Despite assurances by the project's architects that these and all other remains would be left intact, the Antiquities Authority was adamant that the law must be upheld. So, they brought in their own experts to supervise the excavation work across the entire area of the designated construction site.

Volunteers were enlisted to shovel and dig, haul and clean – all of which they undertook with great passion. To be physically in touch with the history of such a place proved for many an intoxicating experience. Student groups from abroad rallied to the cause. A special delegation joined them from Adelaide's Global Dawn campus group, and they eagerly pitched in. The challenge of exploration bonded its participants regardless of nationality or culture. Also among the workers at the site were increasing numbers of homeless and refugees, glad of the opportunity to earn some ready cash. Temporary housing was provided for them in huts and caravans on the edge of the campus.

Spring announced itself with a heat wave extreme enough to drain the spirits of even the most impassioned worker. Lime dust and marl irritated nostrils and clung to sweat-laden torsos; parched throats emitted hacking coughs on the dry air. Portable water bottles were emptied too quickly, and there was no natural fountain from which to replenish them. Catering to the thirst of the excavating troops became a major logistic challenge. Trucks conveyed giant cooling tanks to the site. They travelled there in convoys each morning. The Magen David Adom first aid and emergency team settled into continuous on-site vigilance, and the nearby Hadassah Hospital stood ready to handle cases of dehydration and fatigue. Work began with a three-hour early morning shift followed by a shorter mid-morning one. Then, they shut down operations for a few hours through the noonday heat. The late shift picked up around four and continued through the evening by artificial floodlighting.

The excavation proceeded thus for several weeks until one morning a boy raced down to the edge of the dig calling frantically to the diggers to lay down their trowels.

"This is all wrong," he panted. "You're missing the most important spot!"

Immediately, a security guard strode up to him and demanded his name.

"I'm Shai Porath," he answered, chest puffed out with pride. "My mother's an administrator of Global Dawn."

Shai's credentials did not over-impress the guard who escorted him, protesting, to the on-site administration hut to which Ora had meanwhile been summoned. She was looking distressed and embarrassed at the disturbance he had caused.

"Shai, what on earth is going on?"

"You've got to tell them to stop, Mum! They're digging in the wrong place!" he panted. "There's treasure here, just like you said! Oren and me, we've worked it all out. Look!"

He was holding his aching sides in breathlessness. Shaking with excitement, he waved a piece of paper in Ora's face. She dismissed the guard. Through the window, she saw the excavators pick up their spades and shovels again. The knocking and hammering, tapping and cutting resumed. She hustled Shai over to a chair and motioned him to sit on it. He complied, but was soon jumping about again, too agitated to stay seated for long.

"Shai, whatever's got into you?"

"Look at this drawing. Just look at it, please!"

She took the paper from him. It was a roughly sketched map of Jerusalem, extended to include Nebi Samwil. She sat up in astonishment at the sight of a shape painstakingly ruled across it.

"The Tilted Square?"

"I was showing Omer the theory you taught me. He wanted me to make him a real treasure map."

She stared at the paper, astounded that he had been able to reproduce all the shapes so accurately.

"And?" she prompted absently.

"I took the map of Nebi Samwil off the wall. You know, the one you hung in the corner of the living room? Dad said it was a copy of a really old map – like, from crusader times?"

"And you traced the Tilted Square onto it?"

Slowly, the light was dawning on her. More and more it seemed their move to Jerusalem had been orchestrated by a greater power than chance. It was just as Reuven had said – all part of the Master Plan.

"Shai," she said abstractedly. "I'm taking you home."

Her cell phone rang. It was Gadi.

"They phoned from the school ..."

"It's okay. Not to worry. Shai's with me. Get home as soon as you can, though. We've got something urgent to take care of."

Sprawled on the living room floor, Ora watched her elder son retrace his markings and match them with the map. There was no doubt the tilt of the square followed a straight line from the Holy Sepulchre to Nebi Samwil, and its north-west point was clearly marked at the crest of that historic site. The diagonals of the square intersected precisely below the south-eastern corner of the outer fortress wall.

"Mum? What're those dotted lines by the wall meant to be?"

"Those are the vaults. Look, there's another one, see?" replied Michael over his shoulder. Ora started; she had heard neither him nor Gadi enter the room.

"So, you two," she stammered, "d'you think Shai really could've stumbled on something meaningful?"

"It's possible. The original map looks like a Templar engraving," said Gadi. "Some Templar Knight could have known about the Tilted Square theory and used it as a key to a secret hiding place. The only problem is that Saladin destroyed the fortress and reduced everything around it to rubble."

"Mmm," said Ora. "The last time anyone excavated there, they had to clear away a whole mountain of stones before they could even begin any digging."

"Right," said Michael. "That's when they found the main vaults."

"OK, but there's another problem with the Templar theory, though" objected Gadi.

"Nu? What?"

"The Templars never lived at Mons Gaudii."

"How d'you know that?"

"There's a famous twelfth century story about it. Baldwin offered Mons Gaudii to Bernard, the Abbot of Clairvaux, and Bernard snubbed him. He said 'thanks but no thanks'!"

"Baldwin?"

"Ruler of Jerusalem, at the time?"

"Yes, and the Bernard you're talking about," chipped in Michael, "he's the one who set up the Order of the Knights Templar, right?"

"Exactly. One and the same."

"So, what happened then, after he refused Baldwin's offer?"

"Went off to live at the Temple, I guess – that's the place that really interested him."

"Mmm," interrupted Ora, "all very interesting, but it doesn't prove anything one way or the other. The Templars got to be really wealthy and powerful, didn't they?"

"Right, and they didn't just stay in Jerusalem, they were all over the place."

"It's not as if they had no contact with other Christians, either. There certainly were Christians living at Nebi Samwil, and there could easily have been some Templars there, too …"

"Perhaps they chose it, after all, as a nice quiet hiding-place for their riches?"

She stopped abruptly as Jeanine's words came flooding back to her.

"A treasure trove just waiting to be unlocked …"

Then, glancing at the map again, she snatched it impulsively from the floor, grabbed her keys and sped out of the apartment with Shai fast in her train.

*   *   *

The excavations resumed under the new and animated direction of the Porath family. They began to clear the area just to the south of a reconstructed portion of the original eastern wall. The surface debris was passed in a hand chain out of the pit. Pottery fragments and the occasional complete shard were passed to the supervisor for sorting, inspection and recording. At about five metres, their shovels encountered the hard dolomite bedrock. They had reached the level of the foundations. Between the original fortress and the wall, the ground level had been raised to form a courtyard under which ran the two vaults discovered during earlier excavations. Taking care not to damage the reconstructed wall, they skirted its periphery. Each new section to be unearthed was carefully marked. Centimetre by centimetre, the lifted soil was carried out for screening and sifting.

Shai Porath was becoming a familiar young face on the scene. He followed the work with great excitement, noting each completed area on his map. By the end of the third day, a large new expanse of land close to the eastern wall was clear, but it revealed nothing of notable significance. There was some discussion as to whether or not to continue following the whim of a lad. Excavation so close to the mosque was liable to provoke its religious guardians, and that would serve no positive purpose in the long run. Ora Porath's belief in her son's mission was unflinching, however. As for Shai, he did not budge from the dig as they edged towards the key point on his map.

One afternoon, a volunteer working close to where Shai stood let out a sudden yell and began cursing vehemently. A jagged piece of metal had split from his spade and gashed his leg, just missing the base of his kneecap. A first aid orderly rushed over to take care of him as the supervisor commanded everyone else to stand back.

"Bring a flash-light over here, will you," he called, stooping to investigate the unexpected portion of hard rock. He clambered down into the pit to gauge the size and shape of the rock more accurately. Carefully he chiselled, cleaning as he worked. The rectangular block that he uncovered was evenly proportioned as if purposefully measured and cut out of the bedrock. He set about clearing the impacted earth above it to assess its depth. It was lodged in the ground in such a way as to form a perfect corner with the reconstructed part of the wall. However, where once it would have been held in position by walls on either side, the loosening of the rubble below now gave it mobility.

A small pulley was brought in to lift the weighty cornerstone. As it was being hoisted up, the official camera crew rushed around photographing it from every angle. Theirs was an important part of the site-recording routine, before and after excavation.

The first revelation after the cornerstone was lifted was the extent of the exposed cavity. It stretched several metres under the courtyard along the inner eastern wall, and the placement of the cornerstone at its entrance implied intentional concealment

Shai was beside himself and had to be restrained by onlookers from leaping into the pit to explore the vault with his own hands. The supervisor warned him back, however, and shone his flashlight into the gaping hole.

"There's something down there!" he called. "Could be another hunk of rock. I'm going to take a look!"

Buried in the far corner of the vault was a small, stone chest. Carefully, he shovelled away some of the surrounding rubble, then, with the help of a few extra strong men, manoeuvred it onto a wooden pallet. They placed a crate on top of it, secured it well and used the pulley to haul it up.

In the primary inspection area above, expert brushing and cleaning wore down the defences of the earth-encrusted lid. Then, a blunt-ended spatula was used to lift the lid entirely away from its base. The sight that fell open to view provoked a chorus of "Ooh"s and "Ah"s.

Shai's elation knew no bounds.

"I did it! Real treasure! I found it! Are we rich now, Mum?"

While Ora expounded to him on the subject of state ownership of antiquities, they watched the contents of the chest – mostly a mass of dull-looking old coins – being carted off to a consultant for analysis.

A few days later, an extended *Mabat* television bulletin announced the cessation of excavation work at Nebi Samwil pending evaluation of an important new find.

"... A secret vault discovered at the newly reopened excavation site of Nebi Samwil has revealed a magnificent cache, the value of which has not yet been confirmed. Experts provisionally date the find as First Temple period. The cache is mainly of coins, mostly bronze, some silver. It also includes a few gemstones of still indeterminate colour after initial cleaning. Reportedly, each of the stones is precisely cut and tapered to fit a gold setting. Caught between the settings and the stones are frays of woven linen twined with gold. These gold-threaded textile fragments and the unusually large size of the stones lend credence to a theory that they originally adorned some regal or priestly garment.

Intriguingly, this discovery is attributed to the initiative of a teenager – one Shai Porath, elder son of Ora Porath of the Global Dawn administration. "

*   *   *

The excavations declared complete, building permission was granted and Global Dawn's cornerstone ceremoniously positioned. At last, Global Dawn's foundations could be laid. Immediately, architects, engineers, managers and consultants pitched into the implementation of its magnificent design for harmonious information flow and multi-dimensional experience; a place in which Nature and Technology would join in symbiotic partnership.

The most pressing need was the conversion of the shantytown on the periphery of the park into a permanent residential complex. A frenzied building effort began to accommodate the swelling tide of wanderers and waifs seeking refuge inside Global Dawn's barely raised lintels.

At the same time, on the far side of the campus, construction activity began on a parade of offices and infrastructure to cater for the influx of the project's global sponsors. As these weighty representatives of the world's legal and commercial establishments entered the Global Dawn campus, their stated objectives were harmonisation, unlocking, referencing and reformatting of networks, interfaces, protocols and parameters. They conferred in techno-jargon, and the stubborn barriers between them were slow to surrender. Gradually, nonetheless, agreement was reached on a linkage of resources in readiness for connection to the central information core.

The Global Dawn administration now broached the massive task of building the experiential park itself. It was to be entirely modelled on synergetic principles making respectful use of all the natural resources in the ancient and powerful energy hub that was Nebi Samwil. Its design would preserve all existing orchards and olive groves, water sources and archaeological finds. The landscaping would bow to the beauty of the surrounding hills and valleys, affording natural views for the visitor's enjoyment. Dominating it all would be the geodesic dome – home to Global Dawn's information core.

Mighty shafts of reinforced concrete were driven deep into the bedrock causing the ground to shudder and great energy waves to surge into the air. Huge scaffolding towers were erected to support the several hundred steel and concrete beams that would form the dome's essential framework. Complex plottings and algorithms were displayed on-site via a computer network for on-the-fly verification of every stage. The completed dome would span some eight hundred cubic metres. Its weight would be tremendous. Accurate balancing of its geometric components would be the key to its tensegrity, dictating its ability to be naturally self-supporting. Precision in these calculations was paramount.

The construction method they used was inspired by Buckminster Fuller's original top-down approach. This meant that the main body of the dome was actually pieced together on the ground before being hoisted by cranes onto the foundation shafts. In this case, because of the heavy elements involved, the plan was to assemble it in a series of large segments.

Over the next few weeks, spectators witnessed the lifting and riveting into place of each segment in turn until the vast framework was complete. Finally, cut crystal panes were inserted into each of its geometrical sections. The great open space of the inner dome was well aerated so that little improvised conditioning of the natural environment was necessary. According to the project plan, a computer research facility was installed with hundreds of private workstations in cubicles around the central space reserved for the information core.

As work on the dome neared completion, Jeanine carefully repositioned the plaque in Yoni's memory on its inner wall.

The Disney greats arrived to join the Global Dawn venture, intent on integrating this new enterprise into the daily lives of the region. With them they brought all the paraphernalia, traditional and modern, of a Disney-style theme park, There would be a commercially tenable balance between fun and culture with virtually real interplay between visitors and environment, simulation and holographic immersion – everything needed to provide Global Dawn's visitors with a scintillating tour of their universe ... Money was no longer a constraining factor. The Disney consortium included engineers, architects, landscape modellers, film and video producers, lighting and audio designers, and hundreds of other park design and creation specialists. These were people with an understanding of the human perceptions of space and form who were able to display what should be seen and to hide what ought to be hidden. They took charge of the park concept promising to build a faithful replica of Reuven's original vision.

Meanwhile, finishing touches were made to the dome itself, and the Global Dawn treasure was placed on a rich bed of dark velvet in a specially designed central showcase.

The site was overrun with professional news collectors, each anxious to scoop the latest dramatic Global Dawn story. Michaela struggled to balance her professional desire for the limelight against her concern to keep family matters under wraps. Ora, too, while fielding the throng of journalists, video operators, cinematographers and more, was anxious to protect her son from their harassment.

At last, all was ready for connection of the world's information resources into a single global network. Michael's crew took charge of manoeuvring the technological core itself into its designated position. All the interfaces were checked and prepared for the moment of linkage. There was nervousness in the air, but no expert calculation or inspired foresight could have anticipated what was about to happen.

Michael plugged in the final connector, and instantly massive vibrations rocked the entire grid as the great network sprang to life. Pulsating bands of light burst out of their hardware casings into the energised environment of the dome. Builders, technicians and spectators were flung back against the inner walls. The Global Dawn network, like a misshapen golf ball reflated from within, had begun to reassert the perfect balance of its natural design. At once, a thunderous swelling convulsion ripped from the core into the body of the global grid, blasting aside all man-made impedances, models and formats. Across the great live network in spontaneous convergence cascaded a tide of luminous shapes, flexing and twisting before the stunned eyes of their observers. No longer restrained by conflicting technologies, there was a synergetic confluence of form, colour, sound and vibration. Lightening flares bounced from wall to wall between the crystal panels, then split into rainbow arcs that made the whole dome sparkle like a multi-coloured diamond. A whooshing sound like ocean waves in a conch shell rose to a high-pitched ringing that traversed the dome in echoing cadenza.

More and more onlookers squeezed into the dome, eager to experience the new manifestations spinning in free formation above and around the information core. Their senses were bathed by a symphony of ethereal impressions that skimmed over the live grid, aligning themselves to a new equation according to Nature's own architecture of flexibility and strength. Before their eyes rolled holographic images of all the histories of Jerusalem – people, places, natural events, acts of God, vain words and oracles of wisdom, talismans and magical charms, icons of alarming beauty. It was a levelling of all the battles ever played between good and evil, loveliness and ugliness.

Thus, the Global Dawn dream was emerging – a resilient new vision as foretold in the Master Plan – amid the smouldering ashes of a land verging on collapse.

The constant flow of energy from the central core sent its vibrations through the throne of the gemstones. Erupting from the surface of the stones appeared a halo of white light. It circled, divinely translucent, then rose nobly upwards to the very height of the dome. As if pulled into place by an unseen thread, the stones repositioned themselves in rows, three by four. In the empty spaces appeared a strange pooling of light and an eerie bluish beam above them. The crowd stood in awe as a giant hologram snaked upwards from the throne, hovered above it, and billowed to fill the interior of the dome. It formed itself into the majestic shape of a man, clothed in a long, wide robe with a tunic over it, his head bound in a high turban. He wore a regal breastplate studded with rows of jewels, and across his shoulders, a cloak with wide straps from which gleamed two huge engraved stones.

Ecstatic whispers crowded the air.

"Look, an emperor!"

"No, a priest!"

"A priest!"

"It's the High Priest! Look at his breastplate."

"Oh, my God, see those rows of gemstones – three by four. Don't you know what they are?"

"It's the *Hoshen*!"

"It's what?"

"The holy breastplate the High Priest used to wear in the Temple!"

"The *Hoshen*!"

"The *Hoshen*!"

"Of the Temple?"

"Oh dear God!"

Some people fell to their knees. Others stood stock still, paralysed by the impelling vision. The incredulous whispers continue to circulate,

"It has to be him! The Temple High Priest! That cloak he's wearing, it's the *Ephod*!"

"The *Hoshen*? The *Ephod*?"

"*Hoshen*!"

"*Ephod*!"

"*Ephod*!"

It was a concert of fearful murmuring; a synchronised chant from barely moving lips; eyes were glazed in wonder.

"Those stones on its shoulders – such a size ..."

"And how brilliantly they shine."

Sparks were shooting into the air from the two great stones. Then, from the left shoulder an ancient style Hebrew letter *Bet* curled upwards, its black shape formed by dazzling white fire around it.

The crowd gasped. Next came the letter *Nun*.

"*Ben*! It's the name, *Ben*!" they screamed.

Many were shading their eyes fearfully from the powerful images.

Then, from the right side came *Yud*, *Mem*, *Yud*, and *Nun*.

"*Yemin!*" they called out; *Yemin* was Hebrew for 'right'.

Next, the letters aligned themselves in the air to form *Binyamin* – the name of the most beloved son of Jacob, the biblical patriarch, and the name of the plateau on which Nebi Samwil stood.

Still more letters flew out of the jewel case, coming to rest on the image of the *Hoshen*: *Resh, Aleph, Bet, Nun.*

An anguished woman's cry pierced the air, her voice half-cracked with desolation as she read out the name these letters spelt.

"*R e u v e n , R e u v e n !*"

"Oh, my God, it's Tamar!"

"Catch her, someone, she's passing out!"

She was standing close to the core, reaching up as if to clutch at the letters as they circled in fire above her, and gathered to form Reuven's name. She swayed as if in a trance, unaware of those who tried to steady her. Then, she fell into a swoon and was carried out of the crowded space.

As night fell, the great crystal dome of Global Dawn shone from its central location as a symbol of the project's inherent intimacy with Planet Earth. Holographic projections filled the campus with an air of enchantment. The display adjusted itself to altering subtleties of temperature, light and breeze, each new condition bathing the park with its own radiant light.

Members of The Circle had joined hands in a guardian ring around the jewel case – Ora, Michael, Shira, Jeanine, Ariella, even Michaela and Menashe, too. Ora reached out to Shai and drew him into the circle.

And so, from Reuven to Benjamin came the bearers of Global Dawn to set it at Jerusalem's crest in the place assigned to it in the Master Plan. It was carried by ancient knowledge through the guardian hands of the Knights Templar, concealed in safety until its revelation to Shai.

"Shai," said Jeanine. "Your name means 'gift', and, indeed, you are a divine gift. Only you could have found this key to the future of Global Dawn."

Ora listened to her words and quietly added,

"After all, it was just as Reuven said it would be. The answers were all in names."

*   *   *

The final war was being waged. Those whose strength of spirit was sufficient to ride the ferocity of the storm hid out in forests and in wasteland. Some sought the assistance of a strange man and his dog to cross the northern estuary into safe new pastures.

A young woman with the eyes of an angel and the directness of a ray of sunlight approached the strange man at the water's edge and requested his help. As she thanked him, she asked,

"By the way, what do they call you?"

He answered,

"They call me Reuven."

Epilogue

From East, West, North and South, the followers of Global Dawn are converging on Jerusalem.

Shira has returned to assume her rightful position at the gate to the city. The magical cloak of her spirit stretches from the tip of the horizon to the invisible oceans whence she travelled. It protects the thousands of youngsters who have chosen her to be their guide.

Like Noah's Ark above the floodwaters, Global Dawn stands high above the devastation. As Reuven predicted, a way to Nebi Samwil has been cleared, and a cleansing of the Earth has begun.

At the gates of Jerusalem reside four angels, guardians of the planet:
Tamar – mother of Shahar, Shahar – child of a new global dawn, Michaela – sibling spirit of its creator, and Shira – harmonious soul of Mother Earth.

Global energies beam in perfect unity through the crowning crystal dome of Global Dawn, shimmering in cross-formation over the city and resonating in the four corners of the Earth. Into the cosmos is projected a single ray of harmony – Global Dawn's message of the unity of Planet Earth in a new dimension.

*   *   *

About the Author

First-time novelist, Deborah Gelbard, is a London University honours graduate in literature. She has lived and worked in England, France, Belgium, Spain and Israel. Her professional expertise spans commercial diplomacy, consultancy and marketing writing for the hi-tech industry. She is also an accomplished writer of literary essays and short stories.

LaVergne, TN USA
23 August 2009

155593LV00002B/86/A